Dark Origins

Level 26
Dark Origins

Anthony E. Zuiker

with Duane Swierczynski

MICHAEL JOSEPH
an imprint of
PENGUIN BOOKS

MICHAEL JOSEPH

Published by the Penguin Group
Penguin Books Ltd, 80 Strand, London WC2R 0RL, England
Penguin Group (USA) Inc., 375 Hudson Street, New York, New York 10014, USA
Penguin Group (Canada), 90 Eglinton Avenue East, Suite 700, Toronto, Ontario, Canada M4P 2Y3
(a division of Pearson Penguin Canada Inc.)
Penguin Ireland, 25 St Stephen's Green, Dublin 2, Ireland (a division of Penguin Books Ltd)
Penguin Group (Australia), 250 Camberwell Road, Camberwell, Victoria 3124, Australia
(a division of Pearson Australia Group Pty Ltd)
Penguin Books India Pvt Ltd, 11 Community Centre, Panchsheel Park, New Delhi – 110 017, India
Penguin Group (NZ), 67 Apollo Drive, Rosedale, North Shore 0632, New Zealand
(a division of Pearson New Zealand Ltd)
Penguin Books (South Africa) (Pty) Ltd, 24 Sturdee Avenue, Rosebank, Johannesburg 2196, South Africa

Penguin Books Ltd, Registered Offices: 80 Strand, London WC2R 0RL, England

www.penguin.com

First published in the United States of America by Dutton, a member of Penguin Group (USA) Inc. 2009
First published in Great Britain by Michael Joseph 2009

1

Copyright © Anthony E. Zuiker, 2009

Illustrations by Marc Ecko

The moral right of the author has been asserted

Printed in Great Britain by Clays Ltd, St Ives plc

A CIP catalogue record for this book is available from the British Library

ISBN: 978–0–718–15562–9

www.greenpenguin.co.uk

To Susan Kennedy, my new partner in crime

I t is well-known among law enforcement personnel that murderers can be categorized as belonging to one of twenty-five levels of evil, from the naive opportunists starting out at Level 1 to the organized, premeditated torture-murderers who inhabit Level 25.

What almost no one knows—except for the elite unnamed investigations group assigned to hunt down the world's most dangerous killers, a group of men and women accounted for in no official ledger—is that a new category of killer is in the process of being defined. Only one man belongs to this group.

His targets:
Anyone.
His methods:
Unlimited.
His alias:
Sqweegel.
His classification:
Level 26.

PROLOGUE

the gift

Rome, Italy

The monster was holed up somewhere in the church, and the agent knew he finally had him.

He removed his boots as quietly as he could and placed them beneath the wooden table in the vestibule. The boots were rubber soled, but even those could make some noise on the marble floors. So far, the monster didn't know he was being followed—as far as the agent could tell.

The agent had been chasing the monster for three years. There were no photos of the monster, no physical evidence at all. Catching him was like trying to capture a wisp of smoke in your fist. The force of your action would cause it to dissipate and re-form elsewhere.

The hunt had taken him all over the world: Germany. Israel. Japan. The United States. And now here, Rome, inside a seventeenth-century baroque-style church christened Mater Dolorosa, which was Latin for "sorrowful mother."

The name fit. The interior of the church was gloomy. With his gun in a two-hand grip, the agent moved as silently as possible along the yellowed walls.

A notice posted on the church door said it was closed to the public for renovations. The agent knew enough Italian to understand that the four-hundred-year-old fresco on the interior dome of the church was being restored.

Scaffolding. Gloom. Shadows. It was a natural habitat for the monster. No wonder he'd chosen it, despite its being a sacred place of worship.

The agent had come to understand that the monster knew no boundaries. Even in times of war, churches and temples were considered places of sanctuary—safe havens for those seeking the comfort of God during their darkest hours.

And as the agent made his way around the metal poles and underside of the scaffolding, he knew the monster was here. He could *feel* it.

The agent was no believer in the supernatural; he did not claim to have psychic abilities. But the longer he hunted the monster, the more he found that he was able to tune in to his savage wavelength. This gift brought the agent closer than any other investigator to catching the monster—but it came at a cost. The more he tuned his brain in to the monster's insanity, the more he lost touch with what it was like to be sane. He had recently begun to wonder whether his single-minded pursuit might soon kill him. He'd discarded the thought.

His focus had returned when the agent saw the most recent victim, just a few blocks away. The sight of the blood, the torn skin, the viscera steaming in the cool night air, and the marbled beads of fat hanging from exposed muscles would later send the first responders outside to vomit. Not the agent, who had knelt down and felt a thrilling burst of adrenaline when he touched the body through the thick latex of his examiner's gloves and realized it was still warm.

It meant the monster was nearby.

The agent knew he wouldn't have gone far; the monster loved

to hide himself and enjoy the aftermath of his work. He had even been known to secret himself within the scene while law enforcement cursed his name.

So the agent had stepped into the small courtyard near the victim's body and let his mind wander. No deductive logic, no reasoned guesses, no gut, no hunch. Instead the agent thought: *I am the monster; where do I go?*

The agent had scanned the rooftops, then saw the glittering dome and knew immediately. *There. I'd go there.* There was not a seed of doubt in the agent's mind. This would end tonight.

Now he was moving silently among the wooden pews and the metal poles of the scaffolding, gun drawn, all of his physical senses on high alert. The monster might be smoke, but even smoke had a look, a scent, a taste.

The monster stared down at the top of his hunter's head. He was positioned on the underside of a paint-splattered wooden plank, clinging to the gaps between the wood with his skinny, strong fingers and equally powerful toes.

He almost wanted his hunter to look up.

Many had chased the monster over the years, but none like this one. This one was special. Different.

And somehow, familiar.

So the monster wanted to look at his face again, in the flesh. Not that he didn't know what his hunters looked like. The monster had plenty of surveillance photos and footage of all of them— at work, in their backyards, on the way to fill their vehicles with gasoline, bringing their children to sporting matches, and purchasing bottles of liquor. He'd been close enough to catalog their smells, the aftershave they wore, the brand of tequila they drank. It was a part of his game.

Until recently he'd thought this one was merely average. But then the man had begun to surprise the monster, making leaps no one ever had before, coming closer than anyone else. Close enough that the monster had let the other hunters fall away, focusing in on the one photo he had of this one, staring at it and trying to imagine where his weakness lay. But a photograph wasn't the same as real life. The monster wanted to study this one's face while he still tasted the air, gazed at his surroundings, drew its smells into his nostrils.

And then the monster would slay him.

The agent looked up. He could have sworn he saw something moving up there, in the shadows of the scaffolding.

The dome above him was a strange quirk of seventeenth-century architecture. It was fitted with dozens of stained-glass windows that took all incoming light and shot it to the peak of the dome, as if exalting God with his own radiance. In the sunlight it would be breathtaking. Tonight's full moon gave the windows an eerie glow, but everything below the dome, from the vaults down, was draped in dramatic shadow. A stark reminder of man's place in the universe—down in the unknowing dark.

The dome itself was adorned with a panorama of heaven, with floating cherubs and heralds and clouds, as if to taunt man even more.

Wait.

Out of the corner of his eye, the agent saw a flittering of white and heard the faintest pull of something that sounded like rubber.

There. Over by the altar.

This hunter is goooooood, the monster thought from his new hiding space. *Come find me. Come let me see your face before I rip it from your skull.*

The silence was so absolute, it was almost a pulsing, living thing, enveloping the church. The agent moved swiftly, hand over hand, climbing the scaffolding as silently as possible, gun tucked in his unsnapped side holster, ready to be drawn at a second's notice. The wood was rough and sharp beneath his searching fingers; the poles felt dusted with motes of dirt and steel.

The agent slowly crept around another platform, climbing higher now, looking for any kind of reflection or hint of the monster. But there was little available light. He took a quick, sharp breath and lifted himself to another level, desperate to see over the edge as he exposed his head and neck to the unknown. If only he could see . . .

I see you, the monster thought. *Do you see me?*

And then he did.

The agent saw the monster's face for the first time. Two beady eyes looking out from a blank visage—as if someone had taken a hot iron and pressed away all of its features . . . except for the eyes.

Then it was gone, scurrying up the side of the scaffolding like a spider ascending its webbing.

The agent abandoned stealth now. He tore after the monster with a speed that surprised him, pulling himself up the crossbeams of the scaffolding and around the edges of the planks as if he'd been practicing on an FBI course back in Virginia.

There he was again—a glimpse of a pale white limb, whipping around the edge of a platform, just two levels above.

The agent climbed even harder, faster, more frenzied. The

monster was moving closer to the heavenly dome. But heaven was a dead end. There was no way out other than the exits below.

For the first time in decades, the monster felt true fear. How had this hunter sensed him? How was he so fearless as to pursue him up here?

The face of his hunter looked different now. This was no mere law enforcement officer who'd followed a *hunch* and caught a *lucky break*. This was something new and wondrous. The monster would have tittered with excitement if it wouldn't have slowed his ascent.

For a glorious moment the monster had no idea what would happen next. It reminded him of being a child. Just a few square inches of pressure on his hunter's trigger and the right trajectory could end everything. The monster was many things, but he was not bulletproof.

Will it end up here? Are you the one who will bring death unto me?

The agent had him.

He felt the trembling of the wooden plank above him—the last bit of scaffolding before the dome. The agent whipped past the last two crossbeams. He pulled his gun.

There he was—pressed flat against the uppermost plank. A moment passed as the agent stared through the gloom into the monster's eyes and the monster stared back. What passed between them was the length of a heartbeat, impossibly short and yet unmistakable—a primal recognition between hunter and prey in the climactic moment just before one claims victory and the other collapses in death.

The agent fired twice.

But the monster didn't bleed. It exploded.

It took only a split second for the agent to recognize the sounds of splintering glass and identify the mirror he'd shattered with his bullet—no doubt meant to help the experts with their restoration work. The mistake could have been fatal. But as he whipped around to fire again he knew the monster was already gone, could hear him smashing his way through a stained-glass window and out onto the rooftop of the church. Colored glass rained down, opening a gash under his eye as he lifted his gun and fired blindly through the jagged hole in the glass. The bullet hit nothing, soared away into the heavens. A scampering sound could be heard running down the outside of the dome . . . and then nothing.

The agent raced down the scaffolding, but in his heart he knew it was futile. The monster was loose on the rooftops of Rome, an invisible tendril of smoke wafting up and away, nothing but the faintest lingering trace left to prove he had ever really been there at all.

PART ONE

the man in the murder suit

Two Years Later

chapter 1

The emaciated, ghost-thin man the FBI called "Sqweegel" worked feverishly at his grandmother's sewing machine. The maniacal pecking thundered in the small bedroom on the second floor.

ThwakwakwakwakwakwakwakWAKWAK.

WAK.

WAK.

WAK.

Sqweegel's small bare foot pushed the pedal. His toenails were manicured, as were his fingernails. A desk lamp cast a glow on his intent face. His delicate hands coaxed the material forward, sending the cloth around the zipper directly into the path of the throbbing metal head as it applied the stitches. It had to be right.

No; scratch that.

It had to be *perfect.*

The hot parts of the machine made the room smell of burning dust; the blood smelled like pennies.

15

The piece of material was still tacky with dark, partially dried blood. The material was tough but not indestructible. He'd caught the zipper on something just sharp enough to slice through an inch of the black cloth attaching it to the rest of the latex suit. There was no blood loss; it had scraped away a few layers of epidermis at most. Still, even this was too much. He'd dug the lighter out of his tool kit, then held a flame to the edge of the metal until whatever skin cells had clung to it were gone. He mustn't leave anything of himself behind. Then he'd come home.

And now he was repairing the tear.

It had troubled him the entire way home from the little whore's apartment on the outskirts of the city. Before packing it in its case, Sqweegel had tried to poke the curled flap back into place. But it refused to stay. He closed the case and tried to forget about it. That proved impossible. He saw the tiny cloth flap sticking up off the suit in his imagination, like a black flag frozen midflap on an airless moon. It distracted him so much, he almost drove off the road so he could open the trunk and push the flap back into place.

He resisted the urge. He knew it was silly. And he knew he'd be home soon enough.

The moment he closed the front door behind him, Sqweegel took the suit to the sewing room. This had to be taken care of immediately.

Sqweegel used his grandmother's machine because it worked as perfectly now as it had the day she'd ordered it from the Sears, Roebuck catalog in 1956. It was a Kenmore 58, and it cost $89.95. Sewed forward as well as in reverse, under a built-in light. All it required was a little oil on the moving parts and a good cleaning of the exterior every few weeks. Give something enough attention, it'll last forever.

Like the suit.

His small foot stopped working the machine. The speeding

16

head cycled down to a complete stop. He crouched down until his eyes were inches from the material. He admired his handiwork.

There.

No more tear.

Now it was time to wash all of the filthy whore blood away.

chapter 2

The Bathroom / Dressing Room

S qweegel rubbed his hands with powdered soap and watched the pink water swirl at the bottom of the white porcelain sink. Another sad life down the drain. But this sacrifice would be the herald of something new. Something wondrous. It excited him to think about it.

Now, though, it was time for more practical matters, such as the removal of the hair.

Sqweegel's blade was clean, the water hot. His skin was already moisturized with vegetable oil—never shaving cream. That would be like mowing a lawn under six inches of snow. He needed to see what he was doing. Every square inch.

Top to bottom. Open areas first: Scalp. Face. Neck. Forearms. Chest. Legs.

He paused after each pass of the blade to hold it under the running water. Bits of black stubble and microscopic skin flakes swirled in the drain before disappearing.

Then, his underarms. The backs of his legs. His ankles.

Scraping. Pausing. Rinsing. Swirling.

Next came the most difficult—yet satisfying—part of the process: flensing the hair from his genitals and anus. To do it right required pulling his scrotum until it was perfectly taut, ready for the pass of the blade. The positioning took time—sometimes upward of five or six minutes. The pass of the blade, by contrast, was always steady, deliberate, careful.

The shaving of his anus required even more positioning. His feet pressed high against the tiled walls of the industrial bathroom, his torso leaning forward, for easier access. One hand steadied him; the other held the blade. It was as if the base of his spine was hinged, and he could fold himself in half. The ritual was the same: Scrape. Pause. Swirl in a bowl of warm water. He took his time, sometimes holding the position for a few minutes before another pass of the blade.

The more hair he removed, the calmer he felt, and the easier it was to hold this position. The closer he felt to pure.

The closer he came to salvation.

In the next room, Sqweegel opened the combination lock on the refrigerator—which was kept at the warmest temperature possible—and removed four and a half sticks of butter. He had tried economizing and getting it down to four, but the extra half stick really was necessary. Five was too much and not really a solution, anyway.

Four sticks were the ideal; four sticks come in every package. Which meant that every eight packages required one extra package, to be used for half sticks.

He tried not to think about the half stick too much. Someday he'd find a way around the half stick.

He carefully opened the paper wrapping of the first stick, split it in half with his hands, and began to rub his chest and shoulders—the largest part of his body first—before moving to his extremities. Each limb required a half stick, as did his genitals and anus. The depth of the butter must be consistent over the entirety of his body. No peaks, no valleys.

The last of the butter—about a quarter of the final half stick—was spread on the part of the suit that would cover the soles of his feet. It took a lot of practice to get the amount just right.

Now the suit.

He paused for one last spot check. The suit was spread out on a piece of industrial plastic on the floor of the clean room, which he had been resanitizing for the past few days.

No holes. No thin spots in the material. The parts of all three zippers—the chains, the teeth, the sliders, the tape ends, the bottom stops—were in perfect working order.

It was ready. So was he.

He began to climb into the suit, a process that was studied, slow, and precise. An observer might liken the sight to a five-foot, six-inch, 126-pound stick bug wrapping itself in a thin white chrysalis tailor-made to its insectoid body. That is, if an observer had the patience to watch the entire process, which took the better part of two hours. He didn't time it. He focused on the task at hand. And the half stick really did make all the difference. The cleansing. The plastic. The shaving. The four and a half sticks of butter. The suit.

It all led to this.

He turned toward the mirror slowly, delaying the gratification for as long as he could stand it, but it was hard now, so hard. He raised his slender arms in the air as if to praise something that lived in space.

Turning, turning, *turning*, hearing nothing but the faint beat of his heart against his rib cage.

Finally, the mirror captured his image.

Ah, *there* he was.

No one.

chapter 3

The Library / Viewing Room

Sqweegel walked down two flights of stairs to his dark, damp basement. The plaster on the walls had chipped away in places, revealing the thin wood slats beneath. They had always reminded him of the rib cage showing through the torn carcass of a large beast. An animal that had been gutted by a larger, more savage animal.

He wanted to run his fingers over the wood slats, just as he had as a child, but a splinter at this point would mean another trip to the sewing room. And he was too eager to watch the clip he had in mind. It was more than ten years old, but he'd been fantasizing about it since first light. The footage had just popped into his imagination, unbidden.

Only later did he realize why. How it was a sign.

But that's how Sqweegel's mind worked. Making subconscious connections that would later aid his mission.

The most important mission of his mortal life.

Below ground level, the air smelled not just of death but of many deaths, fighting with one another. It was a sweet cologne of suffering, with aromatic notes painstakingly gathered over the last few decades. No other place on earth smelled like this; no other place could. It was instantly intoxicating.

He stepped into a small room, just off the first landing. The room was lined with custom-made wooden shelves, and nearly every inch of shelf space was filled with eight-millimeter film canisters.

His bony, latex-covered thumb glided along the labels:

Slut Redhead Before Wedding
4/17/92

Just the printed text on the label brought back snatches of memory: the bone-white lacy dress, torn, dirty, rolled up into a ball in the corner of the dungeon. The shivering pale bride, begging to know what she'd done wrong, struggling against her binds. Sqweegel telling her, *You know nothing about purity. It's a mockery to wear that dress, and now I'm going to show you what it's like to stand naked before God. . . .*

And then another label, another set of memories:

Vain TV News Whore
9/11/95

Oh, Sqweegel remembered *her* in vivid detail. She thought this grisly series of unsolved murders would be her big break. Ratings. A book deal. She bragged to her colleagues that she'd be the one to solve it, become her own *brand*. She needed a lesson in humility, and Sqweegel was only too happy to give it to her—her own video camera probing parts of her body she had never seen before. The juicy, dirty, hidden parts, expertly lit and shot and then mailed to the station for her viewers to see . . .

Self-Absorbed Mother Who Ignores Her Boy
3/30/97

You squeeze a life out into this world; then you turn your back on it? Let me show you what happens when God turns his back on you, my child. . . .

His thumb finally stopped on the one he wanted:

Senator's Cunt Mistress
7/28/98

Sqweegel plucked the canister from the shelf and brought it to the viewing room on the next level down. It was a fully sound-proofed home theater, constructed long before such things were in vogue. No fancy digital disc, or even video: Nothing beat the raw rush of images on film, speeding by at twenty-four frames per second.

After loading the film reel onto the projector and snapping it on, Sqweegel sat in a worn leather chair in the very center of the room and let the images on the screen wash over him.

Sqweegel's breath was hot with anticipation. He freed his cock from the murder suit and began to stroke it. Slowly at first.

But as the film unspooled, his fist moved up and down more urgently, violently, his eyes never leaving the screen.

He hadn't watched this one in a while. He'd forgotten how good it was.

He'd forgotten what her *insides* had looked like.

Sqweegel reversed the film and started again. He knew he would watch it dozens of times before dawn. He'd been watching so much surveillance footage these past few months that he needed a small diversion—a mental palate cleanser, of sorts. A reminder of who he was, and what he could do in the name of the Lord.

The film countdown flickered across the screen: 10, 9, 8 . . .

To watch the 8mm film, log into LEVEL26.com and enter the code: snuff

chapter 4

The eight-millimeter film flapped around the reel a few times before rolling out to leave a blank white screen. Nobody said a word, even after a few moments. Dead silence filled the room.

Not that you could blame them.

Tom Riggins scanned the faces gathered before him. A few minutes before, they were pumped. Excited to be called to the fabled Special Circs division at Quantico for this hush-hush meeting, all expenses paid. Some of them acted like they didn't give a shit, but Riggins could tell. The curiosity was killing them. He was counting on it.

And a few minutes before, they were like schoolkids before a midterm exam. Focused. Determined to succeed.

But now . . .

These were not just cops or forensic scientists. The people gathered here were the best of the best, and they'd been summoned

27

by the most elite law enforcement division in the country. But to Riggins—a man in his fifties with the lean, hard muscle of an ex–middleweight champ—they were a bunch of doe-eyed kids, some even bearing the faint traces of acne scars. This was nothing new. Everyone in Special Circs had started looking ridiculously young in the early 1990s, when momentum took over and Riggins realized he'd be a Special Circs lifer.

"You've just watched the handiwork of Sqweegel," Riggins said. "He's a psychopath who has shot, raped, maimed, poisoned, burned, strangled, and tortured upwards of fifty people in six countries over a span of more than twenty years."

Two decades, Riggins thought. The monster had started his work when some of the people in this room were still stuffing lunch boxes in book bags for their first day of school.

He continued.

"Sqweegel is a very patient killer. He takes his time between targets and expends an almost inhuman number of hours preparing. We only see his homework after he's struck. In some cases, the prep work stretches back *months*."

Riggins scanned the room. They appeared to be listening—or at least, they nodded at the right times. But he could tell they were still thinking about the piece of film they'd just watched.

Some of them even blinked rapidly, as if their eyelids could wash the images from their retinas.

Good luck with that, kids.

Special Circs had been born out of the Justice Department's ViCAP—Violent Criminal Apprehension Program—in the mid-1980s. The public knew all about ViCAP, a computerized think tank that attempted to track and compare serial killings. Cops and investigators everywhere could use ViCAP as a resource. But there were certain cases that no city police department—or even the FBI—was equipped to handle. Wanted to handle.

That's when they were flipped up to Special Circs.

Riggins knew better than anybody else that the burnout rate here in Special Circs was stunning—agents lasted anywhere from forty-eight hours to six months, tops. A spectacularly "long" run might be considered a year or two, but that usually ended in suicide, solitude, or sedation. You don't bounce from Special Circs into another career. You bounce into survival mode.

Special Circs was the little-known division that floated below the radar of the American public. Few newspapers covered Special Circs cases. They don't make TV specials about them. Their cases don't come up at cocktail parties in L.A., the Beltway, or Manhattan. They work cases most citizens never heard about, would never *want* to hear about, and certainly did not want to think possible.

If they did, they'd never leave the house.

Not that they'd be safe at home. A high percentage of the really twisted stuff happened behind front doors all over the country. Like the husband who found out his wife was running around with an old college boyfriend, then took a golf club and impaled her with it, from anal cavity to throat. The lab guys marveled at the sheer muscle it took this guy to force the steel rod through her entire body, past tough muscle and bone.

Then there was the fifteen-year-old meth head who searched everywhere in his house for his copy of *Vehicular Homicide*, the video game that he would play for hours on end to offset his tweaking. The kid looked and looked and looked; no game. Then his grandparents got all *intervention* on him, told him that they threw away that horrible game for his own good, and that he was going to a special place near the beach that would help him. The kid left the room, then returned with a power drill and proceeded to irrigate their ear canals, one at a time—right through a hearing aid, in the case of his grandfather, a Korean War vet. *You're not hearing me; you never listen to me,* he reportedly screamed at them as their blood and brain tissue rained down around him.

Riggins could list cases all night. The body parts in fruit jars. The pregnant slaves in the pit. The semen in the baby diaper.

This was all stuff nobody in their right mind wanted to think about for more than a few seconds.

This was the stuff he thought about all the time.

He lived for the dark side of man.

But this case at hand, and this snuff film they'd just watched . . .

Well, he could almost understand the silence.

chapter 5

Tom Riggins had never liked the Special Circs War Room. It looked too much like a college classroom—long, Formica-topped desks on four risers. Riggins stood at the bottom, in front of three screens. They were full-color, HD, next-generation smart screens that could move files, enhance photos, and update field operatives all with a single touch.

Which made him seem like a professor, addressing his students.

At fifty-three, Riggins almost looked the part. He dressed in dark, muted colors that suited his general demeanor. The only flash of color was the white on the ID badge that hung from his jacket pocket at all times. Riggins had been at Special Circs longer than anybody else. And what did he get for it? Three ex-wives, and two kids who hated his guts. An apartment he never saw, full of books he never read and a handful of CDs he never listened to. And a burgeoning alcohol problem.

He cleared his throat.

"Sqweegel is a Level 26 killer—the highest rank we now recognize, and about four ranks above what the rest of the world recognizes."

That got their attention. The CSIs in this room knew all about

31

the so-called Evil Scale, which ranked killers from the lowest ranks (cases of justifiable homicide, jealous lovers, abused teenagers fighting back) to the highest (torture-murderers, terrorists, sex killers). Mark David Chapman, the man who shot John Lennon, was a mere 7—basically, a homicidal narcissist. Ed Gein, who killed, boiled, and ate his victims, then tanned their flesh for use as lampshades, rated a 13. Ted Bundy rated a 17, while Gary Heidnik and John Wayne Gacy both topped the scales at 22. As far as the world knew, that was as bad as it got.

But over the past twenty years, Special Circs had encountered killers so extreme that they had been forced to add three new classifications to acknowledge that their skills and methods were far beyond those of Heidnik or Gacy. Their homicidal predilections ran beyond torture and rape; they believed themselves to be vengeful gods walking the earth, and possessed an almost superhuman ability to stalk and punish the victims, whom they considered inferior beings.

Most of these young agents could only dream about these so-called Level 25 killers. Such beings were so rare and so new, they hadn't even made it into the textbooks yet.

And now Riggins was telling them, essentially, that there was something out there even *worse*.

Someone whose skills *did* qualify as superhuman.

Riggins allowed them a few moments to let the number 26 sink in their brains; then he continued.

"Crime teams from Israel, Egypt, Germany, and Japan have tried to bring him to justice. Quantico alone has sent twenty operatives after him. They have all failed. His intelligence is off the charts, and he's never left a single piece of physical evidence."

This finally prompted the reaction Riggins wanted—skepticism. After all, physical evidence was where they ate and slept; it was the foundation of their professional lives. Saying there was no physical evidence was like telling an accountant *sorry, no numbers*.

A young CSI, female—from San Francisco, Riggins thought—spoke up.

"Not a single piece of evidence in over two decades? How is that even possible?"

"We believe that Sqweegel wears a suit—a kind of body condom that covers every square inch, helping him avoid forensic detection."

"A *body condom*?" San Francisco repeated. "Still, there have to be some trace elements of—"

"Nothing," Riggins said. "Every time a suspected Sqweegel case pops up, we send in a battalion and place everything that isn't nailed down into tiny little baggies. We've been unable to find any piece of him. No blood or body fluids of any kind, no hair. Not even a stray skin cell."

Another CSI—one from Chicago—asked, "How is he linked to his victims, if he leaves no trace? This sounds like a boogeyman somebody cooked up to clear a lot of open cases."

"If only," Riggins said. "No, we know about Sqweegel's activities because he likes to tell us about them. And from time to time, he sends along evidence."

"He's proud of himself. Showing off," offered San Francisco.

"Yes. And unlike some other serial killers, Sqweegel's not looking for media attention. He's happy just to let *us* know what he's doing. It's his life's work, and he sees us—Special Circs, specifically—as his chroniclers."

"Sqweegel," repeated a CSI from Philadelphia. There was a trace of laughter in his voice. "Where did the name come from? That some kind of Special Circs joke?"

"No," Riggins said. "The name came from one of his earliest murders—back around 1990, when he was still experimenting. There's nothing he loves more than an unconventional murder scene. Striking where you least expect it. Say, at a busy suburban car wash on a bright summer day."

All eyes were on him now. Like kids awaiting their bedtime story. *A car wash?*

"Mom pulls in," Riggins continued, "kid, about four years old, sitting in the front seat. He loves the car wash and wants to watch the wipers and the big floppy brushes and all of that. Well, about halfway through, the crew hears screaming. Horrible, anguished screams—and you could hear it over the noise of the machines. Nobody can tell where the hell it's coming from. They stop other cars from going in; they turn everything off. But by this time, the mom and her kid are almost out of the car wash, the driver's door is ajar, and there's soap and blood running down the driver's-side door. Manager freaks, gets his crew to seal off both entrance and exit—clearly, the monster who did this is still inside. They call the cops.

"The mother is just *gone*. Sliced up so thoroughly, we were still finding pieces of her in the car weeks later.

"The kid was untouched. He sat in the front seat and watched the whole thing.

"By this point, he was the only human being who'd ever seen Sqweegel and lived. So we questioned him. Asked him to de-scribe the man in the car wash.

"All he would say was *sqweegel. Sqweeeeeegel*. Imitating the sounds he heard while he watched his mother die."

Riggins looked around the room, then said, "The name kind of stuck."

After a few moments, the San Francisco CSI asked, "You said the staff guarded both exits. How did he get out of the car wash unseen?"

"He didn't."

"Sqweegel stayed inside?"

"We discovered that he'd hidden himself in there the night before. He must have snuck in just before closing, and then wormed his way up among the tubes and hoses. He was able to

34

bend his body to avoid the electric eyes that would normally trigger the next hose or brush to start moving, as well as the car wash's security system. Then he twisted and crammed his body up inside the metal frame that holds the foam applicators and scrubbers in place. There's barely enough room for a house cat up there, but somehow he forced himself to fit inside. And then he stayed there for at least eighteen hours, perfectly still, even as a million moving parts whirled and buzzed around him."

Riggins let that sink in, then continued.

"The attack on the mother took place midafternoon. Best we can tell, Sqweegel was waiting for the right victim to come rolling down the conveyor system."

"You still haven't told us how he got out."

Riggins was feeling a little better about this whole thing now. A few of these kids—San Francisco and Philly—seemed genuinely curious.

"Sqweegel hid in the trunk of the car. Below the pullout floor panel, where you're supposed to keep an extra tire? He curled himself up in there, like a fetus in a womb, knees under his chin, thighs pressed up against his chest, feet bent back at an unnatural position . . . and he waited. We think it was at least a day before he let himself out—right there in the middle of our garage. And the only reason we know is because he left us a note."

Their blank stares were downright unnerving.

What Riggins hadn't told them was that the note was left *on his desk*. Freaked him right out. Still did, to be perfectly honest.

So did the next part, which he shared with the class:

"We received a new Sqweegel message yesterday morning."

chapter 6

Riggins had opened the package personally. An eight-millimeter canister packed inside a standard FedEx box. The label read: "Senator's Cunt Mistress —7/28/98," which was what he'd played for them a few minutes before. The clip showed the brutal torture-murder of Lisa Summers—a woman believed to be romantically linked to a certain U.S. senator back in the late 1990s. An oldie but goodie.

This, too, was how Sqweegel operated. Telling his own tale out of chronological order. The handwritten notes and evidence and audiotapes and—in this case—films were selected and sent in a sequence that meant something to Sqweegel. Even if no one in Quantico knew what that was. What they knew for certain was that the arrival of a new reel of film meant that Sqweegel was signaling the beginning of something else.

"The new mailing included the film you just watched," Riggins explained. "What's worrisome is the timing. He sent us a note a week ago, and another a week before that. Usually, he waits months—sometimes years. For some reason, he's ramping up."

"Escalating," said San Francisco.

"Yes," Riggins replied. "After a few years abroad, we believe he's returned to America. All victims were on the East Coast—three in Manhattan alone. Just a stone's throw from where you're sitting right now. This guy is kicking on our back door, trying to get our attention. Well, we'd like to give it to him before he claims another life. Our *utmost* attention."

What Riggins couldn't share with the class: The shockwaves had reached the top brass at the Department of Justice in record time. And strangely, they had spread to other branches of the government, too.

Within hours the secretary of defense himself was personally applying pressure to Special Circs to wrap this case up . . . *imediately*. Riggins was a little mystified by the muscle. Yes, this was a serious threat. The idea of a Level 26 killer loose in the world was terrifying. And yes, Sqweegel seemed to be ready to do something bigger and bolder than ever. But Sqweegel had been killing for a long time. And the new message didn't explain the offer he had been empowered to make to the operatives gathered in this room.

But he had to make it anyway.

That was the whole point of this morning meeting.

"You are the elite," Riggins said. "The best in this country at what you do. So here's the offer, straight from the top. Take this monster down, and you'll receive full salary for life. A twenty-five-million-dollar bonus. Complete erasure of your identity. A clean slate and the kind of life most of us can only dream of. This is a career maker, and at the same time, your golden parachute."

He paused to let the image sink in.

"So who wants it?"

Riggins waited expectantly.

Again, a deafening silence filled the room. Everyone still seemed a bit stunned by the one-two punch of the snuff film and

Riggins's talk. Blank faces gazed at one another with staggered eye contact.

Everyone tried to deflect—looking at one another like school-children, praying that one of them, just *one of them*, knew the answer to the damned algebra problem. Or more likely, praying that one of them, just *one of them*, wasn't terrified out of his or her mind by what they had just seen on the screen.

Riggins waited, but he knew what had probably happened. Word had leaked. When they were summoned from their home units, they started talking to each other—even though they were on strict orders not to utter a syllable about the trip.

Maybe even the name "Sqweegel" came up—it was quite possible that their colleagues or their bosses had assisted on the earlier hunts for the monster. They were here because they were smart kids; a few of them would have pieced it together.

And at some point in the last twelve hours, one of them had figured out that every agent who took the lead on the Sqweegel case ended up either dead or on life support in barely recognizable human form.

So in the end, Riggins received the result he knew he'd receive—even as his superiors ordered him to go through the motions:

Nobody came forward.

Riggins wanted to yell at them. Hurl his coffee cup. Shatter it on one of their pimply, Ivy League–educated skulls. Ask them *why they're in this if they didn't really want to be in this.*

But no. That wouldn't do any good.

Even Riggins had to admit that the offer was on the absurd side. Just like the government to throw piles of money at problems they only pretended to understand. Hell, all the money in the world wouldn't matter if you ended up dead—or worse. And that was a certainty when it came to Sqweegel.

He was a predator of men unlike any other. As lethal as a knife in your skull, but as immaterial as a phantom.

There was only one man even remotely qualified for this case. The one man who had locked eyes with Sqweegel and managed to survive the encounter.

The same man who would never, *ever* take it.

chapter 7

The classroom was now empty, the students long departed for home. Riggins wondered whether he'd just single-handedly shattered the confidence of every decent CSI from coast to coast. Nobody likes to admit they can't handle something, that a case is too frightening for them.

Riggins had known that this was a bad idea from the beginning. He wished he'd listened to his gut instead of his superiors. It wasn't their fault, either. They were reacting to orders from on high themselves.

Constance Brielle approached, put her hand on Riggins's shoulder, squeezed it a little. "They're ready down the hall."

"Great," Riggins said. "*Awesome*. Isn't that what you kids say?"

"I wouldn't know, Tom. I haven't been a kid for fifteen years."

"Bah. You're still a kid."

"Somehow, coming from you, that's sort of sweet."

She tried to smile at him, and Riggins appreciated that. He liked Constance because she reminded him of Dark, before all of the crazy shit happened to him. Constance was smart. Tough. Drawn to the flame, but agile enough to avoid being consumed by it. She got off on recognition of her skills. One kind word—even a casual *attaboy*—was enough to fuel her for months.

She was also an extraordinarily pretty woman, with full ruby lips and precise little hands that drew your attention. Her dark hair was pulled back behind her head with a no-nonsense clip, revealing the elegant angles of her face. Not that Riggins would ever consider making a move. He'd gone that route before, and it accounted for one of the ex-wives who now wished him dead.

"Come on," Riggins said. "Let's get this over with."

An international conference call had been scheduled for eight thirty that morning.

A consortium of forensic psychiatrists from the top crime-fighting agencies in the world—including those from Italy, Japan, and France—had recently pieced together the criteria for a Level 26 killer and strongly urged immediate action. Those countries had pooled their money and were now awaiting the name and CV of the Special Circs agent who would be leading this new, no-holds-barred task force dedicated to capturing Sqweegel.

The secretary of defense himself, Norman Wycoff, would also be present, at the request of none other than the president of the United States. Apparently, Sqweegel had joined the short list of national security risks.

All eyes would be on Riggins in a matter of minutes. He'd never been more on the spot than he was right now. He could feel the perspiration beginning to collect on the back of his neck and knew it wouldn't be long before he sweated through his black suit.

Constance led the way down the hall, then positioned herself in front of a bank of monitors and slipped on a headset.

Riggins stood behind her, bracing himself.

The world wanted answers but Riggins had none. All he could hear was the pulse-hammering footsteps of Norman Wycoff thundering down the hallway.

To join the U.N. conference call, log into
LEVEL26.com and enter the code: dark

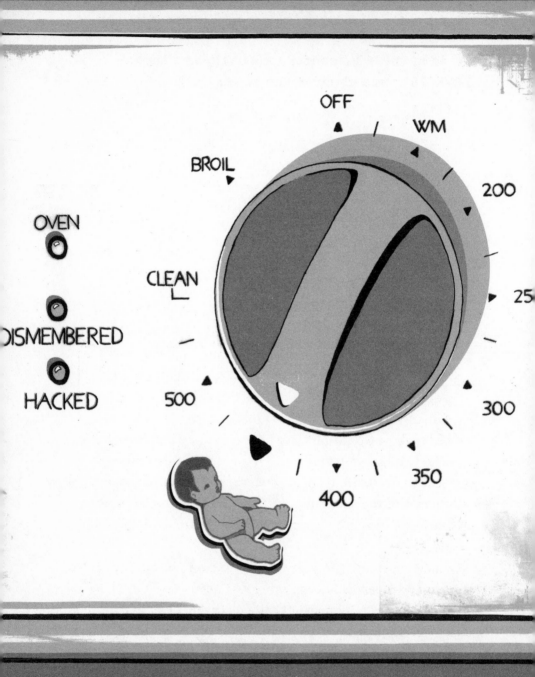

chapter 8

T he meeting had been brief, and exactly the kind of utter and complete abortion Riggins had expected.

Namely because Riggins didn't—couldn't—tell them what they wanted to hear. No one wanted the job of chasing Sqweegel.

But the secretary of defense made matters worse when he pulled rank on Riggins in front of everyone—Constance and the Special Circs support staff, as well General Costanza from Italy, General St. Pierre from France, and Minster Yako from Japan—all of them the top law enforcement officers in their respective countries. It was like being upbraided in front of the whole world.

And as a result, the offer of $25 million pooled from Italy, France, and Japan had been swiftly rescinded.

Now Robert Dohman—the secretary of defense's hatchet man—led Riggins down the tarmac to the Boeing C-32 that was serving under the call sign Air Force Two. Dohman was either

45

doing a poor job of making small talk or doing an excellent job of annoying Riggins.

"So nobody took the offer, huh," Dohman said.

Riggins gave a tight smile. "I'm sure you heard what happened in the teleconference, Dohman. Your boss doesn't keep you on *that* short a leash."

"Did you mention the bonus?"

"Yes, seeing as that was a key part of the offer."

"And nobody bit? Not a single one of your agents could use an extra twenty-five million?"

Dohman had bushy eyebrows, a bad comb-over, melanoma-addled skin. There was a black leather briefcase handcuffed to his beefy wrist.

This fuckhead knew exactly what had happened in that disastrous teleconference. Riggins admitted that nobody had taken the offer. Talks went tits up, and everyone left the room angry, including Riggins.

And of course, General Costanza—Italy's top crime fighter—had to go and bring up Dark's name, which then got the secretary of defense in a lather. How many times could he tell them that Dark was out? Dead and gone, when it came to Special Circs.

Riggins wasn't even sure that Dark shouldn't be arrested, considering the things he suspected he had done after walking away from Special Circs.

No matter—the secretary hadn't believed Riggins. Because a short while later Dohman stopped by personally to escort Riggins to Dulles. The secretary of defense was making a trip west anyway, and it was suggested that Riggins join him.

Suggested, in the same way that an umpire *suggests* that a batter is out.

chapter 9

Air Force Two is not what you'd imagine—all polished wood and leather chairs and scotch in beveled glass tumblers and the lingering scent of Macanudo cigars.

It is more like the floating conference room of a slightly disorganized corporation, cluttered with paper and files and plastic foam cups and discarded sugar packets and a bunch of bleary-eyed guys in shirtsleeves and ties with coffee breath and damp underarms.

And like every other office in the world, Riggins dryly noted, you couldn't even smoke in it.

But at least most companies let you step outside for a nicotine fix. Step outside here, and you'd plunge forty thousand feet to your death, the bright orange tip of your cigarette marking your descent.

Not that he had time for a cigarette. The secretary of defense was in the process of crawling up his ass.

"What was that bullshit in there about you ruling out our best chance of capturing this sick little bastard?"

The country rarely saw this side of Norman Wycoff, America's most passionate defender—and, at times, avenger. Oh, the media occasionally reported stories about his temper, but that was chalked up to being part of his charm. Secretary Wycoff wasn't vindictive; he was passionate about keeping this nation safe from terrorists. He wasn't prone to fits; he liked to make his points.

But they should see Wycoff now. Blue veins bulging out of his ordinarily placid-looking head, and the beginnings of dark circles under his sharp brown eyes. The secretary was famous for looking like the personification of steely confidence no matter the forum, be it an audience of one or one million. Now it looked like whatever taut string holding it all together in his brain had gone *snap*, and he was coming undone.

So here Riggins was, sitting in the cluttered heart of the American empire, being yelled at by the man charged with keeping it safe.

"Respectfully," Riggins said, "I thought we covered this in the meeting, Mr. Secretary."

"Every person I talked to in Special Circs thinks he's the man for the job," Wycoff said. "Why is that? And why are you being so fucking stubborn?"

Riggins sighed. "Dark is not an option."

"You two were close, as I understand it," Wycoff said. "You could bring him back, if you wanted."

Riggins wanted to scream, *How? By laying my hands on his head and exorcising him of his demons? By raising his family from the dead?*

This was exactly the reason he hadn't wanted Dark mentioned in the teleconference. Once Dark was mentioned, then Dark would have to be explained, and once these guys heard about Dark, then of course, hell yeah, they'd want him on the case. Who wouldn't? Dark *was* the man for the job. But it just wasn't going to happen.

Riggins tried to explain it again in a way that would penetrate the secretary of defense's thick fucking skull. Yes, Riggins thought, it was time to break out the visuals.

"Two years ago, Rome," Riggins said. "Dark was the lead agent on the Sqweegel case. We think he came closer to catching him than anyone had in twenty years."

"You *think*," Dohman said.

"We have no evidence, but it soon became clear that Dark rattled Sqweegel. Because Sqweegel retaliated."

"I know, I know," Wycoff said, annoyed. "Against his foster family. It was a tragic loss. But you'd think that would have this Dark itching for payback."

"You don't understand," Riggins said. "Dark had a pretty traumatic childhood. Luckily, he doesn't remember much of it." Riggins remembered what he'd been able to dig up all those years ago about Dark's early childhood, when the man had first started working for him. Stuff Dark himself didn't even know, and never would if Riggins had anything to say about it.

"What he does remember is being raised by a warm and loving foster family in California. Typical story, really—parents think they can't conceive, they adopt, and then boom, they get pregnant, a boy. Boom, pregnant again, a girl. But they loved Dark unconditionally, and Dark felt the same way. They were everything to him. They were the storybook ending every foster kid dreams about. And then . . ."

Riggins reached into his bag, pulled out a manila folder. "It's better if you see for yourself."

He handed Wycoff the file.

"Take a good look at what happened to Dark's foster family. His mother, Laura, fifty-four years old. Victor, his father, fifty-nine years old. Rose, Victor's mother, eighty-three. Younger brother, Evan, thirty-two. Younger sister, Callie, twenty-nine. And her daughter, Emma, eight months.

"Take a look and understand why Dark will never come anywhere near this case."

Wycoff opened the file, flipped through the crime-scene photographs. Riggins watched him carefully. Was any of this getting to him? The children, shot in the face? The baby, discovered in the oven? Riggins was more than a little surprised when Wycoff wiped beneath his eye, sniffled, then handed the file back to Riggins. Good God. Was the secretary of defense crying a little?

"I understand the situation," Wycoff said, voice wavering a little. "But there's been a new development. Bob?"

Dohman leaned forward. He still wore the faint trace of a *Serves you right* smile.

"Last night the White House communications office received an encrypted video recording. NSA decrypted it for us and immediately sent it back, marked 'eyes only.'"

Dohman looked at his boss, who nodded. Dohman placed his thumb on the lock interface of the briefcase. Wycoff's thumb joined his a second later. Something beeped. The lock opened. Inside, fitted in a custom-made cradle, was a single memory stick.

Dohman lifted the stick out of the cradle and handed it to Riggins.

"This clip is designed to play just once. Once it's loaded onto a laptop computer, it will play, then permanently erase. It cannot be copied."

Sure, this message will self-destruct, blah blah, Riggins thought. But it still didn't explain why he was dragged onto Air Force Two for some one-on-one.

"Well . . . you got a laptop handy?"

Dohman frowned. "It's not for you. It's for Dark."

chapter 10

Riggins wanted to scream.

He didn't *care* if he was standing in front of the secretary of defense. One of the most frustrating things about this job, Riggins thought, was dealing with assholes with the unique ability to hear only what they wanted to hear, no matter how loud you shouted. Instead, he took a deep breath.

"I told you before: Dark's out. There is no Dark. As far as we're concerned, Dark is dead."

Wycoff said, "Well, it looks like you're going to have to perform a resurrection, then."

Riggins lowered his head. Wycoff still thought this was a matter of choice, but Riggins knew better. After Sqweegel had single-handedly slaughtered Dark's foster family—*and* set fire to their home in some kind of sick final insult—Dark handed in his papers and went rogue. Dropped off the radar completely. At first, Riggins thought Dark had gone somewhere to disappear, possibly even killed himself.

But then the sightings began—Dark in Tel Aviv. Dark in Glasgow. Dark in Beijing. Dark all over the world, tracking down Sqweegel leads on his own. Always near the scene of a horrific murder that could well have been the work of Sqweegel—*could have been*, but none were confirmed as his handiwork. Yet. Only Dark knew how close he'd gotten the second time, and as far as Riggins knew, he wasn't telling. If Riggins had a nickel for every time during that year he had told a foreign liaison that *no, Dark is not with Special Circs; it must be someone else* . . . well, maybe he would have pulled the plug earlier.

Dark definitely wasn't with Special Circs. Not in name or in mind. Riggins heard he was ignoring police procedure altogether, bribing and torturing his way through various international underworlds in an attempt to find anyone who might have assisted or supplied Sqweegel at any point. Riggins thought he must have come up empty.

Because a year ago, the sightings had stopped. Dark had given up.

So why would he jump in again now?

There was just no way.

"Mr. Secretary—" Riggins started. He wanted to continue with *go fuck yourself.* But again, he held back, took a short breath. You don't work thirty-five years to flame out in two seconds.

Dohman stepped in. "Tom, there's something you don't know. What I'm about to verbalize is classified."

Of course it was. That's why he wasn't even allowed to bring Constance along for this trip—and Riggins trusted her with everything.

"Okay," Riggins said, the stress of the night finally settling in on his nerves. He'd had enough for one day. Where was the guy who filled the drinks around here?

"The video on that stick is of a gruesome murder," Dohman said. "Every second, in high fidelity."

"Sqweegel's done that before," Riggins said. "He likes to—"

"No, Tom. You don't understand. This is *not* like anything that monster has done before."

Riggins loved how it was all *Tom* now. Like they were old college buddies.

Wycoff, meanwhile, was staring out the window, a fist curled up against his mouth. The night sky looked like it had been painted with the darkest hue of blue available. Only a few pinpoints of starlight made it through.

Dohman looked over at his boss, as if for moral support, but Wycoff didn't respond. Bobby D'oh!—as they liked to call him around Special Circs—was on his own with this one.

"The victim was someone of interest to the president."

"What? Who?" Riggins asked, but already his mind was reeling. Good Christ—did that crazy bastard breach White House security and rape the First Lady? Or maybe one of the president's family members back at home in Illinois?

"Can you give me a little more?"

"That I can't do."

Riggins sighed. He really, really could use a gallon of whiskey, some ice. But instead he was stuck here on Air Force Two, playing guessing games with a guy who should know better.

"I can't tell you," Riggins said, "how much this hampers any potential investigation. If you're worried about leaks, let me assure you—"

"We're not worried about leaks," Dohman said.

"Then what?"

"Just bring the stick to Dark. We believe he'll take the case once he sees this."

"With all respect, gentlemen, Mr. Secretary," Riggins said, "fucking forget Dark! I've said it a dozen ways, and I'll keep saying it until it finally sticks."

"Not an option," Dohman said. "We need Dar—"

Wycoff snapped his head around and cut his underling off midsentence.

"Enough!" he barked. "Yes, I hear you, Riggins. But hear *me* now: You have no choice. I'm through fucking around. This is an election year. This thing gets out, even if only a *piece* of it hits the fucking blogs or newspapers, the president kisses reelection good-bye. It also sends one hell of a message around the country. You want to know what message that is, Riggins? It says, in big neon letters, *'You are not fucking safe.'* See, we've come up with this creepy little scale of evil, and guess what: This monster's worse than Bundy, Gacy, Heidnik, Gein, the Son of Sam, and everybody else you use to scare the shit out of your kids when they want to stay out late. This little prick can kill anyone he wants, anytime—even those close to the leader of your country."

Riggins was now dying to know what had happened. Who the hell could it be that nobody would even let him see the recording?

He thought about the oldie but goodie Sqweegel had sent yesterday—the "Senator's Cunt Mistress." They knew the identity of *that* victim: a woman rumored to have been the longtime par-amour of former Senate minority whip Thom Jensen, her de-stroyed body found more than ten years ago. The new tape would send the original investigators—if any had survived this long—back to the case files, revisiting a macabre tale they knew only too well.

But that didn't help them with this new murder. One that struck the Oval Office at point-blank range. If both victims had connections in Washington, was Sqweegel sending Special Circs a hint?

"Anyway," Wycoff said, "that's all for the record. Off the re-cord, Dark takes this mission or we'll have you executed."

The cabin went quiet.

chapter 11

Make no mistake: The secretary of defense *can* wipe out any domestic operative, American civilian, or resident living within U.S. borders. It's not strictly constitutional, but then again, what's constitutional is often a matter of interpretation. The events of 9/11 made sure of that. Made it easier to hide missions and divisions and operations that have been going on for years.

There is a separate division at the secretary's personal command for such removal of unwanted parties. The rumored name: Dark Arts.

Dark Arts has never appeared on the books or in official files. There are no checks cut. Instead, there are billions in cash to rid the nation of such headaches, tucked away deep in the walls of the Pentagon. The Dark Arts unit was couched in the spirit of "national security." A license to kill anyone, anytime, for any reason when it is in the best interests of the Republic.

Riggins had heard of them over the years. He'd come across crime scenes originally thought to be the work of a new gifted serial killer, but then official word would be handed down: "No further investigation required. Thank you for your cooperation."

And that would be it.

Now Secretary of Defense Norman Wycoff was essentially confirming the existence of such a unit.

Riggins sat in dumbfounded silence. It took a lot to flummox a man like Riggins, who had truly seen it all in his years with Special Circs. This, though . . . this was unreal. As if on cue, a broad-shouldered woman in a tuxedo shirt and bow tie stepped forward to refresh Riggins's whiskey and ice.

"I think we understand each other?" Wycoff asked.

"Yeah," Riggins said, still partially numb.

"Good."

Dohman handcuffed the briefcase to Riggins's wrist, then pressed Riggins's thumb to the keypad. Something beeped. There. *His* problem now.

It was up to Riggins to make Dark commit . . . or else.

"Good luck," said Dohman.

I always thought my career would end in death, Riggins thought. *But I had no idea it'd be from people on my own team. Never saw this one coming.* It was a hell of a choice he'd have to make: Bring Dark, the closest thing he had to a friend or a son, back into the fold against every instinct he had—or choose his own death instead.

Riggins took a swig of his whiskey. Ice cubes rested against his lip with every sip. He already needed a refill.

Endless refills.

The secretary of defense split for his private quarters on the plane—borrowed from the vice president, presumably—with several aides trailing after him like lemmings.

Two serious-looking men stayed behind. They eyed Riggins, who eyed them back. Riggins had noted them before and assumed they were Secret Service.

"Hello, fellas," Riggins said.

One, with a buzz cut so short, his white hair seemed to glisten, stared at Riggins. He didn't offer his hand. Riggins didn't offer his, either.

"My name is Agent Nellis," the man with the buzz cut said. "I'll be your liaison with the Department of Defense."

"Nellis, huh," said Riggins, waiting a beat. Then, "Who's your boyfriend?"

The other man introduced himself as McGuire. No first name offered, no exact rank. McGuire simply said he'd be assisting Nellis for the duration of their assignment. Riggins glanced down and noticed that McGuire was missing two fingers—the ring and pinkie—on his right hand. He wondered what that assignment might be, then realized he already knew the answer.

Within a few hours the plane was preparing to land in Los Angeles. Nellis and McGuire remained silent, despite Riggins's sporadic attempts to strike up an innocuous conversation. Even football talk failed—and these two slabs of meat looked like former college linebackers from two different generations. So Riggins gave up and settled in for a long and steady drinking session. He even sweet-talked the rest of the bottle out of the woman in the tuxedo shirt and convinced her to leave the ice bucket as well.

Finally, a few minutes before final approach, Nellis leaned forward and briefed Riggins.

"Dark has forty-eight hours to commit," Nellis explained. "If he fails to commit by the deadline, you're out. Do you understand?"

"Yeah," Riggins said, "I understand."

And he did. Nellis and McGuire weren't Secret Service or regular DOD staffers. *No*, Riggins thought, *I do believe I've just met two agents from Dark Arts.*

He eased back into his airline chair, which was wide and comfortable. A gift from the taxpayers. Then he rested his head back and shut his eyes. Sqweegel had his movies? So did Riggins. In fact, he had a front-row seat to his own life, flashing inside of his eyelids.

He wondered whether he had a chance of convincing Dark. Or whether he even *wanted* to.

These Dark Arts guys, with their obviously fake names—air force bases, Riggins noted dryly—would be immune to reasoning. You don't bargain with stone professionals. You don't try to appeal to their inner children. They were there to do their jobs, not better their souls. Ordinarily, Riggins would have really liked these guys. Guys who don't fuck around, guys who shoot straight.

He wondered just how straight they shot.

Riggins looked down at the waterproof digital watch on his wrist. It had been a gift from his daughter, what—a half dozen years ago? She said she didn't know what he liked, so she picked this up in a mall. Riggins said it was perfect. She told him *whatever*. Riggins thumbed the watch until it reached its countdown function, set the time for forty-eight hours, then hit START.

Funny thing, watching your life slip away by seconds.

48:00 . . .

47:59 . . .

47:58 . . .

Riggins wanted to hole up in a cheap hotel room with a cheap woman and drink cheap scotch until he was sweating the stuff from every single pore. He wanted to forget what he did for a living, because what he did for a living was about to get him killed. But instead Riggins allowed his eyelids to fall, no longer trying to fight the need to sleep, knowing it was futile.

To witness Riggins's fate, log into LEVEL26.com
and enter the code: 4shadow

chapter 12

Waves smashed over Malibu Beach. Dark watched them and took another pull from his beer.

He never tired of looking at the ocean and feeling the salty mist that washed back over his face. It was a little taste of forever, right there on the sand.

The beer helped, too.

Dark had a deeply tanned face, with jagged lines marking the years—especially under his eyes. Squint and you could almost mistake him for malnourished. But his body was all lean muscle, stretched taut over a broad and tall frame. It looked like it had been chiseled from granite. He kept an anchor-style beard—heavier under the nose and mouth, neatly trimmed along his jaw-line. The hair on his head hadn't been trimmed in months. Most of the time, Dark preferred to cinch it up in back and forget about it.

Dark came here—to this particular spot on the shoreline—every morning. He blinked slowly and deliberately. Not in time to the waves, or in reaction to the lashing spray carried by the ocean wind, but to his own heartbeat. He didn't want to become part of the awesome display in front of him—the thunderous waves crashing, spewing foam onto the pebbled shore, the hermit crabs scurrying and digging and hiding. He just wanted to watch.

Dark took another drink. He always started with beer—nothing stronger. When you've retired in your midthirties, you want to ease into your morning. Besides, the point wasn't ripping straight into oblivion. It was maintaining that line between reality and oblivion. He lived in the salty mist between ocean and shore.

And then all of a sudden he knew someone was approaching from behind.

He didn't claim to have batlike radar. But after coming to this crest for 136 consecutive days, Dark had developed a very specific catalog of sights and sounds and smells. If one little detail was off, it stood out like a burst of red in a black-and-white photograph. He'd always been this way, able to tell when the slightest detail was off in any given situation. It was why he was the best. Had been, anyway.

Dark heard shoes—leather shoes on the sand.

The person was walking with resolve, but he wasn't hurrying. As the visitor ascended the crest, he started breathing a bit heavier. An older man.

Dark pulled himself up to a standing position, then slowly turned to face his visitor, who was backlit by the morning sun.

Good Christ.

Riggins.

Dark had another slug of beer and barely had returned the bottle to resting position when Riggins held out his hand. Dark gave him the bottle. Riggins glanced at the label, nodded in quiet approval, then took a good long pull. He handed the bottle back.

Dark looked at his ex-boss, waiting. He mentally crossed off reasons for Riggins being here. Social call? No. Riggins wasn't exactly a social animal. Not a single piece of communication had ever passed between them that wasn't about Special Circs business. If Riggins were to say "Happy birthday," it'd be followed by a manila folder full of photographed atrocities, not a Hallmark card.

Nor could Riggins be here to try to convince Dark to take a case, because he knew *Riggins knew* that was impossible. When Dark left, he had made it clear that nothing Riggins could say—nothing anybody could say—would ever bring him back. Besides, Dark had broken too many laws himself for him to be welcomed back into the bosom of law enforcement. He was damaged goods.

He was also retired. At thirty-six years old.

Dark took another sip of beer. Maybe if he drank enough, the genie would go back into the bottle.

But no.

He was still there. Riggins grinned, then looked out over the surf. Dark could guess what was going through the man's mind: *Yeah. Nice. A little boring. But nice.*

"Beer's great and all," Riggins said, "but I've been all the hell over Southern California tracking down your new address—which was no easy task. Where can we get a good cup of strong coffee?"

chapter 13

Riggins took his black. Dark opted for tap water, to which the waitress decided to add a wedge of lemon. Dark didn't want the lemon; he just wanted to drink something that wouldn't fight the beer in his system.

They sat at a small table near the windows of a casual diner perched at the edge of the Santa Monica Pier. It was impossible to see the ocean from their table. Riggins had chosen the table.

"When you left us," Riggins said, "Sqweegel was at twenty-nine confirmed murders. You know how he got to thirty-five. With what might have happened in the last few years . . ." Riggins paused and looked sharply at Dark but got no response. "He could be up to forty-eight, fifty people by now. And no one's been able to catch this son of a bitch—not even close. But his last string of murders has us all concerned. There's a ton of interest from on high."

This was supposed to be Dark's cue to ask, *on high?* Or raise an eyebrow. Or something. Instead Dark used his straw to push the lemon wedge down to the bottom of his glass. He didn't look at Riggins. He didn't need to. Dark knew the expression that would be on his face.

"They've even come up with a new classification for him," Riggins continued. "You know how it topped out at twenty-five? Well, Sqweegel's now our poster boy for level twenty-six."

Dark said nothing. He continued to examine the drowned wedge of lemon impaled on the shaft of plastic.

"There's something else," Riggins said.

Dark heard Riggins place his briefcase on the table. The twin *clak-claks* of the clasps opening. And even though he kept his attention on the wedge of lemon he was trying to drown, Dark couldn't help but see the small silver memory stick that Riggins was pushing across the table.

"For your eyes only. They didn't even let me see it."

Dark glanced at it, but he didn't touch it. He took another drink of water.

"Which," Riggins continued, "is pretty unusual, wouldn't you say?"

Nothing from Dark.

"You want to know where it came from? Let me give you a hint. He's running for his job again, and if he gets it, he'll be there another four years."

Still nothing.

"Look," Riggins said, exasperated, "this is do or die for me. My last case, either way it plays out."

There was something different in his voice now. Dark looked up.

"What do you mean?"

"Take a look behind you. Three tables back, by the railing."

Dark didn't turn around. Didn't need to. There were two men in suits a few tables away, pushing some egg whites and toast around their plates. They didn't wear black suits—this wasn't a 1950s noir movie, after all—but their Southern California business attire and *Hey, we're just having a bite before the big meeting*

65

attitude didn't fool Dark. He could see the bulges, concealing both firearms and blades. They were operatives of some kind.

Nellis listened to the rough voice in his ear.

"Well?" Wycoff asked. "Is Dark in or out?"

The secretary had been checking in more or less every hour on the hour since they'd left Air Force Two. Riggins had landed and realized that none of his old addresses for Dark were valid. Riggins had made some calls, drove around L.A. deep into the night. Wycoff would ask, "Well what the fuck is he doing now?" Nellis would have to respond, "He's driving up and down the Pacific Coast Highway, Mr. Secretary."

This morning, however, Riggins had finally located Dark's new address and had tracked him to the beach. Now they were here. About eighteen hours into the mission, it looked like Riggins would have his answer, one way or the other.

"Standing by for confirmation," Nellis told a little transmitter on his watch.

"I saw them when we came in," Dark said. "I assumed they were here with you."

"Yeah," Riggins said, then gave a half laugh. "They're with me. They're all the hell over me."

"What do you mean?"

Riggins leaned in closer. "I've got about thirty hours to turn this case around."

"Right," Dark said. "I'm almost finished with my water and I need to go walk my dogs. Just spit it out."

"I am," he said. "And I'm telling you, *I've got thirty hours.*"

Dark looked at the two operatives in the reflection of one of the diner's windows. One of them was pretending to eat, but the other—who had missing fingers on his right hand—glanced over at Riggins a second too long.

"Or what?" Dark asked.

Riggins didn't reply.

But Dark understood all at once.

He talked Dark back into the Sqweegel case, or he was a dead man.

chapter 14

This made no sense to Dark—Riggins being here, the goons trailing him, this ticking clock. Sure, if you screwed up in Special Circs, your career ended in one of three ways: demotion, dismissal, or death.

But death usually came by the hand of the monsters you pursued. Not the people in charge.

Dark sat back in his chair, staring at his former boss. How was he supposed to answer? There was no way he could come back to Special Circs. Not in a million fucking years. But if what Riggins said was true—that his freaking *life* depended on this—then how was he supposed to say no?

Finally, Dark spoke. "Look, Riggins, I don't know what this is about, but I can't. You know I can't. You more than anybody."

"I know what you went through. Believe me. I think about your family every fucking day."

"So how can you expect me to change my mind? Why did you even come here?"

"I came here for *your* sake."

"Oh, yeah? How's that?"

"Let's say you do say no," Riggins said, "and they ice me. Think they're just going to give up and walk away? Please. They're only going to come back and ask you directly. Ask you harder. Maybe even involve your wife. Her family. Whatever it takes."

Dark lowered his head and clenched his fists. This was insane. An hour ago he was on the beach, drinking a beer, watching the waves. Now it felt like somebody had wrapped a leather strap around his neck and was dragging him out to the ocean to drown.

"I'm not asking you to save me," Riggins said. "Promote me, demote me, kill me, poke me in the ass—I truly don't care. I'm a couple of decades past my sell-by date anyway. But see it my way for a second. If you agree to help me, we can do this on *our* terms. You won't even have to be actively involved—you'd just be an adviser. But if you say no, and they get rid of me, they're not going to give up on you. That's because everybody knows you're the only one who has a chance of catching this sick little bastard."

"But I couldn't, remember?"

Riggins paused. "Only because you stopped trying."

Dark stood up from his chair and leaned in over the table, resting his palms on the greasy top, to face Riggins. He thought about his lost year. About the bones he'd shattered. The blood he'd spilled. And he tried to resist the urge to reach out and wrap his hands around his former boss's throat.

Instead he said, "Don't you fucking accuse me of not trying."

And then Dark left, jamming his hands into his pockets and making his way up the pier toward Ocean Avenue. He watched the children run around their mothers, who sipped at oversized iced coffees like they were the only thing keeping them from losing their minds. The sun was already hot and burning off the mist.

As he reached the top of the pier, Dark thumbed the smooth edge of the memory stick in his pocket.

He wondered how long it would be before Riggins noticed he'd taken it.

chapter 15

Malibu, California

Sibby Dark was in the shower, hot water pulsing down her naked back, as she pondered the text message she'd received this morning.

It had been a while since the last one. Maybe a few weeks? She'd stopped keeping track, hoped that maybe it was over.

But this morning, just minutes after Steve rolled out of bed to take his breakfast beer down to the beach, her cell phone had chimed the opening riff to Depeche Mode's "Personal Jesus." The very sound of it made her heart race, even though she was barely awake. She plucked her phone from her bedside table and read the text on the screen:

SOON THE LORD WILL BE WITH YOU

Typical.

For some reason, her little cell-phone stalker liked to send her weird quotes that sounded like they came from the Bible. Which was why she'd assigned the Depeche Mode song to it—mostly as a joke. Her stalker was her own little Personal Jesus, she reasoned, trying to freak her out. Sibby's dad had taught her the best way to deal with annoying pests: Ignore them or laugh at them. Pests are looking for a reaction or validation; silence or ridicule takes both options off the table.

Still, the texts were annoying.

The first text was what . . . eight months ago? At first Sibby had texted back, typing "WRONG NUMBER." But her little Personal Jesus had refused to give up, some days sending as many as a dozen texts, sometimes only one or two:

I CAME TO YOU AS AN ANGEL

DO YOU FEEL MY LIFE, BLESSED MOTHER?

She'd also tried blocking the incoming texts, which were popping up as an "unknown caller." But within minutes he'd text again on a different number, so she'd given up and went back to ignoring them, erasing them as they arrived.

All of the messages arrived while Steve wasn't around—it was as if her little Personal Jesus knew when she was alone. Which, yeah, was more than a little disturbing.

But she wasn't going to let it into her life. And she certainly wasn't going to bother Steve with this crap. Her husband was a former cop; he wouldn't stop until he'd tracked down this loser and threatened to break every one of his texting fingers. And she knew what the cost of losing Steve to a mission like that would be. He might never come back.

He was just finally starting to heal. The last thing Sibby wanted was for her husband to crawl back into his little cocoon of death—especially after she'd worked so hard to coax him out of it.

Sibby turned the water off just in time to hear the familiar sound of Steve's Yukon pulling up and then parking. She heard the dogs barking. Finally—Steve was home. She wondered where he'd been all of this time. He usually didn't spend this much time at the beach.

chapter 16

Dark walked up to the front door of his oceanside home, keys in hand. He waited. Took a slow, cleansing breath. Into his nostrils, out his mouth.

Then he keyed the lock, which triggered the explosion.

The explosion that was Max and Henry.

They were two oversized beach dogs, and they bounded out of the house and spun around Dark, whipping their tails. Max wrapped himself around Dark's leg—his version of a hug.

"Hey," Dark said softly. "All right, now, boys."

He heard the upstairs bathroom sink running. That would be Sibby, preparing for the day.

"Okay," Dark said, then tried to move forward. The dogs wouldn't let him. Not until he dropped down on the floor and rolled around with them a little. It was the same ritual every morning—except this morning he took a little longer, and Max and Henry seemed to know it. So they came at Dark with even more powerful lunges and licks.

Just being in his house reminded him of how far he'd come in the past few years. After the massacre, he'd spent months in a gray hospital room—a few in cloth restraints and heavy sedation.

73

Most of that time was a blur. Then it came time to leave the hospital. Friends made generous offers, but Dark didn't know how to accept any of them. His misery and anguish wracked his body like a lethal dose of radiation, and he couldn't imagine exposing anybody he knew to it. Why would they *want* to be exposed?

So he rented a beat-up bungalow in Venice and furnished it with items from a single trip to a thrift store: mattress, table, chair, pot, spoon, towels. The only remnants of his previous life were a bag full of clothes someone had gathered from his old apartment; he couldn't bring himself to wear them. He had food and booze delivered weekly. With food it was simply the elements for sustaining life; with booze it was a constantly rotating series of bottles in a search for what would help him reach oblivion the fastest. Dark's metabolism seemed to adapt quickly, though, so after a few days the effects of, say, whiskey would wear off, and he'd have to move to triple-distilled vodka, and so on. He tried walks. Mostly he stared at things—the ceiling. The street. The overgrown patch of yard behind the house.

His only goal in those early days was tracking down the monster who'd done this to his family. Everything in his life was just a life-support system for his vengeance. His waking hours were all about poring over the murder books he'd illegally copied from Special Circs, looking for the details he must have missed—or the magic thread that ran from dead body to dead body to dead body to his foster family. The thread he'd discover, and use to strangle the twitchy bastard until his eyeballs popped out of their sockets.

He fantasized about finding Sqweegel and taking his time killing him. Snapping bones until he saw them burst through skin. Ripping out the veins along his arms and legs and cauterizing them as he went along. He'd take his time. One week of pain for every family member he lost . . .

No, a week was far too short. He wanted his vengeance to play out over years . . .

But after a year of fruitless searching, Dark realized that he'd missed no details; there was no magic thread. Your fingers could claw at the walls of your prison cell for years, expecting to find the secret button that would open the door, but that didn't mean you'd find one.

Instead of excising his demons, that year had seemed only to amplify them. When it was over, when he'd hit bottom, he had figured that was it for him, looked for a place to wait out the rest of his life. God willing, he had felt at the time, it wouldn't be long.

Despite what Riggins thought, he'd tried. Oh, he'd fucking tried. And in the end, he'd failed.

Dark had gone back to simple life support. Booze. Sleep. Food, if absolutely necessary.

After a while, he wasn't even sure what kind of life he was supporting.

This was his life until his chance meeting with Sibby.

And now look where he was.

A million-dollar house with a beach view. Spacious rooms with Thomas Moser solid handcrafted wood furniture. Custom kitchen design by Nicole Sassaman. Every time Dark picked up a spoon—designed by Doriana O. Mandrelli and Massimiliano Fuksas—he couldn't help but think of the single, slightly bent utensil he'd use to eat most of his meals before.

Before Sibby.

His bride, and the love of his life.

chapter 17

The three-bedroom home Dark and Sibby shared wasn't furnished for show; it was a cocoon, lovingly assembled. It was a retreat from everything, and every piece was chosen to be pleasing to the eye and to the touch. Dark almost never offered his opinions, but Sibby somehow knew exactly what colors and textures would soothe him. It was almost like precognition. Dark marveled at it every time he returned home from his morning retreat.

Sibby, wrapped in a towel, entered the room and smiled at him. "You were out longer than usual."

She never failed to take his breath away. Sibby Dark was a caramel-skinned beauty with raven-dark hair and eyes so intense, it was impossible to turn away from them. Her body was endlessly fascinating to Dark, but it was her soul that made him feel most at home. He was no longer worried about polluting her with his misery. He hadn't for a long time now—she seemed immune to it. She seemed to have a curative effect on him, too.

Dark struggled to keep his focus trained on her while the beach dogs slammed their sweet faces against his. He loved to absorb every detail of her.

"I know," he said. "Must have lost track of time."

"You missed the show."

"The show" was part of their morning ritual: Dark would return from the beach, find himself crawling around on the floor with the dogs, and then make it upstairs in time to watch Sibby strip, preparing herself for the shower. It started as a joke after they first moved in together, Sibby giving a little seductive twist to the elastic band of her panties before sliding them down her long legs. Dark had smiled and joked about going to find a dollar. The striptease had evolved over the last year and a half to the point where now, more days than not, Sibby didn't reach the shower at all, and Dark would close the bedroom door, and Max and Henry would slam their paws against it, yelping for entry.

Now Dark managed to free himself from the deep pile of writhing canine and climbed to his feet. He put his hands on Sibby's shoulders and took in the scent of her freshly washed hair. It was one of the most intoxicating smells in the world.

"Hey, baby," Sibby said, then smiled.

He leaned forward to kiss her, careful not to press up against her belly.

Her eight-months-pregnant belly.

Yeah, look where he was now.

chapter 18

I t was late. Sibby was almost asleep. The dogs, too. Dark made his way to the balcony six feet away from their bed and carefully slid the glass door open. Out in the darkness he could hear the Pacific taking slaps at the shoreline.

"Where are you going?" Sibby asked.

"Just for some air," Dark said.

"Come back to bed. I want to fall asleep with your arms around me."

"I'll be there soon."

The day had been perfect. A brisk session of morning sex, followed by a light lunch and some reading on the balcony. Wine (for him) by late afternoon, and some music in the living room—Sibby had an extensive collection of pristine cool-jazz LPs, most of them from her father. Charlie Parker, Dexter Gordon. Before long the sun set and Dark rubbed Sibby's temples, hands, and feet. The pregnancy had been smooth so far, and Sibby kept herself extremely fit, but carrying a child takes a toll on even the healthiest bodies.

Soon Sibby was asleep on the couch, and Dark gently carried her to bed. He ended the day as he began it: alone.

This was the hardest time.

The morning was a self-challenge; a benediction; a bracing. Being alone in the morning was tolerable because he knew Sibby would be waiting for him when he returned.

But the nights, and the countless hours until dawn . . .

They were still filled with a slow-burning anguish. And it was only harder now, with Sibby in her eighth month. She was exhausted. She needed to rest as much as possible. Dark couldn't be so selfish as to ask her to stay up and sit with him.

So he tried to distract himself any way he could. Sometimes it was a basketball game. Once in a while, an old black-and-white movie. Most times, it was booze.

Tonight was different, though.

Tonight he had something else.

Level 26, huh?

Dark balanced his laptop on his knees, fired it up. The memory stick was in his jacket pocket, left side. It had been sitting there all day, untouched. He'd done his best to forget about it, drowning himself in domestic life with Sibby, losing himself in her touches, her scents, the sound of her voice. Even when she was doing something as simple as running a fingertip down his face, from his forehead to his chin, everything else faded away.

Still, he couldn't help it. Riggins's surprise visit picked at his mind all day long. It was why he couldn't throw his jacket in the wash and pretend to forget that the memory stick was there.

Dark stared at the screen, absentmindedly twisting and turning the band of gold on his finger.

How could he *not* watch?

To unlock the memory stick, log into LEVEL26.com and enter the code: censored

chapter 19

T he cell phone started ringing and vibrating against the surface of the glass table.

Riggins had put it there on purpose, so he'd hear it, no matter what, even if he was taking a leak in the tiny motel bathroom. Which he had been doing, in fact, when the phone started ringing. Figured.

He shook, stuffed, zipped, and stumbled across the room and reached for the cell, almost knocking his bottle of scotch off the table. The screen read: "DARK."

Riggins fumbled, put the phone to his ear. "Hey."

The phone was silent, but Riggins knew Dark was on the other end of the line. Taking his time, saving his string, gathering his wool—whatever the hell you wanted to call it. There was nothing fast about Dark. Some ops at Special Circs used to joke that Dark moved *so* slowly, he almost went back in time a few days.

You couldn't argue with the results, though. Dark may have been a tortoise, but you should see the collection of mounted rabbit heads on his living room wall. When he focused his mind on a case, it was like nothing else existed. Everything extraneous faded away, and the man pieced together a crime narrative that invariably led back to the culprit. His focus was borderline super-human.

And the fact that Dark had taken the memory stick this morning (even though it took twenty minutes for Riggins to realize it) made all the difference in the world. He could sit in his room and still coordinate the case without looking at his digital watch every thirty seconds. This morning he'd had about thirty hours to live; he was down to about eleven. As long as Dark was still considering the offer, there was hope he'd make it through this.

So Riggins waited. He'd waited sixteen hours already. What were a few more seconds?

Finally, Dark spoke. "I can't do it, Riggins. I've already given everything to find this freak. And I failed. I don't know how this time would be any different."

"Dark . . ."

"No, I'm sorry. Things are . . . different now."

"No, I understand. More than you think."

"You don't need me. You've got good men in Special Circs. Younger and sharper people. One of them will catch him."

"Right."

After that, there wasn't much else to say.

Riggins nodded to himself, then pressed the END key. Looked down at the empty tumbler, with just two nearly melted fragments of motel ice at the bottom.

Funny thing was, he wasn't frightened. Not like he thought he might be. Actually, Riggins was surprised to find he was relieved. He'd been offered a choice: *Do something repulsive, or we will kill you.* Well, he'd tried to do something repulsive—pull the closest thing he had to a son back into a case that had almost killed him. But Dark had just taken that option off the table. It was out of Riggins's hands now, so no more messy moral debates. It was now a simple matter of being on the receiving end of a death sentence.

Nellis and McGuire would be outside, smoking, maybe comparing knife wounds to pass the time. Riggins was certain his calls were tapped, so someone in Wycoff's office had to know what had just happened. How long would it take for them to reach his babysitters and give them the order? Under a minute, maybe?

He pushed aside the cheap, dusty curtains and peeked outside. Nothing but cars in a nearly empty lot, and sodium lights burning holes in the dark California sky. No Nellis. No McGuire. No sign of their black van, either.

There was a knock at his hotel room door.

Riggins briefly thought about his gun, which was hanging next to his jacket in the motel closet. But that would do no good. Nellis and McGuire were basically guys just like him, doing their job, keeping the personal out of it. If he was going to put a bullet in anybody, it should be Wycoff. Right between his bushy eyebrows.

So Riggins would keep the personal out of it. Keep it professional.

He looked down at his digital watch:

11:05:43 . . .

11:05:42 . . .

11:05:41 . . .

11:05:40 . . .

Like sands sliding down the slender glass neck of an egg timer.

Riggins walked over to the thin door and opened it—a formality, really. They could easily have kicked it in. A fourth grader could have.

Nellis was staring at him. McGuire was out of sight—presumably in a flanking position.

No. No funny moves now. Riggins would be professional to the very end. He had about eleven hours to live, and the only sane thing to do was spend them as he pleased.

"Come on in, fellas," Riggins said. "Let's talk."

chapter 20

Somewhere in America

There were shadows down on the dungeon wall. Twiggy, writhing shadows, as if a pack of serpents had decided to band together and approximate the shape of a human being. The shadows doubled, then tripled in size. The snakes were moving closer. . . .

Then, suddenly, they ceased movement completely. Sqweegel stared at his frozen shape on the wall, thinking.

He was thinking about tracking people's movements. Pinning them down to a time. How to affix someone to a specific time and place?

As he pondered the question, Sqweegel began moving again, enjoying the slithering shapes his body cast on the wall. Then he turned and stood at rigid attention, his back to the stone wall. He imagined a giant clock behind him and raised his elbow up at the ten, hand at the three. The moon hung high in the night sky, and its light gave Sqweegel's suit an ethereal, almost angelic glow. His heart pounded out the seconds.

Tick . . .

Tock . . .

Tick . . .

Tock . . .

With every beat more blood rushed through his veins, engorging his penis. Every pump summoned his cock to life. It rose from his body like a third hand, lifting away from the face of the skinny white human clock.

Tick . . .

Tock . . .

Tick . . .

Tock . . .

And then he had the answer.

Sqweegel crossed the dungeon floor to where he kept the giant wooden trunk big enough to fit a human being.

He thumbed the combination lock on the front, then freed it from the latch. Inside were various trinkets he'd picked up over the past thirty years.

After throwing open the lid, he dug through the contents of the trunk with his gloved hands. This was the one little indulgence he kept—aside from the films, of course. These were actual relics of his holy conquests, some pieces still dotted with blood, semen, tears, dust, skin flakes, bile, shit, piss, saliva. Or some combination of the above. This lone trunk couldn't damn him, if ever discovered. No trace of himself could be found inside the box. But it probably would have been safer to have destroyed these things, or left them at the various scenes of his crimes.

But he couldn't resist.

Just *look* at this stuff.

Sqweegel reached in and removed a small stainless-steel device that looked like a tiny harp—an anal spreader. This was relatively new and still tacky with some improvised lubricant. He smiled behind the mask, then placed it to the side.

There was a cock ring with a tiny switch that would release a set of spring-loaded shark-fin-style razors. Trap the penis, bleed it out entirely. He hadn't used one of those in a while.

Black titanium handcuffs that, once locked, could never be opened again. He'd had to recover these from a police evidence locker after the police had been forced to remove them from a scorched corpse. (He just *had* to have them back.)

A Burdizzo—a nineteen-inch set of sharpened clamps originally intended to castrate bulls but co-opted by the transgender community as a DIY device.

So much stuff. So many treasures and trophies and devices for his biographers to pore over and ponder later.

Finally, Sqweegel found the relic he'd been looking for: a stopped wristwatch. It hadn't told time for fifteen years.

It wasn't even a particularly expensive watch—just a Timex 1967 Silver Viscount. Silver band, scratched crystal, with little silver tabs marking the hours between the twelve, three, six, and nine. Self-winding. It was dead when Sqweegel had taken it from the desk drawer of one of his victims.

Something about it, though, made him want it. It was the kind of watch a father might pass down to a son—which was probably the case here, considering the youth he'd gotten it from. The watch had most likely functioned properly when the kid received it, but he'd let it rot in a drawer, never bothering to give it the little bit of attention it needed to coax it back to life.

Sqweegel brought it to his workbench, gathered a small plastic case of supplies, and set to work. Beneath the dial, he saw that the rotor, balance wheel, hairspring, and gears had been allowed to rust.

He disassembled the watch into a series of single pieces, then set to the long task of washing them with a cotton swab dabbed in lighter fluid, followed by another round of washing, this time with commercial lubricant. Finally, the pieces were placed in a small sonic cleaner, and then allowed to dry.

The band required special attention. It was the expandable type, and perfect for trapping tiny wrist hairs and flakes of skin. Every link in the chain had to be cleansed individually, and also soaked and sonic treated.

A while later, Sqweegel reassembled the Timex. There was no need to download an old instruction manual from the Internet; it was a fairly basic timepiece, and sturdy, which made them incredibly popular in the middle of the last century. He worked from memory. Soon, he wasn't even bothering to look down at his hands.

As he worked, Sqweegel wondered about the father, and the son, and why the son had ignored his father's gift. The cheap watch had clearly meant something to the father. Maybe it had seen a war, or a prison camp. Maybe it had seen heartbreak.

And the son had just shoved it in a drawer.

How he'd crossed paths with Sqweegel was another matter entirely, but now Sqweegel made a mental note to dig out the appropriate films so he could relive the experience.

When Sqweegel looked down, he saw that the watch was complete, and ticking again, the rotor spinning smoothly and without complaint.

He strapped it to his own wrist, over the white latex.

chapter 21

Malibu, California

Dark pressed END, then padded his way barefoot through the bedroom, downstairs, and through a set of sliding doors to their walled-off yard. Sibby's touches were apparent here, too, from the hanging lights to the bulbed glass candleholders to the patio furniture—they were all soothing and comforting. This was a place where worries weren't supposed to find you.

He sat on their outdoor couch, let the sharp ocean air fill his lungs, and stared up at the tiny pinpricks of light punching holes in the night sky. They looked like a hundred burning eyes, gazing down at him.

Dark told himself that this was the right thing. Sure, this monster was going to find someone else. Maybe next week, maybe tomorrow. Maybe he'd even found a target tonight, and Sqweegel was tucked up somewhere in a dim, dank corner, ticking down the seconds until it was time to strike.

And maybe Dark could have done something about it. . . .

No. Don't. Don't even think about that. It's not your job anymore.

Don't think about the red-haired girl in the blue cotton nightie with the streaks of blood covering her pale belly and legs.

Don't think about what was crying in the corner. . . .

Was he supposed to feel guilty about it forever? It was too much to ask one man, wasn't it?

Dark had tried to capture Sqweegel. Sqweegel had retaliated . . . and *won*. He'd taken the shot that few men would. He'd hidden his tracks. He'd made sure there was no magic thread. Maybe he deserved to be out there, free. Dark had tried to stop him, broken damn near every law to stop him, and failed anyway. Why couldn't it just be left at that?

So they'd gone and promoted Sqweegel to a new level. Probably what he wanted all along.

There was no scale for what Dark had endured over the past two years.

Dark suddenly hurled his cell phone so hard against the stone patio that it shattered into dozens of pieces.

Inside the house, Max and Henry began to bark. The noise had frightened them. There was another sound behind Dark—the sliding of the glass balcony door one flight up.

Sibby looked down at him.

"Baby? Are you okay? What *was* that?"

Dammit. That was stupid. Stupid for letting it reach him again.

Within a few moments Sibby was down in the backyard with Steve, sitting across from him on their small white brick chimney. She hadn't seen him like this since their earliest days together— the days when his demons were still very much with him, and he seemed utterly defeated.

Sibby had learned to tread carefully then, and she did the

same now. You don't go pushing a man who's already on the edge. You have to coax him back before you can understand.

"You want to talk about it?" she asked.

"It's nothing," Steve said. "Just got carried away. Reception on the beach sucks."

"Who were you trying to call?"

"Nobody important."

"Okay. It's late. Why don't you come to bed?"

"In a little while. I promise."

Sibby thought back to their early days together, and how she quickly learned that there was only one thing that could soothe the pain, even if was just for a little while. The one thing that drove away the demons and brought him back to life.

She moved her legs slowly, and noticed Steve was watching her carefully. The front of her silk nightgown swelled with her pregnant belly, but he couldn't take his eyes off a single square inch of her body. The move was all hers. He was waiting for her to make it.

Sibby knew he loved this, what it did to him. This was what Steve needed now, to take his mind away from the pain.

Even if it was only temporary.

To observe sexual tension, log into LEVEL26.com and enter the code: sibby

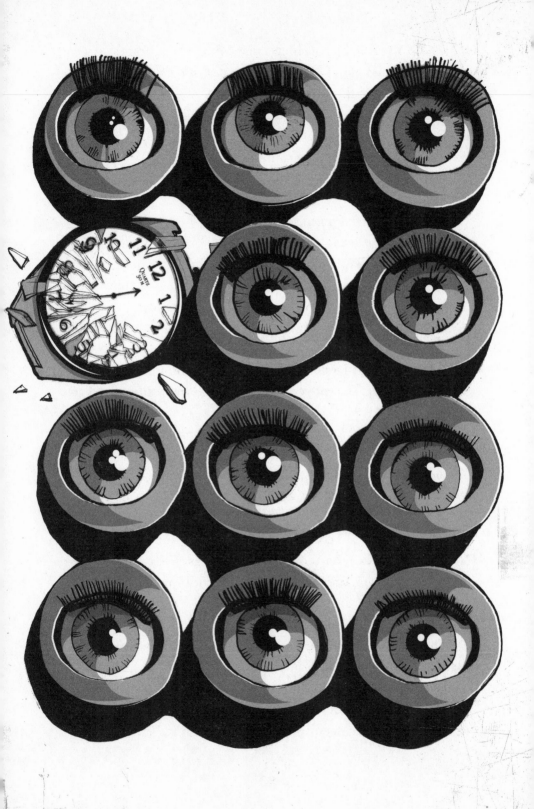

chapter 22

Everything about Sibby—her touch, her taste, her smell, the very sight of her body—was stronger than any narcotic Dark had ever encountered. She knew exactly how to bring him back to earth. And somehow, she'd sensed what he desperately needed.

Their breathing hadn't slowed yet. There was nothing to say. No need to speak at all.

Finally, Sibby whispered in his ear, "Come to bed."

Despite everything, Dark wasn't tired. He was restless. Still thinking about his conversation earlier that evening. Still thinking about Sqweegel. He couldn't get those images out of his skull. The splats of blood on those pale white legs. The razored fabric of her nightgown. The crying in the corner of the room. . . .

Sibby touched the side of his face.

"Hey," she said. "Talk to me."

That was the problem with drugs, wasn't it? They were designed for the moment. And in that single moment they could make the pain disappear. But only for a moment. And then the newfound calm was quickly replaced by an ache for that moment again—a desperate need to scramble back up it. Wracking your brain for a way to remain there forever . . . or at least for just a few more seconds.

Dark kissed her. She rested her head on his shoulder. After a while they left the yard and climbed into bed, lying on top of the sheets and letting the cool ocean air wash over their bodies, wicking away the sweat. Their hands touched, knuckles to knuckles at first.

Then Sibby wrapped her hand around Dark's and squeezed gently. You could smell the salt in the air and the remnants of the candles Sibby had been burning earlier.

Then the house phone rang.

It was strange to hear it at this hour—strange to hear it at all, in fact. Most calls went right to their cell phones. Sibby had wanted to get rid of the landline, but Dark had insisted they keep it. Cell phones ran out of power. Towers could be knocked out of commission by something as simple as a light tremor.

The phone rang again.

"I'll get it," Sibby said softly.

"No, no. I will."

Dark sighed, reached across his pregnant wife, and picked up the receiver from its cradle.

"Just ten minutes," Riggins said. "Ten minutes and I go away forever."

"Dammit, Riggins."

"I wouldn't ask if it weren't important. You took the USB drive. I know you've probably watched it by now."

Dark felt Sibby squeezing his hand a little harder now. A pleasantly cold blast of air washed over both of them. It would be nice to stay in this bed and not move for weeks. Not move until the baby was born. And then they could bring the baby back to this bed and lie here some more. Maybe until the baby was ready for college.

It would be nice, but Dark knew it wasn't going to happen.

He asked, "Where?"

"Same place as earlier."

"That diner's got to be closed by now."

"So we'll sit outside and enjoy the fine California night."

"It's almost morning."

"Whatever."

Dark turned his head to face Sibby. He wanted to ask her to hang up the receiver and yank the cord from the wall mount. It didn't matter if there was a slight tremor because there was no one they'd need to call right now. They were here together, and that was all that mattered.

Instead he found himself telling Riggins, "Fine. I'll be there."

chapter 23

Here it was. Finally.

The moment she'd dreaded ever since she met Steve.

Funny to think she used made a joke of it back in their early days. *Your last name is Dark, huh?* she'd asked. *So I'm guessing you're one of those happy-go-lucky types.*

Steve *Dark*. She had no idea.

It was a chance encounter in the liquor section at Vons in Santa Monica. The man who would become her husband had been piling his cart with booze—mostly whiskeys and scotches, along with some bottles of white and red wine. She assumed he was making a party run. Later she'd learn it was simply his weekly order.

And catching him out in public was a freak occurrence as well. For the past few months he'd called his order in, had it delivered to his beat-up apartment in Venice. That night, though, a strange mood had struck him, and he'd decided to go shopping in person. It had been so long, Sibby learned later, there was actually a thick layer of dust on his car.

Steve was a disheveled mess, but Sibby merely read it as *I had a really late night*, not *I've lost myself for months in a death spiral of depression.* Because despite the tousled bed head, the pale skin, the devil-may-care attitude toward personal hygiene . . . Steve was still a desperately handsome man. Enough to make her pause and try a dumb line—something she hadn't done since college. She spoke to him because she knew she'd kick herself later if she didn't.

"So, when should I drop by?" she asked.

He turned and blinked, unsure that she was actually addressing him. Unsure she wasn't a ghost. Later, she would learn that it had literally been weeks since someone had spoken to him.

"I'm sorry," Steve said. "What did you say?"

"Your party," Sibby said, pointing to his cart. "When does it start? I see you've got a bottle of Cakebread in your basket, and it just so happens to be my favorite Chardonnay."

The next moment, Sibby remembered, was the longest moment in the world. Steve just stood there, staring at her, as if he were struggling to find the right words. He tried a smile, but it came up false. A little scary even. And in that small eternity, Sibby wondered what strange world she had tumbled into.

What was she doing in Vons, talking to a strange handsome guy who looked like he hadn't taken a shower in days? This could be Charles Manson, Jr., for all she knew.

And then she had her hands tightly wrapped around the tacky plastic handle of the shopping cart and was ready to start pushing it down another aisle, any aisle, it didn't matter, just so long as she was able to loop around the store once before abandoning the cart and leaving the store before he noticed—

"Eight," he said. "Tomorrow night."

Steve's smile this time was the real thing. Sibby returned it, her grip on the handle loosening. He wrote down his address on the back page of a paperback novel she had in her purse—Faulkner's *Sanctuary.*

The next night she arrived and was only partly surprised to see a small bungalow with just one occupant—Steve himself. There were two place settings, mismatched, on a makeshift dining room table covered with something that looked suspiciously like a bedsheet.

"Nobody could make it," her future husband explained, a shy smile on his face.

"If the Cakebread didn't make it, I'm outta here," she said, mock-serious.

"After we met I went back and bought three more bottles."

He had, too.

And that was the night the sweet, slow mystery of Steve Dark began to unfold before her. He told her the bare bones up front—he had been a cop, a federal agent, but a case had gone horribly wrong, and he'd quit. It wasn't until their fifth date that he'd mentioned he was adopted, and used to have a foster family, but they'd died in a horrible accident.

And it wasn't until after they were married by a justice of the peace that Sibby learned that the case that had gone horribly wrong and his foster family's horrible accident were the same event.

She knew the year following their death was a living hell.

What was clear from the beginning, though, was that Steve never talked about—and from what she could gather, never even *thought about*—becoming a cop again. But now Sibby could tell something was different. Steve was a haunted man, but not like this. There was something specific nagging at him.

Please don't let it be the job, she thought. *I can take anything but that. Because whatever happened to him in that job almost killed him, and I can take anything but losing him.*

"You seem like you're living in the past today. Can you tell me what's going on?"

Steve was silent. But Sibby refused to let it go.

"You're being asked to do something, aren't you?" she asked him.

"Yes."

"By your old employers."

"Yes."

"What did you tell them?"

"I told them no."

Sibby exhaled. She hadn't realized she'd been holding her breath.

"You did?"

"My old boss, Tom Riggins, showed up this morning and asked me to come out of retirement. He's very good at needling someone until he gets what he wants. You can't ignore them. It's never going to stop on their end. So I'm going to take care of it on mine."

Sibby looked at him, scanning for the smallest trace of a lie. She could usually tell, with the little things, like when he was covering up a birthday present or sparing her feelings. Steve had certain little tells.

But she didn't see any of them now.

"Okay," she said. "Take care of it. But come right back to me?"

"Of course. Where else would I go?" He smiled, but Sibby could tell it was for her benefit.

Steve stared at the ceiling for a few moments. Then he snatched up his keys from the coffee table, checked his watch, and left the house.

Sibby looked down at her cell phone, resting on top of the comforter. The day had come full circle; she was alone in the house again. The only thing that would make this moment perfect, Sibby thought, was for a text to arrive.

And then one did.

chapter 24

Santa Monica Pier
3:30 A.M.

R iggins watched Dark park his black Yukon in the lot next to the pier. Dark drove like he lived: in slow motion. Deliberately. Methodically. If you didn't know better, you'd assume it was some old buzzard behind the wheel, cruising the Pacific Coast Highway like it was 1939, back when Santa Monica was a sleepy little beach town. But that's just how Dark moved. He didn't rush a goddamned thing.

For once, Riggins was glad Dark was taking his time. The longer he took, the more he could enjoy his cigarette.

The more time he had before he was killed. What was it now? He checked the official death countdown on the watch that had been a gift from his daughter:

8:24:08 . . .
8:24:07 . . .
8:24:06 . . .
8:24:05 . . .

Somewhere out in the darkness behind Riggins—maybe near

the children's amusement rides? maybe the carousel? maybe even under the pier?—were Nellis and McGuire. And Riggins was sure they were checking their watches, too.

Back at the Motel 6, the two Dark Arts operatives had refused a drink, as expected. But they'd listened to Riggins, anyway. They were, after all, professional men.

"I suppose you've heard that Dark said no," Riggins had said, sitting on the edge of his sagging bed.

Buzz-cut Nellis nodded. McGuire made no movement whatsoever. Maybe he was thinking about his missing fingers.

"But I've still got time on the clock left, and I haven't played my best card. What I need is some space. Dark was one of our best ops. He made you in *seconds*, and he's always had a big distrust of strangers. If I'm going to make this work, I need him to think we're alone. That this is just between the two of us."

Nellis looked at him. "If you run, we'll find you. And it'll be a lot worse for you."

"I'm not planning on running," Riggins said. "You can even hold my car keys if that makes you feel better. What am I gonna do, skip down to the ocean and try to swim out to Japan?"

Nellis and McGuire agreed to give Riggins his space. But they would be nearby, somewhere they couldn't be "made."

What Riggins didn't tell his babysitters was that he had no intention of talking Dark into the job.

Instead, what he wanted was to spend some of his last hours alive with his friend.

Now Dark was approaching, taking the stairs up to the pier one at a time. Riggins enjoyed another hit from his cigarette and let the smoke flow out of his nose like he was a cartoon bull.

"Dark," Riggins said.

Without warning, Dark smiled and snatched the butt away from him. He took a drag himself before flicking it over the side of the pier.

"Lung cancer," he said. "Number one killer of men."

Shit. Riggins had been looking forward to finishing it. He had eleven smokes left in his pack, and he refused to die until he'd savored every one of them.

"Now you tell me."

"You thought the baby on the video would do it, didn't you? Get me to come running back to Special Circs."

Riggins looked up at Dark, genuine surprise on his face. "Baby?"

"Like you don't know."

"Honest, I haven't watched the thing. I was under strict orders to deliver it to you. Your eyes only."

"Stop bullshitting me. You're the lead agent on this case. Since when are you not allowed to see case evidence?"

"Now you're starting to understand what I've been dealing with here. This isn't just a criminal investigation anymore, Dark. It's gotten political. International. We have D.C. types calling the shots, squeezing us, wondering why we're not walking on fucking water and churning out loaves and fishes."

"That's insane. You don't squeeze and threaten your best agents to catch someone like Sqweegel. You give them resources."

"You want to call Norman Wycoff and tell him that? I'm sure he'd be happy to hear from you."

Dark said nothing. He felt far removed from Special Circs—but he also couldn't imagine it under the thumb of the Defense Department. The world seemed to have embraced the absurd since he'd voluntarily taken himself out of it.

"So what's on that video?" Riggins said.

chapter 25

Dark swallowed, not really wanting to recall the images he'd seen just a few hours ago. But he began describing it in shorthand, anyway.

"A young girl—maybe seventeen or eighteen," Dark said. "Red hair, pale skin, freckled. She's sleeping. No idea that Sqweegel's under her bed, waiting for her to fall into a deeper sleep. Then he makes his move. Climbs over her."

Riggins shook his head. "Fuck."

"She wakes up in time to feel the first slice, which cuts through her blue cotton nightie. She fights back, but every time she lifts a hand he slashes through it. After a while, she stops lifting her hands. He really lays into her now, but he keeps looking over to the corner of the room."

"Why?"

"It wasn't clear at first. You'd think he'd be looking at the camera, if anything at all. But then I realize that he's showing off for somebody in the room."

Riggins got it right away. "Oh, fuck. A baby?"

"Strapped into his bouncy chair, which is the perfect vantage point to watch his mother get sliced to ribbons. Sitting there for

God knows how long, crying to be held and fed. And that's where it ends."

"Jesus."

The two men sat in silence for a while.

Dark thought about the other details he'd gleaned from the video—the everyday objects that were now part of a grisly, blood-soaked tableau. The pink-flower-patterned comforter, soaked and stained red. The stuffed bear with a bow around its neck and flecks of dark crimson on its furry face. A small plastic dental pick, also streaked with blood. In some ways, they were just as hard to look at as the girl's mutilated body. Taken from a safe, ordinary place and dropped down in the middle of a horror show.

"I had no idea," Riggins said.

"Yeah, I'm sure you didn't see it first," Dark said. "If you'd seen it, I doubt you would have shown up here to make me watch, too. But that means someone above you thought they knew how to fuck with my head. Maybe they even know that Sibby is pregnant. . . ."

"Wait . . . what?" Riggins asked. "Shit. Belated congrats, Dad. Though I should be insulted you didn't share this bit of news. How many months?"

"Baby's due in a few weeks," Dark said, annoyed at himself for blurting that out. "Point is, someone's screwing around with my life. And I swore two years ago that it would never happen again. I was out this morning, and I'm still out now."

Riggins tapped another Lucky Strike out of the pack. "You probably think I'm pissed."

Dark shrugged.

Riggins turned and put his hand on Dark's shoulder. "Well, I'm not. Jealous, actually. You've got your life waiting for you back in that pretty little house in Malibu. And a baby . . . well, that changes everything. I guess what I'm saying is—I understand. There's nothing I wouldn't give to be in your shoes right now."

There was an awkward moment, and then Riggins put out his hand.

Dark frowned, then took Riggins's hand and shook it quickly. As he held it, Riggins leaned in.

"There's just one more thing. I don't want to give these assholes the satisfaction just yet. So humor a dead man and walk with me for a while, okay?"

From the inside of their van, Nellis and McGuire watched on a small video monitor as their subjects shook hands, and then headed up the pier.

"Dark's going on the move with Riggins," said Nellis into a tiny mouthpiece. "Still no confirmation."

Their van was equipped with HD cameras and omnidirectional mikes. But the pickup distance was limited; as Riggins and Dark moved, Nellis and McGuire could pick up only snatches of the conversation. They'd have to move in closer, yet stay out of sight.

Sooner or later they would know Dark's intentions. A yes would spare Riggins's life. A no would mean a busy night for them. Syringes. Knives. Acid baths. And sponges.

Plenty of sponges.

And with the endless stalling from Riggins, well . . . Nellis had to admit, if only to relieve the boredom, that he was starting to look forward to that part.

chapter 26

Somewhere in America / Outside

creeeeeeeeeeeee . . .

The sharp blade dug a trench nearly a millimeter thick into the double-paned glass. It made a circle, and then the circle was removed with a suction cup.

A white face appeared in the hole. Pushed its nostrils into the empty space. Sniffed. Looked to the right, then the left.

Satisfied, a white-gloved hand reached in, grasped the lock.

Flipped it.

Click.

Now it was easy. The glass door slid open noiselessly.

Sqweegel was in.

He moved through the house slowly. Quietly. The carpet was soft and expensive, with excellent padding beneath. The floorboards were tight. He knew he wouldn't have any problems, since this house was built just a few years ago. Still, he also knew how to shift his weight and counteract any noise. He knew how to be patient and still, and how to sink into his next step.

He also knew how to avoid the dogs.

He crept by them like a dust mote, lazily floating through the air. He was slow, unworthy of note.

He paused at the bottom of the stairs. Nearby was a credenza on top of which rested a beautiful pewter bowl brimming to the top with metal toy cars. An odd thing to collect among such an otherwise tastefully appointed house. Sqweegel had wondered about it when he first saw it months ago. He'd been tempted then—tempted now, in fact—to take one and add it to his treasure box.

There were also ballet shoes on a small wooden shelf on the wall. Oh, what delicate yet strong feet had once slipped into them, danced with them. He coveted them, as well.

But such thefts would be too much of a tell. Too many voices confusing the message. He was speaking to Dark, and he didn't want the message garbled.

He wanted his hunter to hear him loud and clear.

The message would be left upstairs, on the second floor of the house.

Sqweegel slithered up the stairs, joints and bones like the pistons and gears of a rubber locomotive. He traveled slowly. Languidly. Deliberately. There was no particular cadence to his movements. Just a long, slithering ooze up to the second floor.

His body crawled over the top step, and then he began to move down the hallway on his hands and feet, spine slowly undulating up and down as if it were made of hard rubber. Sqweegel's movements couldn't be described as even remotely human. No person would think to move himself in such a way.

No one had ever captured him on film. No one except Sqweegel, of course, in the early years when he would tape himself repeatedly and learn from his own mistakes on playback.

But if you were to watch the movement on film, you would last maybe a minute before you reached for the FAST-FORWARD button. Mostly because nothing would appear to be happening.

Then you would realize he had moved ten feet without your noticing.

After a small eternity, Sqweegel was outside the door of the master bedroom. The décor suited his needs perfectly. His thin, bony body was camouflaged by the white walls. There was complete silence except for the gentle breathing coming from the bed.

Where she was sleeping.

To follow the intruder, log into LEVEL26.com and
enter the code: sqweegel

chapter 27

Malibu, California
Wednesday / 6:30 A.M.

First thing in the morning is when the world looks the most unreal—bathed in those first blasts of light breaking over the horizon. Darkness has been banished. Everything's going to be all right again.

Dark was exhausted. He'd spent the early-morning hours wandering the streets of Santa Monica talking to Riggins until five A.M., when they finally happened upon a brightly lit diner. They chatted over plates of fried potatoes, runny eggs, toast, and cups of coffee. Riggins did, anyway. Dark abstained.

Riggins shared some Special Circs gossip—or whatever passed for gossip in an organization whose members had no real lives. This, of course, didn't last long; there were hardly any agents still around from Dark's era. In fact, dozens of careers had begun and flamed out in the two years he'd been gone.

So Riggins turned the conversation to the comings and goings of his kids. Dark pretended to care.

But to Dark's surprise, Riggins never brought up the Sqweegel case again. No baby, no president, no Level 26 . . . nothing.

Dark nodded, sipped his own coffee. The same cup of too-strong brew he'd sat down with hours before. It was now cold and bitter. Kept his brain fed with just enough caffeine to keep him awake.

When the first rays of the sun had turned the skies a deep pink, Dark knew it was okay to say good-bye. He'd given Riggins a few hours; now it was time to return to Sibby. To ease back into the calm pattern that was his new life.

And now he would lock the Yukon and walk to his front door. The dogs would smother him with thunderous affection and doggie saliva. And Sibby would be waiting for him. He'd touch her milky white, soft skin. Lean down and kiss the tender spot beneath her chin . . .

Leaning down . . .

Wait.

Dark would have missed it if he hadn't been leaning down, staring at the pavement beneath his feet.

The broken watch, just a few inches from the curb.

It was a cheap Timex, silver coated. Face smashed. Dark took a pen out of his pocket and used it to lift the watch from the ground. The face had been crushed at 3:14 A.M.

Dark looked up and down his block. Birds chirped. Sprinklers spewed. Behind it all, you could hear the peaceful blasts of ocean waves against the shore.

Nothing out of the ordinary.

There was a leather bag holding the Yukon's instruction manual in the glove box. Dark tossed the manual and carefully transferred the broken pieces of the watch into the bag, then zipped it.

Dark keyed their front door—insert, twist, open. The second he stepped inside his dogs started barking. He tried to hush them as he moved toward the staircase.

"Sibby?"

No answer.

Dark's pulse began to bang in his neck. He ran up the stairs, hopping two at a time, hands on the walls.

"Sibby!"

He swung open the door to the master bedroom only to find her perfectly fine. Groggy, but alive.

She blinked, ran her fingers through her hair, then sat up in bed fast.

"Honey? Is everything okay? What's wrong?"

Dark couldn't answer her. What *was* wrong, exactly? The fact that he found a broken watch in front of their home? It didn't even make sense to him. Nothing, technically, was wrong.

But he couldn't stop the tremor that started in his gut and sent aftershocks throughout his entire nervous system. Dark closed his right fist so tight, his fingernails dug into his palm. He needed the pain to ground the live wires under his skin.

He hadn't felt this kind of panic, this kind of dread since . . .

No.

It wasn't happening again.

Or was it?

Wasn't that what you told yourself the last time, Dark? That you were being silly, there was no reason to be afraid, your foster family was okay, perfectly fine, because in the real world, nothing bad happened to families. . . .

Mom. Dad. Grandma. Evan. Callie. Emma.

Sibby supported herself—and her protruding belly—with tired, rubbery arms. Clearly, she had been in a deep, dead sleep.

"Steve! Please tell me what the fuck is going on!"

Dark, though, was busy opening a drawer, pushing aside folded sweaters, and wrapping his hand around a Glock nine-millimeter. He popped in a clip.

"Stay here," he said.

chapter 28

Dark checked the closets first—the two downstairs. He pushed aside jackets, stomped the carpeted floor, tapped the closet ceilings with the Glock, listening for any kind of hollow sounds that would indicate a secret compartment or burrowing space. Dark was halfway across the living room when he had a second thought, then returned to the closets. On his hands and knees, he ripped up the carpet to check the floor beneath—there could be a false door or hinge there. But no. Nothing.

He ran his fingers along the walls, especially in the corners. A tiny fissure could reveal a door . . . or it would just be a crack in the drywall.

Out of the corner of his eye, Dark saw curtains flutter—over by the back patio doors. He made his way across the room cautiously, gun in a two-handed grip. He watched the curtains like they were the torso of a fallen beast and he was waiting for the slightest indication of a breath.

Dark pushed the Glock between the two curtain panels, then slowly pulled to the right and . . .

Nothing.

Their home wasn't large by Malibu standards, but it still took

Dark a good thirty minutes to feel like he'd given it a thorough search. No room, cabinet, closet, shelf, vent, plumbing recess, or gutter was left unchecked.

Still, he knew he could be overlooking something obvious. Something that Sqweegel would spot in an instant—and exploit.

He also looked for anything—like the broken watch—that was out of place. Left there either on purpose, or not.

There *was* something off. He could feel it. Some little detail he'd seen a thousand times in their home that was now askew. But if there was something, Dark had a hard time pinpointing it.

He was exhausted beyond words now. The shock of Riggins, the sex, the bad diner coffee, the watch . . . it all blurred in his mind. He wondered, idly, if maybe this was just a bad dream, and soon he'd roll over and smell the pungent perfume of Sibby's shampoo and know everything was okay.

Dark slid the weapon in the back of his jeans, then leaned against their bedroom wall.

Sibby was sitting in the middle of the bedspread—legs crossed, wrists on her knees. As if a peaceful yoga position could help her deal with the insanity that had broken out in her home.

"Sweetheart," she said calmly, "I want you to know how much you're scaring the living shit out of me right now."

"I'm sorry," he said after a while.

"What's going on?"

Dark looked at her a long moment, as if to remind himself that this was Sibby, not his foster mom. He hadn't traveled back in time. He wasn't in the middle of a gruesome replay. This was here. This was now.

He went to his dresser and picked up the leather bag he'd carried into the house. After unzipping it, he handed it to Sibby.

"I found this in the driveway. It's not mine."

Sibby looked inside the bag.

"Whose is it?"

"I don't know. Could be that someone just dropped it. But sometimes, people use them to tell when a target leaves his house."

"Target?" Sibby asked. "Are you saying someone's tracking you?"

"Not someone serious. It's an old trick. Almost a joke."

Sibby thought about this. "And whoever left it didn't pick it up."

"Exactly," he said. "It's someone playing a joke. Or trying to distract me."

Dark looked at her. But not with warmth in his eyes. Now he regarded her clinically, looking her over head to toe. Examining her skin for unusual marks without trying to alarm her.

"What?" Sibby asked, looking suddenly uncomfortable.

"You didn't hear anything while I was gone?"

"If anyone would have come within ten feet of the house, Max and Henry would've woken me up."

"Right," Dark said, then walked to the bedroom window.

"Besides—who would be targeting you?"

Who, indeed.

Riggins had mentioned Sqweegel's name not twenty-four hours ago, and already Dark was seeing him in every shadowy corner.

Maybe the broken watch outside could be explained away by Riggins's two babysitters. Maybe they were seriously old-school. Maybe their budgets had been slashed, too, and all they could afford were a bag of cheap Timex watches to track America's most dangerous enemies.

Right.

No, it was someone sending him a message.

But who?

And what was he trying to say?

chapter 29

To be perfectly honest, Sibby *did* feel a little strange.
Lightheaded, like she had skipped a meal last night.
And her body was stiff in places it hadn't been the day before. Her joints were sore. Mouth dry.

But she wasn't about to tell Steve that. Not with him prowling around their home with a broken watch and a loaded gun.

No wonder she hadn't told him about her Personal Jesus. If a broken watch on the street could set him off, imagine what would happen if she told him she had a cell-phone stalker.

Besides, her stiffness was probably just another surprise from the pregnancy, which had already wreaked havoc on her body over the past eight months. Friends told her the worst was yet to come, as her body would physically transform to deliver the child. Her joints would be flooded with a chemical relaxant that would cause her hip bones to widen, like she was a child's Transformer toy or something.

Maybe that's what was happening now. Her hips felt like someone had been pulling on them.

This was no reason to worry Steve. He was already panicked enough for the both of them, even though he did his best to hide it.

He was sitting on the edge of the bed now, close to her but not facing her.

She fought the urge to cry. Her emotions had been a volatile cocktail her entire pregnancy, and the closer she drew to the nine-month mark, the worse it got. Overwhelmed with sadness one minute. Furious the next.

Sibby tried to push it away. She said, "I can't help you if you don't talk to me."

"I've put a lot of people away," Steve said calmly. "People who might want to pay me a visit."

"Is there someone specific, Steve? Someone you think is coming after you now?"

He didn't reply.

"Is that why you were out with your old boss last night?"

Still nothing.

Max and Henry were both sitting at attention. Panting. Waiting for their walk on the beach. They didn't understand why they weren't going for their walk. Wasn't it time for their walk?

Sibby had oceans of patience when it came to Steve; she had to. He was slow, methodical, guarded, secretive. Yes, it could be maddening.

But it was also what attracted her to him.

Steve was the quintessential man of stone, and Sibby was always amazed when she was able to break through the hard exterior and feel the little bursts of warmth locked inside.

The little fragments of his past that he'd shared with her throughout their relationship—he was an ex-Fed, his foster family had died, he blamed himself for their deaths—had been enough to sustain her. Sibby didn't want to take a crowbar to the rock and lay bare all of his secrets. If anything was worthwhile, it had to be given willingly.

"You're not telling me everything," Sibby said, as calmly as she could.

Steve seemed to struggle with the words.

"I put a lot of bad people away, Sibby. People like that wouldn't think twice about hurting me or you if they had the chance. I freaked, okay? I'm sorry. . . ."

They held each other for a while. She felt his lips on her forehead. All was calm. Safe.

Then something shattered a downstairs window. Steve and Sibby jumped as though electric currents had coursed through their bodies.

chapter 30

Dark grabbed the Glock from the small of his back and told Sibby, "Dial 911."

He sidestepped down the stairs, gun ready.

On the oceanside patio he saw curtains flowing. His heart was pounding again with every step. His brain screamed one name: *Sqweegel.*

But this wasn't like Sqweegel at all. He didn't waste time placing watches under tires or smashing windows. He didn't announce himself. For him, the thrill of the hunt was hiding in the last place you'd expect to find him, and you'd see his dark eyes at the very last moment. And by then it would be too late.

Finally, he saw what had shattered the window: a rock the size of a baseball. Shards of glass surrounded it on the hardwood floor.

Dark stepped over the glass, careful not to disturb a single fragment of it, and looked up and down the shoreline. Nothing.

He pulled the cell phone out of his pocket and texted Riggins.

Dark's text was simple: his address, followed by "GET HERE NOW."

If this were Sqweegel related, there was no better person to have on their side now than Riggins.

Text sent, Dark looked out of his broken patio window again. Across the way there was a Los Angeles Sheriff's Department cruiser, cherries flashing. Two officers were talking to his neighbor.

The man was reportedly a self-made millionaire, originally from the Bronx. A breakthrough in plastics had transformed his life, brought him out to the most scenic stretch of the West Coast for retirement, and he never stopped complaining about it. He openly flirted with Sibby, even when she became obviously pregnant. Sibby thought he was sweet.

"I want those little pricks killed on the spot," the neighbor was saying. "Can you do that? Can you bring them out here so I can watch them be executed?"

"Is everything okay?" Dark asked.

The neighbor held up a rock in his hand—very similar to the size and shape of the one Dark had found in his home. He shook it angrily at Dark.

"They get you, too?" he asked.

Dark shook his head.

"Oh, wonderful—just me, then." The neighbor turned his attention back to the sheriff's deputies. "Can you do something with this? You know, stick it in some kind of machine and let the DNA pop up like they do on *CSI*?"

Dark wished them luck catching the culprits and walked back toward his house. Sibby was already out on the front balcony, looking for him. She had a *What the hell?* expression on her face. Dark shook his head.

"Just kids," Dark told her, once he'd stepped back into the house. "Throwing rocks through people's windows."

"It's unbelievable," she said. "We can live in a million-dollar home, in a great neighborhood, and we still have to deal with this kind of thing. What if the baby were here, playing under that window?"

"I know," Dark said quietly.

Sibby stormed off to the kitchen closet and pulled out a broom.

"I'll clean it up," Dark said.

"No, I'll do it. I need something to do, or otherwise I'll go out looking for those little brats myself. They haven't seen fury until they've seen a pregnant woman with raging hormones."

There was a knock at the door.

Riggins.

"Hey," he said. "I got here as fast as I could. Everything okay?"

"Yeah," Dark said. "We're okay."

Riggins meanwhile was pacing the room, scanning the floor, the walls, the things on the walls, the ceiling, before finally settling back on the broken patio window.

"So what's the deal with that?"

"Just some kids with rocks."

"They let kids up here in Malibu?"

"Apparently." Dark looked behind Riggins. "Where are your dates?"

"My men in black? Outside. I still have them thinking that I'm on the verge of convincing you to take the case. I figure they owe me until the very last minute."

Sibby appeared behind Dark. "Hi. You must be Tom." She extended a hand. "Dark talks about you . . ."

"*Never*, I know. Good to finally meet you, Sibby."

Dark had mentioned Sibby only once to Riggins last night—when the news about the pregnancy had slipped out. If nothing else, Riggins knew how to be polite.

It was a strange moment for Dark—two very different worlds colliding. Riggins was the past, a character actor from a long-canceled series. Sibby was the present, the focus, his reason for everything. They shouldn't be shaking hands. They shouldn't even be in the same room. The universe could explode.

Sibby broke the tension. "I'll put some coffee on. Tom?"

"Yes, please."

"Nothing for me," Dark said. "I'll clean this glass up off the floor."

Riggins looked at the shattered glass strewn across the floor, then locked eyes with Dark.

He whispered, "Any chance it's him?"

chapter 31

"I don't know," Dark said. "This kind of juvenile behavior isn't part of his profile—is it?"

"No," Riggins said. "Not in any of the cases we've studied."

"Even if it was him," Dark continued, "why break my neighbor's window? It's not like Sqweegel to get an address wrong."

"Well, sure."

"And Sqweegel doesn't announce. He'll just pounce."

"Of course."

Riggins clasped his hands together and pursed his lips like he was about to whistle. But he made no sound. Part of him was having fun listening to Dark go on. He was being downright chatty.

Finally, Dark asked, "Okay, what?"

"Oh, nothing," Riggins said. "Just that none of this feels right."

"We've been up all night, and you're a few hours from the end. Of course nothing feels right."

Riggins didn't even need to look at his watch now. High noon, and that would be it.

"Touché," he said instead. "But look at it from where I'm standing. I pop back into your life, and a few hours later, you've got a shattered patio window. Tell me—how many acts of vandalism does the city of Malibu suffer each week? You and Sibby ducking rocks all the time?"

Dark ignored him and broomed the shards into a rubber dustpan, then began to carry the pieces over to the plastic kitchen trash can. But something in the jagged mess caught his eye. He stopped and carefully picked out a single shard, held it up to the light.

"What is it?" Riggins asked.

Slowly turning the shard in the bright sunlight, Dark examined the piece like it had Sanskrit on it.

"Well? Christ, don't leave me hanging here, Dark. I might be dead by the time you get around to telling me."

"This edge. It's perfectly cut. Look."

Riggins saw that he was right. The edge of the shard resembled a perfect half-moon crescent, and that was something that didn't naturally occur when you tossed a rock through a plate of glass.

"Is Banner still over in trace?" Dark asked.

Riggins nodded. "What else is a guy like that going to do? So what, you want to use the LAPD's top crime lab to track down a bunch of punk Malibu kids?"

Dark told Sibby that Riggins would be having his coffee to go and he'd be back in a few hours.

Outside Dark's house, and a professional distance away, Nellis sat in the passenger seat of the van, listening to the secretary's voice bark into his ear again. "What's the status?"

"Riggins and Dark are meeting now. There's been an act of vandalism at Dark's house, as well as his neighbor's."

"Vandalism? In fucking Malibu?"

"Rocks through windows."

The secretary paused to consider this. "Probably fucking Riggins. Stalling for time."

"No, sir," Nellis said. "We've been on him the entire time."

"Okay," Wycoff said. "Fuck this. I'm en route to you now. If Riggins can't do his job, maybe I'll have to do it for him."

Dark rapped his knuckles on his neighbor's door. Riggins stood behind him, a few feet away. This should be interesting—Dark interacting with other human beings. In all of their years together at Special Circs, Riggins had known Dark to avoid most other people. He worked his cases like a scientist, preferring evidence already prepped, dyed, and pressed between two pieces of glass. Not alive.

"What now?" the man asked; then he saw who it was. "Oh. You again."

"Didn't mean to bother you," Dark said, "but I was wondering if I might have some of the broken glass from your window."

"Huh? Why on earth would you want that?"

"My friend here," Dark said, pointing his thumb at Riggins, "works for the LAPD. Seems there are some skater punks who have been vandalizing the area for a few weeks now. If he can take some of your glass, the guys in his crime lab can analyze it."

"For what?" the neighbor asked. "A fingerprint? They threw a goddamned rock at the glass, not their fists. You should give your friend the rock. Let them do their DNA thing on it."

"But the glass would be very helpful, too."

The old man looked at Riggins, then back at Dark. "I don't get it. Why the glass? I watch those shows. I know what crime labs can do and what they can't do. What the hell would they do with a bunch of broken glass?"

Dark said, "Sir, it would help us a lot."

"You—what's your name?" The neighbor was now pointing a thick fingernail at Riggins. "You work for the city; is that right? Tell you what: You can have my broken glass if the city buys me a new sliding door."

Riggins said, "Okay, sure thing, bud." He pulled out his wallet, thumbed out five hundred dollars, and held it out to the old man.

"What's this?"

"Five hundred bucks."

"You're going to pay me five hundred dollars for a bunch of broken glass?"

"We're serious about crime in Malibu, sir."

"No wonder the city's going broke," he mumbled, then gestured them inside the house. "All right, c'mon. I'll give you your glass. I'll even throw in the rock for free."

Riggins saw Dark watching him as he brushed past him and into the house. Riggins smiled to himself. As good as Dark was at understanding people, sometimes he didn't have the first clue when it came to interacting with them.

chapter 32

When you die a violent and mysterious death in Los Angeles, your body goes to the morgue. Your possessions are divided among your loved ones. Perhaps even your soul goes to another plane of existence.

Everything else ends up in Josh Banner's trace analysis lab.

If your death involves a police investigation, tiny fragments of whatever surrounded you at the time of your demise would eventually find their way to Banner.

There was a lot of death in Los Angeles. Which was probably why it was a good thing that Banner was a bit of a pack rat.

Riggins hated coming to Banner's office. Every little fragment seemed to have this *eau de death* about it.

Dark, however, had always loved coming here. Banner was one of the few kindred spirits Dark seemed to have in local law enforcement; they were like two thirteen-year-olds geeking out over the same comic book.

"I thought you retired," Banner said.

"I did," Dark said. "But I could use a favor."

"Sure, sure. You got it."

Riggins could do nothing but hand over the two boxes full of broken glass and watch the boys go to work. He checked his watch and hoped Banner would put these windows back together before too much longer. Because his forty-eight hours were going to be up fairly soon. He knew that much.

Two boxes of broken glass. This was going to take a long time.

And that was fine with Josh Banner.

He was happiest when it was just him and the evidence. People were mercurial, moody, annoying. Evidence didn't change. Didn't flake out on you. Didn't throw a temper tantrum. Didn't play mind games with you.

Evidence just sat there and waited for you to figure it out. Silently. Patiently.

Banner pulled on his plastic gloves, donned his lab safety glasses, then plucked a pair of tweezers from the side pocket of his white lab coat. He set to work, patiently reassembling the glass pieces on a giant light table that cast a soft blue haze over the clear fragments. This, at least, gave Banner the illusion that he was working on a giant jigsaw puzzle, and all of the pieces he needed were on the table in front of him. And like a jigsaw puzzle, it would tell a story when it was complete.

He worked peacefully, swiftly. Hours later, he noticed he was about halfway done; another hour, and three-quarters of the shattered windows were reassembled. The closer you came to completing a puzzle, the faster the work became. He was just assembling the final pieces and beginning to understand the story they told, when Riggins and Dark walked into the room.

"You're just in time," Banner said, smiling nervously.

Riggins shoved his hands into his pockets and shuffled toward the light table.

```
To enter the crime lab, log into LEVEL26.com and
enter the code: shards
```

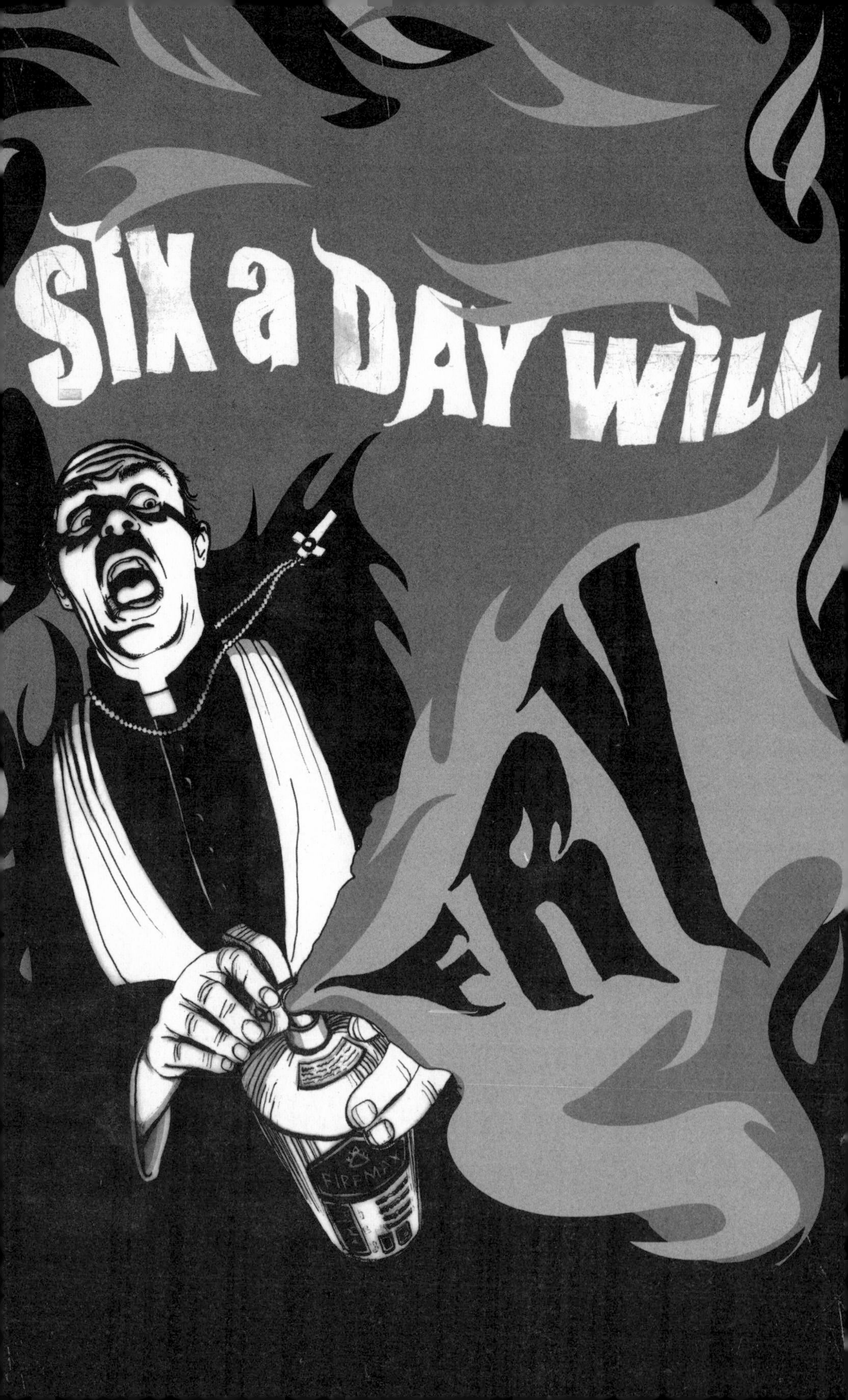
SIX A DAY WILL
FRY
FIREMAX

chapter 33

Banner was finishing his explanation just as Wycoff entered the room flanked by two Secret Service agents.

"Riggins, it's time."

Dark could barely focus on what was happening. His mind was still reeling from Banner's revelation.

"Goddammit," he said. "I checked every room. Every closet. I pulled up the fucking carpet . . ."

Riggins pressed his fingertips down on the light table like he was intending to crush it with the sheer force of his hands. He glanced at Wycoff, and then back at Dark. "This is not what I wanted to happen. You have to believe me."

But Dark wasn't listening. He was already calling Sibby.

"Everything's okay, honey," she said. "The cops are still here, fielding lawsuit threats from our lovely neighbor. But what about you?"

"Everything's fine," Dark said.

"Don't lie to me. What's wrong? I can hear it in your voice."

Banner's trace analysis had shown that, yes, rocks had struck both windows. But shards from only Dark's window showed a circular

133

pattern—proof that a glass cutter had been used on it first. There were traces of a suction cup used to pop out a small disc of glass.

Which was how he'd gotten in.

"I swear, honey," Dark said, "I'm fine. I'll call back in a little while. But let me know the minute the police leave."

Dark ended the call and turned to deal with the situation at hand.

Time was nearly up; Nellis and McGuire were waiting in the hallway, and they were prepared. Prepared. Hoods were shoved in their pockets. Wrist bindings and syringes were ready. The safe house and dumping grounds were standing by.

Their orders had changed slightly a few minutes before when Wycoff had arrived. Once the secretary gave his final ultimatum, the decision would be in Dark's hands.

A yes meant their mission was over; Nellis and McGuire would be reassigned after a brief furlough. Nellis wondered, idly, whether it would be in the Los Angeles area again. He didn't relish the idea of sleeping on the plane.

But a no from Dark would mean the mission would double. Wycoff had made it clear: Grab Dark and Riggins; subdue them both; transport them to the safe house. Riggins wouldn't be brought back, and Dark's forty-eight hours would begin.

Maybe it would be only twenty-four hours. Or twelve. Wycoff was becoming very impatient.

Maybe they would have to grab Dark's wife as well, a thought Nellis didn't relish either. But that was part of the job. He'd known agents who said *no women, no kids*, but they just weren't willing to go the distance. Frankly, they were pussies.

"Riggins," Wycoff said again, pointing to his watch. Riggins looked balefully in Dark's direction and sighed.

Dark noticed that the watch was an MTM—favored by Navy SEALs and no doubt part of Wycoff's constant efforts to appear as hard as possible. Dark knew a little of Wycoff's background; he knew the man had never set foot in a combat zone.

So the threat *was* real, coming straight from the top, and Wycoff was here to deal with Riggins, and then throw a little hissy fit and try to convince Dark personally.

Dark hated these fuckers. All of them.

He glanced over at Riggins.

Riggins realized that, sadly, once again, he was right.

Even after they killed him, they wouldn't leave Dark alone. Not with Wycoff here personally. All the secretary had to do was change his mind and apply the same pressure to Dark. Why wouldn't he? The man was a spoiled brat in an expensive suit who was used to getting what he wanted. All of the fucking time.

Wycoff looked down at his watch and saw the second hand sweeping toward the twelve. Fuck Riggins—he'd had his shot. Wycoff realized he should have applied the full-court press to Dark right from the start.

He refused to walk out of this police station without the answer he wanted.

Needed.

Nellis watched from the hallway and quickly ran through the options in his mind.

If they ran for it, Riggins would make the first move, probably taking something from the top of the lab counter and winging it at them. Dark would tune in a second later and try a flanking move, or perhaps even grab the secretary as a hostage. It would be awkward for a few moments but easily resolved. Maybe it wouldn't be time for syringes; maybe it would be time for guns. He didn't care one way or the other, as long as something happened soon. He was dying of boredom.

They were in the middle of a police station, so lethal action would be difficult to cover up, but then again, Riggins and Dark would have tried to assassinate the secretary of defense. The LAPD would shut the fuck up and like it.

Nellis felt the excitement and adrenaline creep into his bloodstream. This could be good. This could be *real* good.

00:03 . . .
00:02 . . .
00:01 . . .

Dark looked at Wycoff.

There was only one thing he could do.

"Mr. Secretary," Dark said, "Riggins told me about the escalation. I want you to know that you'll have my full cooperation with the case. I'm in . . ."

Riggins and Dark locked eyes. The weight of the world seemed to roll off Riggins's shoulders. An unspoken test of loyalty, one neither man would be able to explain, had finally been passed.

Wycoff looked stunned, as if he'd swallowed a peach pit. His security detail looked taken aback, too. For that matter, so was Riggins.

"Hey," he said. "Dark, look, you—"

"We've discovered something at my house. You want to take a look?"

Dark started walking them through the evidence, one piece at a time.

This was the only option that made sense. If they were going to take Riggins out over this, then it was clear they wouldn't stop at him. They'd hound Dark, day and night, quite possibly bringing in Sibby and her family—and years of their income tax filings, and work records, and medical records, and whatever else they could dig up—and keep hounding, pressuring, needling, until it would grind their lives to a halt. What was worse, Dark would be left without an ally he could trust in Special Circs.

No, sparing Riggins's job was the only way to take control of the investigation.

Because it was clear that this monster had taken an interest in Dark again, and Dark wasn't going to get him to go away by ignoring him.

And Dark wasn't going to give up until he a put a bullet in the real thing, not an image in a mirror.

The job was over. Nellis and McGuire returned to their van. Sleep awaited, then their new assignment. Nellis wouldn't admit this to anyone, not even himself, but he'd been looking forward to sliding that needle into Riggins's meaty neck and watching the life flutter out of his eyes. Watching that smirk fade from his lips. His body turn cold, and then still. Leaving now, to be honest, was a little disappointing.

But then again, who knew? Maybe they'd be back to clean this mess up some other day.

chapter 34

Somewhere in America

Sqweegel patrolled his basement naked, sawed-off shotgun in his left hand. Cinnamon grit dusted his sweaty, wiry body.

He watched his row of monitors as he paced. It was too exciting to sit still and watch passively. His nerves twitched with excitement, his very muscles telling him to *move*. He breathed quickly, excitedly.

There was much more to be done, now that the hunter was finally starting to listen. But first things first. Now it was time to feed the finches.

The monster made his way over to a wooden table—the same one his grandmother used to keep up in the kitchen. Its surface was crisscrossed with slash marks going back decades. The grooves were deep and black. Sometimes Sqweegel would stick his tongue down into one of them to see whether he could still taste the remnants of long-since-cooked ingredients. To see whether his tongue could bring back a forgotten sensory detail.

Not today, though. Today he busied himself with loading the shotgun.

He rested the stock on his hip, shoved a round into the magazine tube, then racked the action bar, slamming it into the chamber. The *clack* echoed off the basement's stone walls.

The finches in the cage across the room reacted to the sound, fluttering up and down in a panic.

Sqweegel lurched over to the makeshift aviary, and then squeezed his thin fingers between the wire bars. He had built the cage himself, fashioning it from old refrigerator shelves he found at a junkyard. The base of the cage was an old steel baking pan.

He longed to pet their heads, to rub the tiny soft feathers over their bony little skulls, but they never let him. In fact, they didn't seem to like their home at all. There were several broken eggs at the bottom of the makeshift cage, as if the male finches were unable to bring themselves to mate.

"Why do you fly?" Sqweegel purred to them. "Why don't you sing? Set you free and you die. In a cage with no wings."

In one lightning-quick move, Sqweegel raised his loaded shotgun to the cage and pressed the barrel right up to the wired bars.

The movement terrified the finches all over again.

But then he stopped.

Lowered the gun.

"I know," Sqweegel said. "You're hungry."

He sucked on the tip of his index finger briefly before tapping it into the birdseed dish—a soap dish from his grandmother's bathroom. He kept it outside the cage so he could control the finches' diet plan. It had been a day; they would be hungry.

Several half-ripe grass seeds clung to his saliva-coated fingernail. Sqweegel gently rubbed his finger over the edge of the black gun barrel, leaving a few seeds behind.

Then he placed the barrel flat against the edge of the cage.

"Tweet, tweet," Sqweegel said. "Time to eat, eat."

One brave finch, eyeing the seeds, ventured over to the edge of the cage. His clawed feet gripped the wire bars, and his head

139

cocked toward the barrel. He seemed curious. What was this? A new way to eat?

After a few moments, the finch let its hunger overcome its trepidation. It pecked at the seeds.

"There you go, little one. There you go . . ."

Sqweegel smiled, revealing his black teeth. The very sight should have been enough to frighten the bird back to the other side of the cage, but somehow the bird was assured. Nothing to worry about here. Just another way to feed.

Soon the finch finished the seeds and poked its head farther up the steel cave to see whether maybe—

Klik.
Boom.

The entire finch—as well as much of the cage behind him and his former roommates—was pulverized by the blast. Feathers and pieces of steel wire flew against the stone wall of the basement. Tiny chunks of bird meat clung to the remnants of the cage, tiny wisps of smoke curling from them.

Sqweegel bent down and picked up a few feathers, stroked one of them softly against the skin of his cheek. There was no way to know for sure, of course . . . but Sqweegel had a feeling the finch never even heard the click.

PART TWO

dark rising

chapter 35

p here you could see everything—all of Los Angeles, in
infinitesimal detail, all the way out to the Pacific.

Dark had never bothered with the observatory until
Sibby had dragged him here a few months after they had started
dating. *How often,* she'd said to him, *do you have the chance to feel
like God?* Dark, much to his surprise, had to admit that he dug
the view, even though he'd grown up in L.A., and dismissed the
place as a tourist trap.

Early in their relationship they would bring a picnic lunch up
here, along with a cold bottle of wine. They'd drink and let their
brains go fuzzy and joke about being God and what they'd smite
first, down on the sinful streets of L.A.

But they weren't here for a picnic. Not this evening.

Ever since telling Riggins he'd join the hunt for Sqweegel,
Dark had felt the day spin wildly out of control. There were fran-
tic calls to Sibby after realizing that the wriggling little worm had
been inside their house—but she didn't answer the house or her

cell phone for an agonizing half hour. Finally she'd called back to tell Dark that she'd been shopping and hadn't heard the ring. She'd had to get out of the house for a while.

Dark had thought about it for a second, then said, "Good. Stay out all afternoon. Don't tell me where you're going; don't tell anybody. Keep it random."

"Are you serious?" Sibby had asked, a laugh in her voice.

"Humor a crazy ex-cop," Dark had said, wincing as he spoke the words. *Ex-cop*. Technically, his retirement was thirty-five minutes in the past; he was back on the job.

"Okay, okay," she'd said. "See you at home tonight."

"How about you meet me at six thirty tonight at our old place. Up in the hills?"

Sibby had started to say the words. "Old place? Wait, do you mean the Grif—"

"Exactly," he said. "Buy good stuff. I love you."

"I love you, too, even if you're weird."

Dark had arrived an hour early—mostly to scope out the place. The backlit walls and dark golden domes made the observatory look more like a religious gathering place than a tourist attraction. Then again, that description also seemed to apply. Human beings gathered here to gaze at the heavens and consider their place in the universe. Almost like a church for atheists.

Sibby had arrived at six thirty sharp and quickly shot down Dark's attempts at small talk and light conversation. She knew him too well.

"Okay, stop," Sibby said. "What am I missing here? You drag me up here to one of our favorite places, we haven't talked all afternoon . . . Are you leaving me or something?"

Dark looked at her. This was just like Sibby—right to the point. No pretense, no games.

144

"Yeah," he said.

Sibby smiled at first, until she looked at his face and knew he was, in fact, telling the truth.

He was leaving her.

The angry look on her face slammed a thousand hot needles in his heart. It knocked the breath out of him until she turned away, staring down at the Los Angeles basin below.

"You know, if this is your idea of a joke . . ."

"No, it's not."

Sibby turned back to face him again, scanning his tired eyes for the little tells that only lovers—*soul mates*—can see. She saw that he was telling the truth, and then her own eyes went dead. Cold.

Dark reached out and touched Sibby's arm. It was stiff. Unmoving.

"We took the broken glass from our home to the forensics lab this morning."

Nothing on Sibby's face. It was like the frozen-over surface of a lake.

"The reconstructed window showed that someone had use a glass cutter to break into the house, then smashed it later to cover it up."

Still nothing. Her face was Arctic permafrost. Were any of his words penetrating?

"This guy . . . this sick son of a bitch . . . was the one who left the watch. Who broke our window. He got in with a glass cutter, made it past the dogs, and somehow hid for more than an hour. You must have slept the whole time. He was inside when I came home."

"No," she said coolly.

"No? What do you mean no?"

"I'm a light sleeper. There's no way someone could have been inside our house."

145

"Sibby, the forensics don't lie. Someone broke in. And he might have been in your room."

"Did you hear yourself say that, by the way, Steve? *Your* room? Like you've already left me?"

There wasn't time to talk her through this. And now he saw his mistake. He'd wanted to leave her with a happy memory. The happiest memory *possible*, anyway, given the circumstances. Her favorite place. Dark, though, supposed he knew what would happen all along. He could have done this anywhere and the result would have been the same: a momentary flash of confusion, quickly masked by a fierce and powerful self-defense mechanism.

What made Sibby strong was the same thing that enabled her to throw up her mental shields. And God help anything that tried to break through.

It was how she dealt with her parents' divorce, when she was only thirteen.

How she dealt with a dorm-room rape, when she was only seventeen.

How she was able to love him now—freely, unconditionally, because she knew how to guard herself in case the world came crumbling down. Like it seemed to be doing right now.

Sibby stood up, even as Dark continued speaking.

"I've packed our things and had them sent somewhere safe," he was saying. "The dogs have been boarded . . ."

But Sibby wasn't listening—she was leaving. She took a few steps before Dark realized it and was walking toward the concrete stairs, moving surprisingly fast. He cleared the distance between them and took her hand. She pulled it away.

"Please listen to me, Sibby. Your life is in *danger*. That's the only reason I'm doing this . . ."

But it was too late. The shields were up, and Sibby was gone.

chapter 36

G o, Sibby thought. Just walk away from the observatory. Across the lawn. To the car, then down off the top of this damned mountain.

A few steps away she almost stumbled, her right ankle on the verge of twisting, but she caught herself. She was not going to fall down now. She was going to find a way out of here. Hole up for a while—maybe at her father's. He was only an hour away, up the coast. Sibby surprised herself by how quickly the plan formed in her mind, even as she strode across the plaza to her car.

What bothered her wasn't the fact that Steve wanted them to separate. He wanted to protect her; she got that. She knew how his mind worked. It was completely wrongheaded, and she wanted to scream at him for even thinking it, but she understood.

Your life is in danger. Is that what he'd said? Didn't he realize that when crisis strikes, you don't pull apart—you come together?

But honestly, that wasn't what made her uneasy now. It was the fact that she had *lied* to Steve that morning.

She didn't tell him that she *had* been in a strangely deep sleep.

She climbed into the driver's seat, turned the key in the ignition.

She hadn't been able to bring herself to confess that her hips *had* been sore.

She shifted gears and took off back down the mountain.

And she hadn't even let herself remember, until right this very moment, as she shifted in her seat and felt the fatigue in her core muscles and her back, the very worst part—it wasn't the first time.

Dark gave her a few moments, then walked across the lawn, climbed into his Yukon, and hurled it down twisty Hollywood Drive after her. Not so much to intercept her or change her mind—frankly, that didn't matter now. All that mattered was getting Sibby away from L.A., out of the reach of the twitchy little freak who seemed to be fixated on her.

Look at you, Sibby. Trying so hard to keep your emotions in check, even in private. You won't even indulge yourself when nobody's looking.

Well, Sqweegel thought, watching on a monitor in his basement lair, *I happen to be looking. But you don't know that, do you?*

Sibby rocketed down the 101, changing lanes at every given opportunity. It was still technically rush hour—then again, it always felt like rush hour in L.A. She saw a gap; she pressed down on the accelerator and slid into it, then raced forward and looked for the next gap. She wanted to be as far away from Steve, from the observatory, from *everything*, as possible . . . for now. Think about it later.

Especially the soreness. And what it meant.

Dark followed her down the 101, then through downtown on the 110 and over to the 10, all the way out to the Pacific Coast Highway. Could go either way from here. She could take the exit to their place in Malibu, or she could continue north. If she blew past their exit, Dark could relax a little. That meant she'd be heading directly to her father, who'd watch over her like a hawk.

There was a sea of red eyes in front of him, blinking with varying degrees of intensity. L.A. traffic was a living thing, and Dark was the first to admit that Sibby was much better at negotiating its circulatory system. It took a lot of concentration just to keep up.

Sqweegel stared at Sibby's face on the monitor, entranced.

Human beings reveal their emotions through not only words but also a symphony of facial tics and movements. You could watch most movies without sound and follow the story almost perfectly. The details didn't matter; it was the hesitation, the fear, the pain, the confusion, the agony that played out on the faces of the actors that told the real story.

Actors were no match, however, for the real thing.

And to enjoy that particular show, you had to be clever.

Modern car gadgets have made it easy. GPS units are increasingly common, and Sqweegel found it simple to attach a remote camera—piggybacked on the existing wireless signal—to such a device. Like the one Sibby Dark kept in her car.

Enough watching, though. Now it was time to step into the movie himself.

Sibby was stunned when her cell phone started playing the opening riff of "Personal Jesus."

149

Now? Of all times, this creepy son of a bitch texts me *now*?

She knew she should ignore it, focus on the road, but she couldn't resist. She plucked the cell from her purse and glanced down at the screen.

GOOD SEEING YOU AGAIN LAST NIGHT

Sibby had to read it twice to comprehend, and the second time the implications exploded like little bombs in her brain. *Last night? Again?* They distracted her from the pulsing, weaving traffic of the 10 for just a few seconds.

One second, though, was all it really took.

chapter 37

Sibby's foot hammered the brake, but it was too late, the gap too narrow. The front bumper and her grill collapsed from the force of the impact, followed a tenth of a second later by the hood, which was ripped from its moorings and sent smashing into the windshield. Glass exploded. Her instincts were to continue to press down, make the brakes *work* already, as if pressing them any harder could minimize—or somehow undo—the damage still playing out around her body. But the car had been going fifty-seven miles per hour, and the gap was too small for braking systems to even matter.

A tenth of a second later the airbag exploded in Sibby's face, smashing into her nose and mouth. The steering wheel bent under her grip, the brake pedal snapped free beneath her foot, and the column beneath the wheel rushed forward as if to impale her. The impact, however, had caused her body to shift to the left, and the column missed her—as well as the baby inside her—by inches.

The column slammed into and through the passenger seat, ripping fabric, crushing springs.

Her door and the passenger doors were ripped from their hinges. The backseat was wrenched from the frame and slammed into Sibby's seat from behind. By this time, she was already being thrown from the vehicle, tumbling through the air toward the concrete barrier that separated her lane from the horrified drivers in the eastbound traffic.

All of this took less than a second.

Sqweegel's thumb, in fact, was still on the SEND button.

Dark was a quarter mile away, but it might as well have been a thousand.

He hammered the pedal and rocketed down the 10 until he was like a kamikaze pilot dead set on reaching the ground faster than anyone else, weaving around other drivers, whose red taillights blazed as they tried to come to a stop.

Dark's Yukon fishtailed. He leapt out before it came to a complete stop and began running to the scene, a few dozen car lengths away. Each step felt like it touched down on a treadmill speeding backward. The soles of his feet burned as they slammed down and rose from the asphalt again. His breathing seemed to stop. No matter how hard he pumped, he couldn't run fast enough.

Please don't let it be Sibby's car was the prayer running through his head, but Dark knew it was in vain. It was as if his blood knew first, had already received the information directly from the crash site: *Yes, it was Sibby's car.*

Dark finally reached the crushed vehicle a few seconds later.

God help him, it was Sibby's car.

The vehicle was like a broken toy in the middle of a messy toddler's playroom. Chunks of plastic and metal and glass had been sprayed all over the road.

Sibby was lying there among the wreckage—not moving.

Not breathing.

Dark leapt over the back of the car and crouched down next to her. His hands shook until he willed them to stay calm. Then he tilted her head back, pressed his lips to hers, blew, started the chest compressions—but then he saw the large stain spreading across her belly. Oh, God, no. He ripped off his shirt, feeling the seams burst when it didn't yield quickly enough, and pressed it to her stomach.

Dark knew the muscles surrounding a fetus were extraordinarily strong. Women developed a virtual ball of armor to protect the life form inside, and it took a lot to break through that armor.

But the blood continued to spread, like a spilled inkpot across a pristine white tablecloth . . .

The remote camera in Sibby's car was completely obliterated, but Sqweegel had expected that. So he tapped a few keys and within a few moments found the I-10 traffic cameras he wanted. When the image resumed, an ambulance and fire engine were fighting their way through the traffic to the crash site.

"Don't worry, Dark," Sqweegel said softly, watching the man's tiny image on the screen. "Los Angeles Socha Medical Hospital is nearby. They'll get her there in time."

He reached out a latex-wrapped finger and rubbed the blurry white image of Sibby, imagining he was soothing her.

"After all," he said, "we've got to do everything we can to protect that baby."

chapter 38

Malibu, California
9:14 P.M.

S o this is what people have when they have real lives,
Riggins thought. A lot of nice stuff. Riggins could have
nice stuff, he supposed. If he didn't mind it sitting in a
house collecting dust.

The movers were hauling away the last of the boxes. Riggins had
hired them personally—a local outfit he'd found online called Starving Students. Seemed goofy enough to be honest. Riggins made the
call, told them that it was a rush job and that they'd be hand-
somely rewarded for their speed. Who knew whether these guys
actually were students, but they wouldn't be starving that night.

They also were unlikely to be connected to Sqweegel in any
way; Riggins had found them at random in a Craigslist ad.

"That everything?" Riggins asked.

"Yeah, I think so," said the lead mover.

"Okay," Riggins said. "Follow that car. He'll escort you."

The car was unmarked—FBI. Two guys Riggins knew and
trusted as much as he could trust anyone.

Not that it ultimately mattered; this stuff was going to a private storage facility—again, chosen at random by Riggins. If Sqweegel wanted to work hard to trace Dark's stuff, then let him have a field day. Let him jizz all over the fancy Crate and Barrel crap, shove a Restoration Hardware candlestick up his ass.

Because there was only one way Dark would ever be reclaiming his belongings—and that was if Sqweegel was dead. Otherwise, Steve would be. And he wouldn't be giving a crap about his furniture.

Sibby, on the other hand . . . well, she might mind.

Riggins felt a little weird about all of this—even though it was the right thing to do. Even though it was his goddamned idea.

Part of it was genuine concern for Dark and Sibby. If that maniac had found his way into this beachfront home once, he would do it again and again, with impunity. There was no way either one could spend another night here.

But honestly, part of Riggins wanted Dark completely focused; otherwise, this thing really would kill him. And Dark couldn't focus with Sibby in the frame. No, it was best to have her stashed with her father while Dark concentrated on the task at hand.

The moving truck pulled away. Riggins took one last tour of the house with a flashlight, just to make sure he hadn't missed anything. Or overlooked something.

But no—he had been thorough. He was about to lock up for good when he heard a noise upstairs.

Dripping water.

No. Don't be surprised. It would be just like him. Hole up in a goddamned shoebox and wait for everyone to leave, and then, at the last possible moment . . .

Well, fuck him, Riggins thought, and drew his weapon. He almost hoped the little bastard was up there.

Almost.

He headed upstairs slowly, veins pounding with every heartbeat. There wasn't just a drip now; it sounded like a steady stream pouring from a faucet.

Moving down the hallway now. Closer to the sound of the running water.

What if it was one of those starving students, up here washing his hands after taking a leak? Could have been lost in his own little iPod world as his buddies pulled away. He didn't deserve a bullet in the head for being a dipshit.

So Riggins called, "FBI!"

No answer.

Farther down the hall, Riggins realized the source: the master bathroom. The water was louder now. Gushing. Riggins put his ear to the cold wood. Listened.

It was a bathtub, filling. Familiar sound, back when he was still married. His exes loved their Calgon moments.

Riggins stepped back. Now or never. He smashed his foot through the wood, just to the right of the knob. The door popped open. Riggins darted inside. Whipped his pistol left, right, center.

The bathroom was roiling with steam rising like a fog. He checked the only space left: the closet.

Nothing.

He nudged the hot faucet off. Let the steam settle a little. Some water dripped into the tub.

Drip.

Drip.

Drop.

The sound made Riggins look at the floor. There, on the smooth white tile, was a tiny bird feather. Steve and Sibby didn't have any birds. The dogs would probably never stop trying to eat them.

So then, what was it doing here?

Riggins carefully took the thin, hard shaft between the tips of his fingers and lifted the feather to eye level. Dull gray, with tinges of pinkish brown along the edges. Riggins was pretty damn far from a bird expert—he knew some flew, some didn't, and some tasted great with gravy and stuffing. But there were people in Special Circs who could track this thing down to its order, family, genus, and species.

The kind of bird, however, wasn't what bothered Riggins. Was this possibly left by Sqweegel? That didn't seem right. The freak who never leaves so much as a skin cell behind suddenly drops a *bird feather*, of all things? No. It had to be something else.

Maybe a bird flew in through the broken patio window, flapped around here for a while, then escaped to another part of the house. But if that was the case, then why didn't Riggins find any other traces of a bird or its feathers anywhere else? He'd packed Dark and Sibby's things personally.

Maybe it *was* Sqweegel. Maybe he was finally slipping up.

As Riggins pondered this and scanned the room for more feathers, the steam cleared. As the steam cleared, the writing on the mirror began to appear.

It was a phone number, written with what looked like a child's fingertip.

Riggins stood, flipped open his cell phone, and snapped a photo before it could disappear. Then he started thumbing digits.

To call the killer, log into LEVEL26.com and enter the code: oneaday

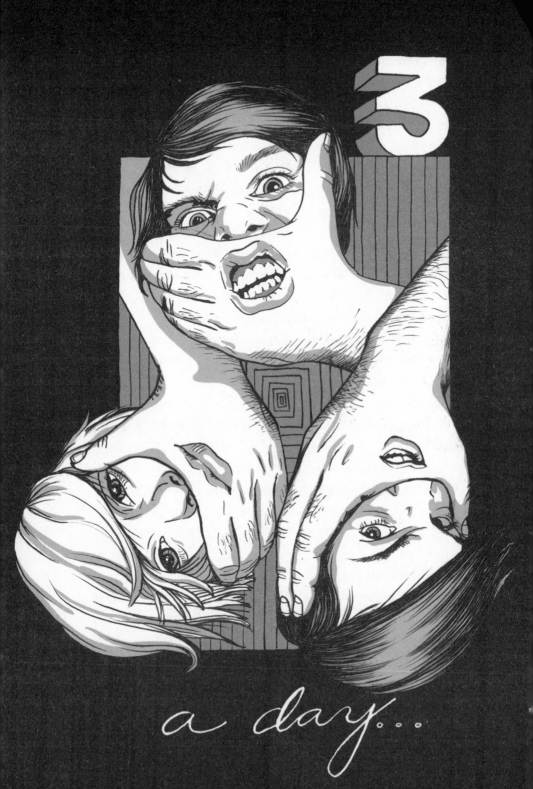

chapter 39

D ark was sitting in the waiting room when Riggins returned, looking sweaty and out of breath. Clearly, he'd raced here after getting Dark's text with the news of the accident, and had made some phone calls on the way.

"We'll have two cops on her, twenty-four/seven," Riggins was saying, "and I've already got a team combing the wreckage for trace."

But Dark was only half listening. He knew Riggins was trying to reassure him. *Don't worry. We've got this covered. Nothing will happen to her. Everything will be all right.* In other words, the usual lies.

Instead, however, Dark's mind was on the procedure being performed behind his back, in another part of the hospital. Past the blinds, through the drywall, across another hallway, and through another pale wall . . .

. . . where Sibby had IVs in her arms, white bandages on her legs, a plastic tube down her throat. They'd stripped her, and they'd set to work immediately. There was much to stabilize: her head, her heart, her lungs, the internal bleeding . . .

The love of his life was on an operating table, and surgeons and nurses were swarming all around her, all of them focused on the same task: saving her and their baby.

Dark breathed in slowly, and his nostrils filled with that harsh stuff they used to clean hospital waiting rooms. He tried to will himself into that room with Sibby, just to be with her. Let her know she was not alone.

But he couldn't get the recording he'd just heard out of his mind. The words he'd heard at the other end of that phone number were a distraction from Sibby. The childlike yet sinister tone. Something he'd never heard before.

The voice of his adversary.

One a day will die.
Two a day will lie.
Three a day will cry.
Four a day will sigh . . .

He recited the sickly little taunting nursery rhyme, something other kids in the playground would chant just to freak you out or make you cry and run home to Mommy. It sounded vaguely familiar, yet Dark knew it wasn't something he'd heard on the playground. Where did he know it from?

Back when Dark was still on the hunt for Sqweegel, there were only second-class relics to examine. He remembered the distinction from Catholic grade school: Second-class relics were objects touched by a saint. Holy books. A crucifix once held by a saint. A fragment of a shirt or a robe.

Sqweegel's relics were a little different. Dead, mangled, tortured bodies. Messages scrawled in his victims' blood. Closets he'd chosen to hide in.

Nothing of the actual man himself. He was too careful, too methodical for that.

In other words, no first-class relics—pieces of the saints themselves. A fragment of bone. A strand of hair. A toenail clipping. A strand of muscle tissue.

But now, finally, they had a first-class relic of Sqweegel: a sample of his voice.

After hearing it, Dark found it difficult to *unhear* it. The words seemed to dig through the pulpy mass of his brain, creating their own little echo chambers. You could silence the source, but you couldn't stop the relentless echo:

> *Five a day ask why.*
> *Six a day will fry.*

He should be focused on Sibby. On their child. Not wasting mental energy on this.

Riggins was going on, too, about how he personally had briefed the cops on Sqweegel's capabilities. He wasn't going to be sneaking into this room under a gurney or inside an X-ray machine. They were going to check everything larger than a Jell-O cup. Hell, they'd even check the Jell-O cups, just to make sure.

Dark nodded as if he were listening. But he was actually trying to stop hearing the words of the poem.

It was as if Sqweegel's voice had been genetically designed to create a severe physical response in Dark, like an influenza virus attacking a host. There was too much to block out.

> *Seven a day . . .*
> *Oh, my.*

Riggins's fingertips touched his arm.

"Hey. The doctors say she's going to be in there for quite a while. Why don't you go somewhere for a while to clear your head? I'll be right here."

After a few moments Dark finally nodded, then wandered off down the crowded hall and out of the hospital. There was only one place he could think to go.

chapter 40

Somewhere in Los Angeles

S qweegel twisted off the metal lid, placed it on the floor next to him. Then he turned the red metal canister upside down. The white powder—sodium bicarbonate—dropped to the ground with a dull, dusty thud.

A few quick swipes of the rag cleared away most of the sodium bicarbonate. It didn't have to be perfect. Normally, this would bother Sqweegel. He'd fixate on every remaining speck of powder, and he'd end up wiping the interior for hours.

But not today. There wasn't time. He reassured himself that he was simply being prudent, then moved on to the next step.

Next, he fed a length of clear tube into a rusty metal drum, then placed the other end of the tube in his mouth. He sucked three times, quickly, until the liquid partially filled his mouth. He pressed his thumb over his end of the tube, held the tube over the canister, then released his thumb.

The liquid poured freely. Sqweegel loved the tin-pan sound of it, hitting metal. The powerful fumes, enveloping his nasal cavities.

It reminded him of lying in the back of a station wagon, listening to the father or mother or college senior or somebody filling the tank of the old family truckster for a long highway trip. A trip they'd never complete.

Enough for now. Sqweegel knew he could easily become lost in his own memories. All it took to trip the breaker was a simple sound, or smell, or texture.

Besides, there were four more canisters to go.

And when the process was complete, and the tops with the pressure gauges and hoses were reattached, there were five modified fire extinguishers resting on the floor.

Sqweegel still had a little liquid in his mouth, left over from the last canister. He took a Bic lighter from his tool kit. Thumbed it to life. Spat the liquid over the flame and—

Whoooosh.

The fireball briefly illuminated the room around him. The wheelchairs. The metal cabinets. The tile floor. The wooden chairs. The drabness of a storage room that was all but forgotten, under the everyday bustle of the floors above.

The kind of storage room where you'd keep old fire extinguishers. Or metal cans of gasoline for the backup power generators.

The kind of storage room that didn't have good locks or competent security.

chapter 41

D ark stared up at the immense, backlit cross. For a moment,
it made him feel like a little kid again. Back when he'd
first learned about God.

He remembered being three years old, standing in the middle
of the pews at church, his birth father telling him, *As long as you
pray to God, everything will be okay*. He thought of Sibby on the
operating table, Riggins standing guard nearby, and he wondered
where his father was now. He hadn't seen him in more than thirty
years. He had very few, hazy memories of him. But his old man's
trust in God had always stayed with him, and he hoped to hell
his faith would be rewarded now.

His foster father had also been a religious man. Faith, he had
once explained, was everything. And there were plenty of Bible
stories illustrating the power of faith. Abraham, on the brink of
slaughtering his own son. Jonah, in the belly of an impossibly
large beast. Job, enduring torments that seemed without end. But

in the end, faith and prayer were what had saved them all. And that's what Steve had grown up believing.

They didn't tell you about all of the *catches*, though.

They waited until you were a little older for that.

Dark walked away from the black Yukon, thumbed the security lock, then walked toward the front doors of the Hollywood United Methodist Church on Franklin Street. He hadn't grown up Methodist, but he liked coming to this church from time to time.

Maybe it was because it held its own in the middle of Hollywood itself, several blocks away from Grauman's Chinese and the flashing spotlights and open-air malls with huge Babylonian-style elephants reared up in worship of the Great God Film. If you wanted to stand on a balcony and catch the best view of the Hollywood sign, you couldn't do it without the United Methodist Church in your frame of view. *That* was holding your own. Dark admired it.

This church was also a place that allowed him to be truly anonymous. He wasn't a regular worshipper here. Neither was anyone he knew.

Dark didn't usually attend during a service anyway. He preferred to be here alone. Only in the solitude could he sit and sort out his mind.

Inside the church it was tomb quiet. Every footfall echoed off the marble walls. Toward the front, six priests kneeled in front of the altar, heads bowed, praying in silence. On the left side, a lone man in an overcoat was standing at a row of candles, lighting them one by one with a narrow wooden matchstick. He finished, placed the matchstick to the side, bowed his head for a moment, then exited the church. Maybe he was one of the last in Hollywood. One of the last true believers.

Dark still believed.

He truly did. Nothing that had happened in his life could shake him from the fundamental idea that there was a God.

But Dark's jury was still out on his benevolence.

You could pray. You could have faith. You could live a life with the single goal of doing good. You could do your best to balance that goal with the goals of being a good father and a good husband.

You could brush your teeth three times a day and floss. You could help old ladies across the street. You could refrain from vice and other excesses.

And yet God could still take it all away.

Or worse: let it happen.

This was not a three-year-old's God. This was the real God, his mask torn away to reveal supernatural indifference.

That was the catch.

Still, Dark reached out to him.

He chose a spot in the middle of the sea of pews, fell to his knees, and began the Our Father, trying to concentrate on the words. Because a mumbling recitation of something you've memorized isn't prayer; if so, a robot would be capable of worship. But the more Dark tried to focus on the words, the more he thought of Sibby. *Thy will be done.* Was that thy will? Her broken body lying in the middle of the steaming Los Angeles asphalt? *Give us this day our daily bread.*

Lead us not into temptation . . .

But deliver us from evil.

Dark prayed the best he could, then let his mind go blank. Maybe God would finally talk to him now. Maybe there had been enough indifference, and God would realize what had happened, and he'd say, *Oh, you. I haven't thought about you since you were three years old. . . .*

But nothing. Still deathly quiet in the church. Dark could hear the sound of his joints softly popping as he shifted his weight on the wooden kneeler.

God wasn't paying attention today.

Dark stood up and watched the six priests continue their vigil. Maybe they'd found the direct line. Maybe that was how you did it.

He moved to the back of the church and stared at the row of candles the Last True Believer had lit. They illuminated a nearby statue of Jesus Christ dying on the cross. It was at least fifteen feet tall and hand carved.

Was that how it worked? Did you have to suffer like no man had suffered before just to receive a nod from the Father?

Maybe, Dark thought, *he could put a good word in with the son.*

All at once, without conscious thought, he found himself falling to his knees and breaking down. Not in tears, and not in prayer, but in plain words.

"Please don't take her from me," he said softly. "Please don't hurt the baby. They're innocent. If you want to take anyone, take me. Don't have mercy on my soul. Have mercy on theirs. . . ."

The words tumbled out of his mouth. After a few moments, they stopped.

Dark made the sign of the cross, then left the church.

chapter 42

A few minutes later, Jesus's feet were on fire.

All it took was one match, placed to his divine left toe. Paint over wood. No miracle in that. Easiest thing ever.

And then the flames traveled down the accelerant-soaked line that led to the row of offertory candles, feeding the flames at the base of the cross.

The fire started just after Dark departed the premises. This was planned, of course. If Dark smelled smoke, he'd only stay until he could find a way to stop what had to happen. And that wasn't the point—to have Dark fight a fire.

No, he wanted Dark to turn around and see a trail of fiery hell in his wake.

Sqweegel dropped the match into the metal offering box, then crept up the marble stairs to the choir loft, which would give him a God's-eye view. He was still wearing the overcoat, so he stripped it off now. He wanted the Maker to see him as He made him:

Glorious.

The priest on the far left in the row of six noticed it first—the crackling sound. He looked to his right, then up to the ceiling for some reason, then finally . . . *Ah, there you go, Father. So courageous of you. The funny sound is coming from the back of the church, near all of the rows of votive candles. We are the light of the world, they proclaim.*

But they were also fantastic accelerants.

By the time the priest had risen to his feet and tapped the shoulder of his nearest companion, the hand-carved statue of Jesus was completely engulfed in flames.

Here's your sign, Sqweegel thought.

The view from the choir loft was perfect for the ballet of panic that followed. Three priests running around one set of pews, two around the other. All drawing closer to behold the miracle. Only one of them was thinking practically. And he ran into the sacristy for the nearest available fire extinguisher.

Meanwhile, the five other *servants of God* drew closer to the fire, as if they could stop the flames with a few drizzles of holy water.

The sixth priest ran down the center aisle with a fire extinguisher in each hand. This guy was really thinking. He yelled to his colleagues, handed one of the extinguishers over.

Now faith and mystery and holy terror gave way to cold logic: They had to put this thing out before the whole church—which featured many tons of wood—caught fire.

The sixth priest was the first. He pulled the safety pin, aimed the rubber hose at Jesus's feet, and squeezed the trigger. But it wasn't sodium bicarbonate that sprayed out of the hose. It was gasoline.

A thin line of fire traveled back up the line of gasoline and into the extinguisher—

FA-FOOM.

The metal canister exploded in the sixth priest's hands, and the resulting fireball engulfed the two priests standing closest to him.

But the other priest with the extinguisher hadn't put it together yet. He saw the awful explosion, saw his brothers' bodies consumed by white-hot fury. But in that split second, he assumed it was a gas leak. Or a bomb.

No reason at all to suspect the extinguisher in his hands, which the priest knew was the only thing that could save the lives of his colleagues. He pulled the pin, screaming, then rushed over to the first burning body he could and squeezed the trigger, trying to recite an entire prayer in the same moment.

He got as far as "Oh, Heavenly Father" before he was blown apart, head and shoulders heading toward heaven while his torso flew backward into the nave.

Sqweegel watched from twenty feet above. He felt the heat wash over his face, cleansing it. The sweet scent of burning flesh soaked into his pores.

Oh, this was better than he'd imagined.

Now he watched the remaining two priests—the ones whose flesh wasn't fusing to their bones—try to find their way out. Oh, this was amazing, the logic crumbling under pressure. The frenzy setting in.

They immediately ran for the front entrance. Which made the most sense, of course. Why run the long way back through the church, then duck through the sacristy, then down a flight of stairs, then finally through the rectory lobby and out the side door? Why not take the exit that was mere yards away?

Because the front doors were locked with industrial-strength chains; that's why.

Sqweegel had put them there, just after Dark left.

But see, here's where logic broke down. One tug, and you should be able to understand that these doors weren't opening. You hear the rattle of the chains, the dull thud of the links against the wooden door, and you realize: *Okay, the doors are chained. Let's find another way out.*

Not these priests, though. They were too panicked to make

this simple leap. They pulled at the doors and howled as the thick chains banged against the wood. As if their shrieking cries would be interpreted by God as *prayer* and a request for divine intervention. One touch from the heavens and the chains would disappear.

God, though, didn't hear them. Or maybe refused their request. Because the chains remained looped around the ornate brass door handles, as secure as ever.

And by the time the two remaining priests realized their folly and ran back into the church proper, it was too late.

Sqweegel drove away from the church, muttering to himself:

"Hell hath enlarged itself.

"And its fires were *ravenous*."

chapter 43

As promised, Riggins was sitting in the painfully bright waiting room, keeping careful vigil. Dark took the seat next to him, and then pressed his forehead against the tips of his fingers.

"Anything yet?" he asked.

"No. She's still in surgery. Doc popped his head in for a second, but he wouldn't talk to me. Let me page him again."

"Okay."

"Oh, and Wycoff called. Asking why we hadn't caught Sqweegel yet, now that you were on board. I swear to God, give me a few minutes alone in a room with that officious little prick . . ."

"Ignore him," Dark said. "We just need to focus on the mission."

"Well, you can ignore him. I have to deal with him calling every hour."

Dark sat down. Nothing in the waiting room had changed. The same faces. The same stack of unread celebrity magazines. The same cocktail of sweat and burned coffee and desperation.

The same TV, tuned to the same channel . . . which was now playing the local eleven o'clock news.

The white block text at the bottom of the screen hit Dark first:

HOLLYWOOD UNITED METHODIST

Then the words of the chief of police of North Hollywood, speaking into a KCAL9 mike:

"*. . . know six people have died inside. The fire department said the doors were locked. Now, there's been a lot of theft in the area, but instead of keeping the bad guys out, they kept the good people trapped inside.*"

Dark didn't understand. He had just been there. What did the drive take, from there to Socha? Twenty minutes, this time of night? Half hour, tops?

"Reporting live from North Hollywood, this is . . ."

Dark's BlackBerry chirped. He took it out of his pocket, scrolled down. One new message. He clicked the button and his blood ran cold.

To receive a text from Sqweegel, log into
LEVEL26.com and enter the code: crossout

chapter 44

Socha Medical Hospital / Intensive Care Unit
Thursday / 12:09 A.M.

Dark watched the machines beep and throb and monitor and inject and calculate and display. They did their job efficiently, dispassionately, mindlessly. Their job was keeping his love alive.

Sometimes Dark wished he could be just a machine. Consider it: Your day could be little more than carrying out basic functions, with no messy emotions clouding the daily routines. Do your job; feed and exercise your body until it eventually broke down. But that was okay, too, because new machines were being born every day. The machine that was *you* wasn't vital. Not in the grand schematic of things.

Then he would think about Sibby and remember that only with her could he let himself go, let himself feel again. And how good it felt to feel. How life was more than a series of basic functions carried out by anonymous cogs in a machine too big to see. Without her . . . Well, without her Dark knew he *would* revert to being little more than a machine.

The head surgeon, a barrel-chested man with strangely slender hands, interrupted with a quick knock on the door.

"Mr. Dark?"

"Yeah," Dark said. He looked down and realized he had been clinging to Sibby's fingers. That was all he *could* cling to, thanks to the IV butterfly needles taped to the backs of both of her beautiful hands.

An hour before, in the waiting room, the same surgeon had told him that the surgery had been a "success." Somehow, the word sounded wrong in the context. The surgeon explained that all of Sibby's internal bleeding had been stopped and the baby was stable . . . for the time being. But there was another problem they were monitoring—a toxic buildup in her blood. They'd know more after a few tests. Until then, Dark was told, wait and pray.

Like those priests in the church? Had they died because Dark had just so happened to choose that church for a few minutes of peace?

Had Sqweegel been watching from inside the church, just like he did in Rome, waiting for Dark to leave? Or was he tucked away somewhere else, triggering the fire by remote, then crossing the item off his sick little poem:

Six a day will fry.

Now the surgeon was back, startling Dark, who'd been lost in his own head.

"We just received the blood work from the lab," the surgeon told him. "Sibby's liver is failing."

"What?"

"We believe it was damaged in the accident."

Dark looked down at Sibby, eyes closed, surrounded by tubes and tape and machines.

"Ordinarily," the surgeon continued, "we'd want to get the

baby out of there right away—it's far enough along and would have excellent chances of survival outside the womb. But a cesarean is out of the question right now. When your liver fails, your body can't deal with the stress of surgery. There's an extremely high risk of Sibby bleeding to death."

"What are the options?" Dark asked.

"Not many good ones, I'm afraid," the surgeon said. "The clock is ticking. We could do the cesarean followed by the liver transplant—if we're lucky enough to find a donor in time. But let me stress that this is a very complicated procedure, and not performed very often."

"And when it *is* performed?"

The surgeon lowered his head. "It's rarely a success."

Dark looked at Sibby's unconscious face. He knew what she'd say: Get the baby out of her; forget about her; the baby was all that mattered.

But he wasn't going to make that call. Especially if there was a chance she could fight back on her own. Not that the surgeon had indicated this was a possibility. But the surgeon didn't know Sibby and the fighter she was.

"Should I place her on the urgent transplant list?" the surgeon asked. "If we're even thinking about trying it, we have to get on that list immediately."

"How long does she have?" Dark asked.

"We have a window of about seventy-two hours. Unless she goes into labor first."

"Put her on the list," Dark said, and with that, the surgeon nodded and made his way out of the ICU.

Dark went back to watching the machines watching Sibby. Machines never had to make decisions like these. For machines, it was all ones and zeros, simple computations that carried no moral or emotional weight. A machine never has to choose between the love of its life and an unborn child.

Forget the machines. He had to know what Sibby wanted. Dark took her fingers again and rubbed them gently. Her skin was smooth and frighteningly cold.

"Hey," he said quietly. "It's me. I only have a few minutes, so . . . I wanted to say thank you. Thank you for making me the happiest man in the world. None of this is your fault. We built a beautiful life together. We're going to have the most amazing baby. We're going to get through this. And I'm going to do everything I can to make this up to you."

Dark paused a moment and gathered his thoughts.

"I love you. You're the only thing worth dying for. And I know that because you're the only thing I'm living for."

Sibby *was* in there, and she could hear Steve. It was frustrating because she couldn't move. She didn't exactly know where she was. She couldn't even find her own arm to try to move it.

. . . I only have a few minutes, so . . .

She listened to him struggle to find the words, and she could imagine his face. Mouth opening, then closing. Eyes darting away. So afraid of saying the wrong thing. He was still so very cautious around her, and she never understood why. She wanted to cry out: Steve, you could never say the wrong thing. Just talk to me.

But she had something she was desperate to tell Steve, too.

Help me wake up.

I so badly want to tell you about the texts from Jesus and everything else I didn't want to bother you with . . . only now I understand; now I realize I shouldn't have kept it from you.

You're probably out there worrying, wondering what happened on the highway, and, God, does that kill me. Because I know what this is about. Someone's after me, and I was too stubborn to tell you.

And now he got to me, and our child, too. . . .

chapter 45

S qweegel idled in the convenience-store parking lot, rubbing his fingers on the steering wheel. The latex covering
his fingers adhered to the plastic for the briefest of moments before pulling away. The previous owner of his vehicle—for
it was his now—probably gorged himself with take-out hamburgers, licking his fingers and driving the car and applying meat grease
all over the wheel. When Sqweegel burned this car later in an
abandoned lot, he would be freeing the vehicle from such filth.

Just as he was about to free the children.

The four of them had been beer pimping for a half hour now, but
no dice. Too many uptight asshats, going inside the 7-Eleven for
their smokes or water or milk or their own beer, totally avoiding
eye contact. Nobody stayed parked for long, except for one bat-
tered Pinto parked in the last spot on the left. Maybe the idiot
pulled up and fell asleep. Maybe he'd already had his beer and
passed out on the way to buy more. Fucker.

Rob bounced once on his skateboard, then let it roll to the edge of the pavement. This was getting old. If they wanted to sit around and do nothing, they could do that back home.

Finally Rick said he'd had enough, this was lame, he was out of here. Bumped fists with all three, left on his skateboard, rolling his way home.

The others called him a pussy, but it would only be a matter of time before they packed it in, too. Who were they kidding?

Rob bounced again on his skateboard. *Epic fail.*

But then the door to the Pinto finally opened and a slender figure stepped out. A real Michael Jackson–looking motherfucker, hoodie up, face all covered. Could *be* Jackson, for all they knew. Maybe he cruised Hancock Park for new friends. Maybe he'd invite them all back to Neverland to play with Bubbles and drink chocolate sodas. And they'd tell MJ, fuck the soda pop yo; let's get some beers up in this shit.

It wasn't Michael Jackson, of course.

But maybe he was worth a try anyway. It was always worth a try with the freaks, the tweakers, the stoners. They were kindred spirits. They were the people the world wanted to ignore until they grew up or straightened out or sobered up or whatever.

Rob rolled up first. Shoved his hands deep in the pockets of his shorts and walked along the curb in dirty kicks, stepping around the broken glass like he didn't give a shit.

"Yo, mister. You buy us some beer, we'll buy you a six-pack."

The guy turned his head oddly, like his neck was the only part of him that moved. Rob stood there, waiting for a reply, and after a while, he began to think the guy was deaf-mute or something. Maybe that's why he wore a mask. Like his throat and mouth were all rotted away or something.

Finally, though, he spoke. Told him:

"I don't drink beer. I drink gin."

"Okay, so—"

"So I'll make you a deal," the guy said. "I'll buy you the beer. You buy me the gin."

"Awesome," Rob said, then caught himself. *Too eager, fool. You're buying this deformed bum some booze. Don't sound so grateful for buying him free shit.* "Deal," he quickly added.

Sqweegel walked into the corner store and sailed into the beer aisle. He loved shopping for things in person. He did it so rarely.

His white suit was completely hidden away from the world behind a trench coat, gloves, trousers, hat, sunglasses. Glance at him from behind, and you wouldn't think anything of him—just an ordinary man. Glance at him from the front and you *might* catch a glimpse of white that would give you pause, but then you'd remember this was L.A. There were plenty of celebrities who ran around town incognito. This was the city of sunglasses, of masquerades. Sqweegel fit right in.

He was pleased to find that the store stocked plenty of bottles of mass-produced lager with twist-off caps. Very easy to open— and reseal—with a small amount of torque. Especially if you're wearing rubber gloves.

Sqweegel eyed the surveillance cameras, then selected two six-packs of the brand he thought would impress the children the most. He used a palm to quickly twist the tops off all of the bottles in succession. Then out of a small sewn-in pocket of the hoodie he produced a medicine dropper full of a yellowish liquid.

Drip.

Drip.

Drip.

One for each bottle. More than enough. The liquid was highly illegal and incredibly potent.

Caps went back on, twisting hard, then sealing with a small push of the palm. The children would never know the difference.

Sqweegel carried the six-packs to the front, handed over the cash with a gloved hand. The counter jockey gave his face a quick glance, but then took the money without comment. This was California, after all.

Within minutes, the freak was back outside, big brown paper bag in his hands.

Score.

The guy stopped, though, and stared down into the bag. "Seems they don't sell hard liquor here. Let's take a drive, shall we? Find some other liquor emporium so you three can hold up your end of our bargain?"

Then he looked back up, locking eyes with each of them. Creepy little black eyes like marbles. Rob heard his buds saying *yeah, okay*, but he wasn't sure this was the world's best idea.

"Dude," he whispered to his friend Chris. "We actually going to get into the car with some strange guy?"

Chris shot him a withering look. "What, are you five? You afraid he's going to offer you candy?"

"No, man, it's just—"

Chris leaned in close, hand on Rob's shoulder.

"Don't be a pussy. We'll get this guy his gin; then we'll bolt. Fuck him. We'll get our party on."

Which his how Rob found himself in the passenger seat of the beat-up, musty Pinto, next to a skinny dude in a mask who it turned out was wearing rubber gloves. No, he hadn't noticed them at first. If he had, maybe Rob wouldn't have even given him the money for the beer in the first place.

chapter 46

Chris and Tom were rolling around the backseat like two idiots, laughing and elbowing each other, making the springs squeak under their weight. They were already halfway through their first beers. Glad *they* could relax.

Rob had his bottle of Yuengling resting between his legs, cap in his hand. The surface of the beer tilted left and right like the liquid capsule in a carpenter's level. He was hesitating and not quite sure why.

Maybe it was the smell in the car, which was a little too much like raw sewage. Rob tried to find the button that would lower the window but instead found a crank handle. Figured. When did they stop making cars with freakin' window handles? The 1980s or something? But the crank didn't do anything. It jiggled a half inch up and down but otherwise stayed locked in position.

Fuck it. He took a large sip of his beer. He was slipping into a sour mood, and that would pretty much kill the night.

Rob watched the lights and shop windows and people along Olympic speed by. The beer was cold and good. Nothing like a beer on a school night.

All the while, the driver said nothing.

"What's with the face mask, dude?" Rob finally asked.

"Yeah," Chris called from the back. "What, do you go out with Batman at night and fight crime and shit?"

Chris and Tom started howling in the backseat, the pricks. They weren't up here in the front. Sitting just a few inches away from *him*.

If the guy was bothered, though, he didn't show it. He kept his eyes on the road, stopping at the lights and changing lanes now and again. Slowly, he reached over and turned the car's heat up as high as it would go, like it wasn't already stifling in here.

Finally, he turned to look at Rob. The two black beady eyes regarded him from the eyeholes.

"You mean, do I don a costume and apply my own brand of justice to evildoers in the night?"

"Uh," Rob said, "something like that."

"I have a rare skin condition," Sqweegel said, and let the words hang in the air.

"Oh," Rob said. "That sucks."

"Yes, it does *suck*. If any part of me is exposed to sunlight, I'll shrivel away to skin and bones, and birds will pick at my flesh with their bloodthirsty beaks."

That right there killed the laughter in the backseat.

Birds?

Pecking at flesh?

Say whaaaa?

Rob turned his attention back out of the passenger window, watching L.A. roll by. He blinked. A long blink. The kind where you find yourself nodding off for a second before pulling yourself back up out of the dark. *Whoa*. What the hell was that about? It wasn't even nine yet.

He turned around and the world suddenly vibrated, like someone had just kicked a bass drum buried deep in the earth's crust.

This wasn't an earthquake, was it? Rob's vision swam out of focus before clicking back.

In the backseat, Tom was already passed out, head on Chris's shoulder, bottle of beer slipping out of his long fingers before banging to the foot well and foaming out at the top. Chris, meanwhile, looked like he was having trouble moving his hands. He fumbled at the bottle near his lap but couldn't quite pick it up.

Rob wanted to warn him, *No, dude, don't drink any more beer, something's wrong with it—*

But then he was out, too, and his head slipped down between the two seats.

Sqweegel gently pushed the one next to him back into his seat. His head rested against the passenger window. Drool had already formed in the corners of his mouth.

Now his gloved fingers found the ancient radio and fiddled with the knob until he found the classical station. Something bombastic and German was playing as he took the on-ramp to the freeway. There was a little bit of driving ahead of them, and he didn't want to get caught up in traffic longer than he had to.

If you were looking carefully, you might have been able to see the white plastic over Sqweegel's face shift, right around where his mouth should be.

He was *smiling*.

chapter 47

Somewhere in Southern California

Rob's brain reloaded. The smell hit him first—a foul toilet smell. Then the cold concrete pressed to his cheek, which didn't make sense. Wasn't he in some dude's Pinto just now? What the hell . . . ?

And then he realized he was naked, and somebody had bound his wrists and ankles with plastic ties, and his skin went dead cold, quickly followed by an explosion of ice in the pit of his stomach.

God, did it smell in here. Wherever he was.

He wished like crazy that he could go back in time and tell Chris and Tom, *No, I don't care if you guys think I'm a pussy; we just shouldn't get in the car with this friggin' freak. We shouldn't even be here, pimping for fuckin' beers. We should be home preparing for college, just like our parents keep trying to drill into our stupid little skulls.*

The room was dark, but Rob could hear moaning next to him. Sounded like Chris waking up. If Rob hadn't been so terrified, he would have started cursing him out and telling him what a moron he was.

Then, all at once, the room was full of harsh light.

The freak in the face mask was standing next to a floor lamp. No hoodie or jeans now. The same material that Rob thought was a mask was now revealed to be a suit, covering his entire body. Well, *almost* his entire body.

The thing that protruded from a zippered hole in the front of the suit was uncovered.

Rob hadn't seen many other guys naked. He was only seventeen. Your curiosity gets the best of you and you take too many glances in the gym shower room, you're liable to get your face smashed in. But even to Rob's untrained eye, this guy seemed unnaturally large. Disproportionate on any human being, let alone this underfed-lookin' guy.

The freak padded toward them now, something in each hand, cock bouncing slightly as he walked. Rob craned his neck around for a better view—oh, shit, what if it was a gun?

The man unzipped his mouth as he placed the objects on the floor in front of them:

A broom.

A baseball bat.

Then he stood up again and began stroking himself, massaging it into full tumescence.

"What are you going to do to us?" Rob asked, immediately sorry the moment the words left his mouth.

"I think you know what I'm going to do to you," the freak said. "But I want to give you some options. The options are . . . me. This broom handle. Or this baseball bat. You three decide. By who or by what. Or shall I decide for you?"

Rob glanced down. The guy's dick, it turned out, was wrapped in the white plastic, after all. Wrapped so tight, you could see the veins. Holy shit. What the hell was going on? And what was he talking about, options? By who and by what . . . *Oh, God, get us out of here. Someone fucking hear us and get us out of here. . . .*

"What are you doing, man?" Chris screamed. "We didn't do anything to you."

"I'm ten inches at full erection. The broom handle is thirty-six inches long and two inches wide. The wooden bat is only thirty inches long, but the width is six inches around. But don't worry. I do have certain tools, should you require further assistance."

Tools? Who *was* this guy?

"If you can't decide," Sqweegel said, chiding them, "I will decide for you."

Rob hated himself for the choice he blurted out, but he knew he had to choose first, before the others beat him to it.

Rob tried to tune out everything that followed. The howled complaints from Chris and Tom, who quickly realized what he'd done to them. The feel of the skinny freak's cold, gloved hands on his hips. The gross breath over his shoulder. The grunting noises. After a while, he began to imagine that his body had split all the way up to the middle of his throbbing, wracking chest.

After more endless agony, it all stopped. Rob heard the sound of the man rubbing his palms together.

"Just getting you warmed up," the freak said. "Now let's *really* have some fun."

Then it resumed.

And seemed to last forever . . .

Sqweegel pushed the first boy down to the ground—Rob—and watched him go into shock. It was an education he'd never forget, and Sqweegel was pleased with himself for being able to provide it.

"Now for you two. Who wants what?"

The two boys squirmed away like freshly born maggots.

Wriggling across the dungeon floor, white, pale, limbless things trying to avoid a fate they were powerless to stop.

"I suppose you are leaving the decision to me."

Rob closed his eyes tightly and prayed to God harder than he'd ever prayed before that this was just the worst fucking nightmare of all time and he was going to wake up any second now.

But, of course, he didn't.

chapter 48

The afternoon bell rang.

Some students had dismissal down to a science—a way to hit the lockers (if necessary) and make their way to the nearest exit in the shortest amount of time. Last to the buses is a punk.

So they were the first to see the three boys—naked, bound, and gagged on the front steps.

At first they all thought it was a joke. Some kind of senior prank, where you fuck with the freshmen and embarrass them in front of the entire student population.

But by the time more students had gathered, pouring out of the front doors, someone pointed and screamed. Blood. There was blood pooled around them, and they were squirming and shaking and screaming with their eyes.

Riggins stood in the hallway, waiting for the doctors to finish up. They'd brought the kids here, the closest hospital.

He couldn't imagine what must be going through their parents' minds right about now. The kids had been missing since the night before. Riggins could imagine the parents up all night, praying, making bargains with God to bring their kids back alive, no matter what; it didn't matter; they'd do anything.

Their prayers had been answered. But most likely not the way they'd wanted.

Question now, of course: Was Sqweegel responsible? Riggins had asked to be notified of any particularly horrific assaults or murders in the entire Southland area, and this certainly qualified.

When he told Wycoff about it an hour ago, he'd gone off on a rant. *Fuck the kids! This monster doesn't abduct. He tortures. He kills. Stay focused on the case. Nothing else matters!*

But Riggins couldn't let it go. Socha Medical Hospital was quickly becoming their satellite Special Circs office—what with Sibby, and news about the priests nearby, and now these kids. It bothered him.

Why those kids, from that particular neighborhood? Was it the proximity to Socha—which was only a ten-minute drive down West Third? Was it just the kids' bad luck to run into a Level 26 killer as he cruised the streets of Los Angeles?

Or was it the fact that Dark had lived with his foster family in Hancock Park and had attended the same high school?

Riggins hoped the kids would be able to shed some light on the thing. Even the smallest detail about their tormentor, or where they'd been held, could be the key to everything.

The three of them would soon be transported to the nearest

LAPD station house. Riggins knew better than to push his way into the station and start waving his jurisdictional cock around; it was a fight he didn't need.

But it had worked out anyway. The cop, a beefy, no-nonsense man named Jack Mitchell, had agreed to allow Riggins and Dark to observe the interviews. Especially after he was made to understand that this was exactly the kind of case Special Circs dealt with on a daily basis.

Dark approached, seemingly out of nowhere. "What's the story?"

"In a second," Riggins said. "What's the latest with Sibby?"

"No change." He seemed to want to change the topic back to the case. "And these kids? They say anything yet?"

Dark had seen the kids as they were wheeled into the ER an hour before. He'd been outside for some air and asked one of the uniformed officers what had happened. Christ, the therapy they were going to need. From the stigma as much as the physical stigmata they'd be carrying around in the months to come. Dark was stunned to hear about how they'd been discovered, naked and bleeding, right outside Hancock Park High School.

His alma mater.

Coincidence? Very well could be. But he'd asked Riggins to look into it anyway. After the dead priests and the fire at the church—*his* church—Dark was starting to not believe in coincidences anymore.

"I made a deal with Jack Mitchell from the LAPD," Riggins said. "Parents signed consent forms—we can watch the interviews. And if need be, I'm sure I can sweet-talk our way in there for some follow-up. The parents want the guy who raped their boys caught—and his balls floating in a jelly jar, if possible."

"I know how they feel," Dark said.

To see the interrogation, log into LEVEL26.com
and enter the code: violated

chapter 49

Up a long, narrow flight of concrete stairs, Dark made his way to the front door of the apartment.

This was a *new* place—the one Riggins had arranged for him, mostly as a place to store his essentials. Things he'd need to access quickly.

He paused in front of the door, key in hand, paranoid thoughts running through his head. Had Sqweegel followed the moving company? Had he followed Riggins, who'd personally hauled the boxes up to this third-floor apartment?

Was he somewhere inside, tucked into a corner, or under a sink?

Dark almost hoped so. He'd like to get his hands on him, even for just a few seconds. Even if he died in the process. He just wanted to dish out a little payback for breaking into their home. The one safe place. The place he and Sibby had made together.

Never mind that now. Focus on the task at hand.

Dark was still wearing the shirt that he'd had on at the crash site, and it was still stained with Sibby's blood. Back in the waiting room, Riggins had looked him up and down and urged him to go to the apartment, take a shower, put on some fresh clothes already before he started to offend. Probably made sense.

But Dark could do that later. He had to tackle something else first. Something that had been tugging at his mind for a few hours.

He started peeling up masking tape and digging through brown cardboard boxes. Riggins had said he'd packed up the old place on his own; Dark hoped he'd thought to include his laptop somewhere in there. He was a methodical thinker and needed to lay the pieces out in a particular way. The computer helped him do that.

Dark opened the third box, where he found a square object wrapped in blue tissue paper. He pulled away the paper, and the sight made him pause.

A photo of Sibby, before they met, back when she was still a professional dancer. It was the first photo she'd given him, but only after he'd begged. Dark loved to watch her dance. Frankly, he just loved to watch her move across a room.

When she'd finally relented and given him the photo, he'd studied it for hours, trying to figure out what exactly drew him to it. There was no single detail, though, or bodily feature. It was Sibby as a whole. Sibby dancing—the most beautiful sight he'd ever enjoyed.

Dark carefully rewrapped the frame, his fingers shaking a little. He tried not to tear the paper or leave any suggestion that it had been opened. Then he placed it back in the box, letting his fingers graze Sibby's old ballet shoes, which rested amid the memories of their happy life. He pushed the flaps down and pushed his fingers over the strip of tape until it held firm.

He dug further into a fourth box and found something else—a framed photo of the two of them from the previous summer, just after they'd first started seeing each other. Sibby was wearing a sheer yellow dress. He loved that dress, loved it on her, loved what it did for her body, loved taking it off her body when they returned to her place later that same day . . .

The same body that was now bruised and cut and abraded and suffering on a hospital bed just a short distance away.

Dark caught himself. He could easily see himself getting lost in these reminders of her. That wouldn't do her any good.

He needed to get back to the case, if only to distract himself while he waited for Sibby to wake up.

A short while later he found the box that contained everything he needed: Laptop. Wireless printer. Ream of paper. Pens. Dark sat with them, cross-legged, in the middle of the living room, which was illuminated by a single desk lamp. Everything else in the world could fade away for the moment. Now it was just Dark and the evidence.

Dark knew he'd find the answer in Sqweegel's little "poem."

chapter 50

Dark transcribed it quickly, increased the font, then printed a copy.

One a day will die.
Two a day will cry.
Three a day will lie.
Four a day will sigh.
Five a day ask why.
Six a day will fry.
Seven a day . . . "Oh, my."

Dark crossed a line through

~~*Six a day will fry.*~~

The priests at Hollywood United, obviously. And the kids from Hancock Park that he'd tortured:

~~*Three a day will lie.*~~

Despite the obvious severe trauma to their anal cavities, the three boys had stuck to their story: they were skateboarding, beer pimping. Some guy offered to buy them beer in exchange for some gin. That store didn't have gin, so they hopped into his car and headed out to another liquor store. And that's all they remembered—or so they claimed.

Jack Mitchell had pointed out that the nurse at the hospital had found evidence of blood and trauma around their genitals. The boys nervously explained that away as just some stupid drunken antics—slamming their asses down on ketchup packets.

But then one of the boys slipped. Mentioned the guy was wearing a "white suit."

Mitchell pounced on that. What kind of white suit? What was it made of?

Cloth, the kid said. Three-piece suit. With a vest.

The other two backed him up. Yeah, cloth. With buttons and everything.

Lying.

Just like Sqweegel had said they would.

Three a day will lie . . .

Now Dark stared at the remainder of the list, trying to puzzle it out. Not so much the individual messages, but the pattern. Was Sqweegel checking things off his list at random, or did he have an order in mind? Did it mean something that he started with six, then halved it?

Had he already carried out some of the other lines? No, that wouldn't be Sqweegel. Not this time. This time was all about the grand gesture. And the fact that he'd targeted Dark's house within hours of Riggins's showing up meant that Sqweegel wanted him to pay attention. *Well, I am now, motherfucker. You've got my complete attention.*

To think that just a few days ago, Dark had been free of this.

The pain of what had happened to his foster family would never go away, but it had been a long time since he'd tried to put himself inside a maniac's mind. It simply hadn't made sense anymore. His family was gone, and no amount of Special Circs profiling or empathetic reasoning would bring them back.

And now he was back. Trying to worm his way into a sick little fuck's mind, once again. It was like breaking a leg, *badly*, then breaking it again just to remind yourself that you know how to do it.

The trick to this was seeing the world through his beady little eyes.

Eyes . . .

Wait.

Dark pulled out his cell, speed-dialed Riggins.

"What is it? Everything okay?"

"The video server from my house—did you pull it?"

Dark knew the small server had a built-in monitor that could display what was on the hard drive in his pocket. He'd nearly forgotten about it with everything that had happened today.

"If you say that again in English, I might be able to answer you."

"Surveillance cameras in my house," Dark explained. "One in each room. They're all wired up to a little white box in the top of the front closet. Did you pack it?"

"If it had a wire attached to it, I packed it."

"Where?"

"Maybe one of the boxes full of shit with wires attached to it? I'm sorry, Dark. I packed fast. Listen, let me come over there and help—"

Dark pressed END and started ripping through the remaining boxes.

chapter 51

Sqweegel handed the cab driver the money, told him to keep the change. The dirty yellow Crown Vic peeled away a moment later, leaving its passenger standing on the last sidewalk on the western edge of Manhattan. The driver had been listening to filthy garbage on the radio. If Sqweegel hadn't had other plans, the driver would have paid for his indiscretion. Maybe strap him down somewhere and drill some holes in his ears, freeing them to hear divine sounds. Divine *silence*.

No time for that now, though. The horses were waiting. And his hunter, still spinning his wheels on the other coast, would be lost without another message soon.

Out over the Hudson, lights twinkled on the Jersey side. Sqweegel liked turning his back on the ziggurats of New York City. So many worshipped them, so blindly. They were useful to Sqweegel only in that they gave him countless places to hide. If he wanted to, he could disappear in the concrete slabs of Manhattan for ten, twenty years, without anyone knowing where he'd gone. And all the while, he'd be watching. Like an angel.

Tonight, though, wasn't a night for hiding.

Sqweegel stepped off the sidewalk and made his way down a dirt path. He was decked out like a soldier home on leave from Afghanistan, one weekend only—combat boots, camouflage pants, flak jacket, hoodie, black cap, sunglasses. A little U.S. Army, a little Brooklyn. No one would give him a second glance.

Nor would they wonder about the rectangular white cardboard box tucked under his arm. Flowers for Mom, or maybe a sweetheart. A dozen fresh-cut roses to say *I hope you haven't been screwing somebody else while I was getting my ass shot off in the Hindu Kush*.

At the end of the path was a wooden fence topped with barbed wire. On the front was an etched wooden sign, the grooves painted a faded gold:

MOUNTED POLICE NYPD

A little bit of rustic class in an island of glass, plastic, and shiny metal. Sqweegel admired that, despite himself. People did try so hard to rise above themselves sometimes.

He slid the flower box under the last rung of the wooden fence, pushing it all the way to the other side. Then he peeled off his flak jacket and draped it over the barbed wire. Quickly, he scaled the fence, cleared the wire, and pulled his jacket free as he touched down on the other side. It was a movement so fluid and so fast, anyone watching—not that anyone *was* watching—would rub his eyes and insist on a playback, just to make sure he wasn't hallucinating.

Sqweegel ran his fingers under the tape holding the box flaps together. No need for the pretense now. He was inside.

The lid came off, and inside was a long hand cannon. Ammo. And a plastic bag full of carrots.

All three came from Brooklyn, just like the box. The box, from a florist on Court Street. The carrots, from a corner market on Smith. And the gun? From a small-time arms dealer in Red Hook he'd found online. No more than an hour's worth of shopping.

The gun was loaded in under a minute, each of the silver bullets fed into the chambers one at a time, *click click click click click*.

Sqweegel continued down the path, following a bend to the main stables. The thick smell of horse shit and wet straw assaulted him. This was where the mounted police kept their horses. Their riders may now be kicking back with beer and pizza in Brooklyn, Queens, Jersey, or Long Island, but their noble steeds never left the island. They were forever on duty, on this tiny scrap of nature Manhattan had saved for itself.

Anyone could take a tour of the stables and visit the horses. Sqweegel had, nearly a year before. He'd taken careful notes.

Now he slid the notepad out of his back pocket and began to check the names. Each horse had a nickname. The names on Sqweegel's list, however, were special:

Dalia
Runner
Coach
Beemer
Sampson

First up: Dalia.
A whore's name, Sqweegel thought.

chapter 52

Nothing but white screen, with the occasional flash of dark around the fringes and pixilated distortion.

This was the footage taken in their master bedroom the night before.

What the hell?

Dark fast-forwarded for about ten minutes, then closed the window and clicked on the living room file. The footage shot here, by contrast, was intact. Crystal clear.

The lighting wasn't ideal, but you could see exactly what was going on—just like Sqweegel wanted. He wanted Dark to see how easy it was to break into their house, creep through the room, literally under the noses of Max and Henry, then strip at the foot of the stairs before ascending. Making his way to Sibby . . .

I'm in your house, Dark. Do you realize how easy this is? You, with all of your experience and training?

Did you promise Sibby you'd keep her safe, no matter what?

Didn't I teach your foster family anything about home security?

The time signature at the start of the break-in matched exactly with the time Dark had peeled away in his Yukon, on his way to meet with Riggins in that diner on the Santa Monica Pier.

Son of a bitch had probably been holed up outside, hidden in some dank little crevice, waiting for Dark to leave.

And then he made his way into their home and right into their bedroom, easy as walking up a flight of stairs.

It looked easy, of course, with Dark's laptop playing it back in fast-forward. Watching it in real time was maddening, Sqweegel's inhuman body oozing across the floor at such an incredibly slow speed. Such controlled, measured movements were almost imperceptible to Dark—you had to keep staring to make sure Sqweegel was, in fact, moving.

All while he'd been nursing his cold coffee, listening to Riggins go on about budgets, about his ex-wife, about his life.

Sqweegel, making his way up to where Sibby lay sleeping, completely unaware . . .

Which was why the white screen was infuriating. It made no sense. Every other camera in the house worked fine that night— except for the bedroom?

What line was it? Dark wondered. Which line in the goddamned poem was about Sibby? Not "one a day will die," because she was left alive. Untouched, in fact—she'd said so herself. Two a day will cry? Something about Sibby and the baby? Oh, Jesus fuck, did he do something to the baby?

Dark double-clicked on the REWIND button. Maybe this camera had been faulty for a few days, and somehow he hadn't noticed. But this was unlikely. It was a looped system; any faulty feeds would result in the main server alerting him through a series of quick, annoying beeps.

Something else was going on here.

On-screen the white suddenly cut out, and the image returned. Dark clicked PLAY.

There he was. Next to their dresser, placing something on its polished top. Some little device, and then—

White screen.

The little freak had jammed the signal somehow. He didn't want Dark seeing what happened next.

Or did he? Dark's thumb hovered over the click bar on the touch pad for a moment, then pressed down and began to fast-forward. Minutes on the time counter ticked by, and suddenly the white was gone and the footage resumed.

Oh, God.

Oh, God, no.

chapter 53

New York City

The horses weren't happy.

There was an intruder in their stalls, and he made them nervous. He looked different. Smelled different. Acted different. Didn't act human at all. Annoyed, the beasts neighed and stomped around in their stalls. Some were nervous and pissed in gushes.

Shh, now, Sqweegel wanted to tell them. *I'm not here for you. I'm here for Dalia.*

And there she is.

The metal sign tacked to the front of the stall explained her story:

DALIA WAS DONATED BY MRS. DAHL
ON BEHALF OF HER FALLEN HUSBAND,
A MEMBER OF THE FDNY, ON 9/11/01

Sqweegel's bony hand pushed up the metal latch. He crept inside the stall, moving slowly, calm enough to put Dalia at ease. Nothing that moved this slowly could be a threat, right? She was half asleep anyway. Sqweegel came face-to-face with the brown paint horse, who was ten hands high. Her glistening black eyes blinked methodically.

He reached inside the bag, pulled out a carrot. *A nice succulent carrot, Dalia? It's all yours.*

Dalia sniffed it once, then took a quick bite. The remainder fell out of Sqweegel's hand and landed on the dirty bed of hay below. Sqweegel bent over to pick it up, but the horse spooked. Reared back. Bucked. Sqweegel froze and remained that way until the horse calmed down again. A few more minutes passed before Sqweegel slowly raised a hand, inching closer. Finally the horse allowed her visitor to pet her warm head. Sqweegel leaned in close and whispered, "It's not you, girl. No, it's never the children. It's your mother. Always the mother."

Sqweegel raised the gun, jabbed the silencer between two ribs on the horse's side, then squeezed the trigger once. No need for remorse; he had explained himself to the horse.

Dalia's legs immediately buckled. One leg, followed by another, and then the final two as she went down, snapping a hoof along the way, the weight too great to bear.

The horse tried to breathe, but a lung was already collapsed and her heart was failing. There wasn't even time to make a sound. Her dark eyes grew heavy. The hay beneath her body was soaked with blood. She had no idea what was going on, why her body wasn't working properly. The only comfort, Sqweegel thought, was that it wouldn't be long now.

Sqweegel waited, then reached out and closed the horse's eyelids. Even through the latex fingers of his glove he could feel the fading warmth of the animal. Soon, silence would overtake its exhausted body.

"It's not me," he whispered. "The fireman's whore did this to you."

Four more to go.

Now it was time for Runner.

chapter 54

Dark stared at the image of Sqweegel, leaning over the sleeping body of his pregnant wife. Part of him knew it was just an image on an LCD screen. But the other part of his brain, the animal brain, was overwhelmed with the need to reach through the computer and seize the intruder and rip him apart, muscle by muscle, joint by joint, bone by bone.

All he could do was watch the soundless horrors unfold.

First he unzips the top of his head, revealing a strange patch of white with a yellow spot on it—making it look, strangely, like a fried egg. But then Sqweegel removes it, revealing it to be a small washcloth.

And now he's pushing it onto Sibby's face.

She snaps awake for a moment, arms flailing, but only for a moment. The chemical on the rag—most likely chloroform—is fast acting, and Sibby is unconscious in seconds.

She is all Sqweegel's now.

Dark knew she hadn't woken up and didn't remember any of the attack, but he found himself begging her image on the screen to please wake up. *Don't let him do this to you. Please.*

Sqweegel pulls back the summer-weight top sheet. Gently pushes on the backs of her knees to spread her legs. With one gloved hand, he inches his fingers underneath the waistline of her panties. He suddenly stops; then he hops on the bed.

Dark didn't have words to describe quite what he did with his body then. He pulled something from within his suit.

The screen went blank again. . . .

Dark screamed from the bottom of his soul as the white screen continued for several long, excruciating minutes. He was desperate to know what was happening in those moments, but he also couldn't bear to imagine. Even though some parts of him *could*, in gross, vivid detail. Dark had studied the Sqweegel case file for three years before he'd quit Special Circs, and the freak's perversity knew no bounds. Human bodies were playthings to him, nothing more, and he delighted in bending and prodding and ripping and biting every available part and orifice.

To think of him alone in that room with Sibby, what he was capable of, where his sick, fevered mind wandered . . .

And then the image returned.

The attack seemed to be over. Sqweegel drew back, then moved across the room—into the master bathroom.

There was no video surveillance in the bathroom. But Dark already knew what Sqweegel had done there. Riggins had told him about the phone number on the mirror. They had no idea, however, what Sqweegel had used to write the message . . .

Until now.

chapter 55

Sqweegel's exit from the Dark home looked simple. Effortless. Dark watched the freak's ghostly image float down the stairs, dress himself in the street clothes he'd left in a pile on the floor. Completely at ease. Like he owned the place and was preparing to leave for his nine-to-five.

But then Sqweegel returned to the glass patio window and carefully retrieved the smooth disc of glass from the floor. Using a tiny bottle he had in the front pocket of his pants, Sqweegel coated the edge of the glass with what Dark presumed was adhesive, then placed it back in its hole. He unlatched the patio door, slid it open, then left.

Fast-forward fifteen minutes.

Sqweegel returns with a rock in his gloved hand.

Dark recognized the rock.

He hides behind the curtain, posed like a department-store mannequin.

Fast-forward sixty-five minutes.

The first rays of dawn are visible.

Dark returns home. Races through his own living room, unaware that Sqweegel is standing just a few yards away.

The son of a bitch was still inside when he returned from his late-night talk with Riggins.

Dark watched the footage, amazed.

Sqweegel stands there, motionless, not even seeming to draw breath into his lungs. Arms at his sides. Head down. It's as if he put himself in place, then flipped a kill switch in his brain that froze all biological and electrical activity.

This was a combination of patience and brazenness that no one else would have been able to pull off. It also spoke of Sqweegel's massive confidence.

Confidence . . . or knowledge.

Sqweegel knew he'd been out.

Knew who he'd been meeting with.

Knew that he'd be too eager to see Sibby and that he would rush in to make sure she was okay.

But how? How did he know all of that?

How was Sqweegel able to keep a God's-eye view on all of them—the people who were hunting him as well as the man who was being recruited to hunt him? And his wife?

It was more than confidence, Dark thought. Sqweegel had some other advantage. Partners? It was a possibility.

The surveillance evidence, however, indicated that he was a one-man show.

Look at him now.

Using the rock to shatter their patio window.

Leaping over the patio gate and strolling across the shared lawn to the neighbor's property, then doing the same to his patio window.

What had Dark told Riggins at the scene? That this wasn't like Sqweegel?

Just kids, throwing rocks through their neighbors' windows.

Dark realized that he had been making serious mistakes with Sqweegel—not just underestimating him, but failing to engage his own special skills and think like him, refusing to push himself to inhabit Sqweegel's mind the way only *he* could. He wasn't going to catch him with cold, deductive reasoning. He wouldn't make the same mistake countless other operatives had over the years. Dark was going to catch him by embracing his gift—his ability to tune in to his target's wavelength and follow him beyond the boundaries of reason, into the depths of Sqweegel's darkest fantasies, wherever they led.

chapter 56

R iggins was nursing a crappy cup of coffee in the hospital
waiting room, pad and pen in his lap. He'd just finished a
series of calls that woke up at least two dozen people on
the East Coast. But fuck 'em. This was the nature of the beast.
And the job at Special Circs was about to get a lot more chaotic
in the next twelve hours. They'd have to learn to deal with it.

At least Wycoff seemed satisfied for the moment. Mobilization
was something the secretary of defense could wrap his mind
around. *Finally*, Wycoff had mocked. *You should have brought
everyone out here hours ago.*

Dark walked into the room and sat down next to him. Riggins
looked him up and down, then shook his head.

"You didn't shower, did you?" Riggins said. "What part of *go
home and shower* didn't you understand?"

"Any word from Sibby's doctor?"

"Nothing. I cornered a nurse a little while ago. She told me the
minute she knew something, I would."

216

"Thanks."

"You don't have to thank me."

The two men sat in silence for a while, pretending to look at the same smudge on the opposite wall. But their individual brains were running at full speed, turning the case around in their minds.

"Let me ask you something," Dark said finally.

"What's that?"

"After two years, why is this little fucker suddenly so interested in me?"

Riggins sighed. "I've been thinking about that a lot. You know how I always say sometimes, the only right answer is the simplest answer?"

"Yeah. So what's the simple answer?"

"You just said it: You were on the case two years ago," Riggins said. "You retired . . . left . . . whatever. I think he just misses you. Realizes how much fun you were. And now he wants to bring you back into the game."

"Sqweegel was the one who took me *out* of the game."

"Maybe he thought it'd have the opposite effect. He thought doing what he did to you would . . . *intensify* things."

Dark shook his head. "Still doesn't make sense. Hundreds of investigators have chased Sqweegel. Why is he spending so much time on me? Why push me out, pull me back in? I'm nothing special."

"You came the closest to catching him."

"Maybe. We have no proof."

"You were the only one to lay eyes on him, and I think that rattled him. And now he's throwing a tantrum like a child, trying to get your attention."

"And he knows exactly how."

Riggins turned, a confused look on his face. "What do you mean?"

217

As Dark explained to Riggins what he'd found on the surveillance footage, Riggins stared blankly into his coffee, which now looked like a cardboard cup full of liquid shit. He listened to Dark's dispassionate encapsulation of what Sqweegel had done to his pregnant wife.

That son of a bitch, Riggins thought. And then the writing on the bathroom mirror with her . . .

Good Christ.

The thought of him doing something like that to his daughters—hell, even his ex-wives—would have sent him into a blind rage. He was amazed at how well Dark seemed to be keeping it together. Picking at the case rationally. Calmly. As if it didn't have a personal component. Fuck, if it'd happened to Riggins, he'd already be drunk and ranting about how he'd want to paint the walls with the freak's blood.

But that's not how Dark operated.

Maybe that was why Sqweegel wanted him back in the game. Agents and operatives who blew their tops at the slightest hint of pressure probably weren't much fun to a professional monster. Maybe he wanted to play with someone more durable. Who could take a Job-like licking and, somehow, keep on ticking.

Not that Riggins would tell Dark any of this.

Someone's BlackBerry chirped. Riggins patted his pants—wasn't his. It was Dark's.

Dark pulled out his phone and looked at the screen. One new text message.

To get an e-mail from a "friend," log into
LEVEL26.com and enter the code: headline

chapter 57

Since its creation in the late 1980s, Special Circs had never moved from its home base in Quantico, Virginia.

Until Riggins made a series of phone calls from the Socha Medical Hospital waiting room.

And within hours of those calls, Special Agent Constance Brielle found herself on a plane to L.A. with a dozen of her colleagues—from forensics analysts to computer techs to full-on agents and operatives. At first, she'd asked Riggins whether he was kidding. He assured Constance he wasn't. Then she asked, *Wouldn't it be a little easier for you to, you know, head back to Quantico?* Riggins assured her it wouldn't be.

"What's going on, Tom?" she'd asked him. "Seriously."

"Rhymes with *beagle*," he'd said. "Now go call the airline and get out here."

Constance would have killed to have eavesdropped on Riggins's phone calls to his superiors in the Justice Department, just to see how you could convince them to temporarily move an organization like Special Circs clear across the country.

She hadn't seen Riggins for three days now—ever since their disastrous teleconference with the secretary of defense and Robert Dohman and the rest of the international crime community. Later that night, Riggins had disappeared, leaving little more than a hasty e-mail—*Constance: Be back in a few days. Keep after the pissants. Riggins*—and a stack of case files left on her desk.

With no hint as to where he'd gone. Or why.

But that changed when Riggins had called her that afternoon and told her to join the crew that was already preparing for the trip to L.A. Wheels up in an hour.

And now she was inside the Federal Building at 11000 Wilshire Boulevard, sandwiched between Beverly Hills and the concrete ribbons of the on-ramps to the 405. Here Riggins had commandeered a War Room, a crude simulation of what they had back in Virginia. Later, Constance would learn that this was basically a high-tech show area—a series of rooms meant to impress Hollywood types and foreign dignitaries when they wanted a tour of the world-famous FBI. It would be embarrassing to walk them around the real desks, with broken phones and PCs that barely limped by with operating systems at least six years out of date.

Again, Constance marveled at what Riggins had assembled with just a few phone calls.

The centerpiece of their new War Room was a huge LCD screen attached to a state-of-the-art control panel—everything connected to the computers back in Quantico with the most insane encryption and cybersecurity they could muster. It even smelled like a new car.

Constance fully understood the sudden relocation only when she saw who was seated at the controls.

Steve Dark.

You don't ask Mohammed to take a red-eye to the mountain;

you move the mountain to Mohammed. Especially if Mohammed had retired after the case that got his entire foster family slaughtered.

Riggins nodded at her. "Glad you could make it, Constance."

"Sure, Tom." Like she had a choice?

Dark turned slowly in his chair, then turned his head to look at her. There was a strange blankness on his face, like he was trying to place her. *C'mon, Dark,* she thought. *It hasn't been that long.* It wasn't contempt, or anger, or guilt, or surprise, or anything. To Constance, it was like Dark floated on a different plane of existence than the rest of them, and it took some effort for him to tune in to normal reality. "Hi, Constance," he said flatly.

"Steve. I'm so sorry," Constance said. "How is Sibby?"

"Still in critical condition."

"Oh." Constance fidgeted for a moment, trying to think of the reassuring thing to say, the thing that would comfort Dark, make him open up to her, for even a second. Instead, she heard herself repeating the words: "I'm so sorry."

And she was.

Did Riggins catch that moment? She sure hoped not, but it was hard to tell with Riggins sometimes. Sometimes he seemed like he tuned out, but she would find out later that he could recall every word as accurately as a court stenographer.

Constance tried to focus on the case, not Dark. In just a few days, Sqweegel had escalated his kill pattern, which was highly atypical. What's more, he'd decided to focus on a single geographic area—Greater Los Angeles—which was also unprecedented.

Of course, this was a new level of killer they were dealing with, Constance reminded herself. You've been spending your days and nights thinking about Level 24s or 25s. This was a new kind of beast. The old criteria didn't apply right now.

She also had a hard time separating the case from Dark himself.

He was Holmes to Sqweegel's Dr. Moriarty; the near apprehension in Rome was the closest anyone had ever come. And now, suddenly, Dark was involved again.

How had this happened? The last time she saw Dark he'd made it perfectly clear: it was all over. There was no going back. This was it for him.

And how did Riggins go from *No, never, not going to happen* to *Oh, Constance, you remember Steve, right?*

Constance decided to puzzle it out later. She watched over Dark's shoulder as he typed:

mounted police horses kill

Dark chose the first article that popped up. It was a *New York Times* piece titled, "9/11 Widows Donate Horses to NYPD Mounted Police."

"Horses?"

"He killed five of them," Dark said. "Fed them carrots, then shot them at point-blank range. One by one, one stall at a time."

"Jesus. We sure it's him?"

"He more or less told us he did it."

Dark quickly told her about the murder poem. Constance immediately jumped to the fifth line:

Five a day ask why.

Five horses, with no idea why they were being slaughtered. Is that what the line meant?

"Are the horses asking that?" Constance asked. "Or is that supposed to be us?"

"Nothing is ever that clear with Sqweegel," Dark replied. "There's always a meaning behind the meaning."

Then Dark showed her the news story that Sqweegel had sent,

and Constance skimmed it. She'd always been a fast reader. This, coupled with a flash-drive-style memory, had enabled her to ace both college and grad school. Growing up she was called "genius." But to Constance, it was just a strong ability to recall any fact she'd previously read or heard. Powerful memory, nothing more. A computer could do the same thing. Everyone seemed fixated on that—not her other cop skills.

Real genius was the ability to take the same facts and see the hidden connections between them. Constance was often quite good at it, something no one seemed to notice.

The story, however, didn't present any obvious connections to Constance. Seemed like little more than an extremely cruel act of vandalism—the destruction of city property. Of course, New Yorkers didn't see it that way. The local papers were all over it that morning, bemoaning the loss of five members of New York's finest, featuring black-and-white photos of their uniformed riders, sobbing openly, not even an hour after the bodies were discovered by a maintenance man.

"So the question is, why kill the horses?" Dark said. "Everything Sqweegel does is symbolic. What's he trying to tell us?"

"I don't know," Constance. "What did the widows do wrong? They're just looking to turn their loss into something positive."

"Doesn't fit Sqweegel's usual MO."

"He has an MO?"

Dark turned to look at her. "Oh. Most definitely."

chapter 58

Riggins, meanwhile, found it hard to focus on the horses when he knew that Air Force Two would be arriving in a matter of hours. And with it, King Asshole Norman Wycoff.

He'd thought the mobilization of Special Circs—the most elite crime-fighting team in the country—would have chilled the son of a bitch out.

It hadn't.

The message from the Pentagon had been terse . . . and weird. Wycoff was flying to L.A. to personally deliver a piece of evidence from the murdered teenaged mother's apartment—the one he only knew about thanks to Dark. Wycoff wouldn't say what kind of evidence he had. But clearly it was too important to consign to the hands of FedEx or even an undersecretary of defense.

It was a "new development," Wycoff had said.

Oh, the suspense was killing Riggins.

But frankly, he was also worried about Wycoff and his goons hanging around. The head of the Department of Defense was no longer content to kick back in D.C. and wait for results. No, he was most likely going to second-guess every operational move, which, yeah—would do wonders for catching this psycho. Riggins had thought he could avoid this kind of suffocating *oversight* by relocating Special Circs to L.A. Not the case.

Even worse: If Dark was right, then Sqweegel seemed to have jumped to the East Coast.

Dark turned to face Constance. The War Room monitors blinked with information behind her. Back when he still worked at Special Circs, he'd assumed a mentor role with her. Okay, maybe he didn't so much *assume* the role as Constance kind of *pushed* him into it.

She hadn't taken a position with Special Circs with blinders on. She knew the burnout rate. So early on, she had decided to align herself with one of the best. A few days later, she'd realized that Dark wasn't one of the best—he *was* the best.

He'd taught her a lot. She desperately wanted him to continue to teach her now.

"Take it from the beginning," Dark said. "What do we know about Sqweegel's victims?"

"I've reviewed each of his murders since the first in 1979. Up until now, they seemed without rhyme or reason. Spaced apart. Like he took his time and chose his victims at random."

"And now?"

"Now there's some other element to them. A kind of frenzy. And a new purpose. Where things seemed random before, now little details jump out at me."

"Like what?" Dark asked.

"I'm thinking of the priests especially," Constance said. "Organized religion. And those kids—that's school. Or education. The horses—police?"

Dark nodded, barest hint of a smile on his face. "You're seeing it now, too."

"Honestly? Not exactly."

"I think what motivates him is moral righteousness."

Constance squinted. "How did you come up with that?"

"Priests fuck little boys, so Sqweegel pays them back."

"But those men haven't been accused of a single thing. We did a thorough check. If that's the case, then it's a ridiculous form of misplaced aggression."

"Maybe actual guilt doesn't matter to Sqweegel. A few examples represent the whole. And to him, the entire Church deserves punishment."

"It's a little more than an eye for an eye, though, isn't it?"

Constance had seen the crime-scene photographs. The priests' bodies were so severely burned, forensics workers had to rely on dental records to make identifications. This, of course, was nothing compared to what the forensics team would be taking home in their nasal cavities. Constance had been around burned bodies. You don't forget the nauseating sweetness that comes back every time you inhale.

"You mean," Dark said, "molestation versus immolation?"

"Yeah," Constance said. "It's not the same thing."

"But in the Catholic Church, mortal sin is punishable by the fires of hell."

"Which makes Sqweegel the devil?"

"Actually," Dark said, "in some twisted way, he might think he's Saint Peter."

"So what about these horses? Are they a symbol of the corruption of the horse-racing industry?"

"I know you're trying to be funny, but think about it. Who do those horses represent? The New York Police Department. Perhaps he's judging them for some kind of sin."

"And the kids from Hancock Park are the symbols of something else," Constance said, running with it. "Maybe their parents' greed, or lack of parental interest. We should go back and talk to them again, see if we can pick up the thread."

"Riggins already has agents over there," Dark said.

"There's also the number thing," Constance said.

"Go on."

"From the poem. Six priests. Five horses. Three kids. He's ticking down a list."

"Right. But not in order. His through line isn't numerical. Something else is guiding him."

"There are seven lines in his poem," Constance said. "Seven's an interesting number. You know, as in deadly sins?"

"No," Dark said. "I don't think he'd be that straightforward. He's trying to tell us something with the numbers. Daring us to be clever enough to read the pattern."

Constance realized how much she'd missed this back-and-forth. Anyone else would have laughed if she'd said it out loud, but it was like good sex. Give-and-take. Two minds working toward the same goal, be it catching a psycho or pleasing each other. Both, Constance thought, were as close as two minds could get. In some ways, she felt like she knew Dark better than anyone else.

And that explained a lot about what had eventually happened between them.

"I need to go to New York. The sooner the better," Dark said.

"Maybe that's what he wants you to do," Constance said. "He could have had somebody else do the horses."

"No. Sqweegel's a hands-on kind of killer. In thirty years there's not been a single indication that he's used a partner or hired someone to carry out a task. I've considered whether he's changed up now, but I don't think so. He's a control freak. No one else is worthy of working with him."

"Freak is right. But still, I don't think now is the time for you to be hopping a plane and—"

Just then Dark's BlackBerry chimed. He picked it up, held it to his ear. Nodded silently. "Uh-huh. Okay."

"What is it?" Constance asked.

Dark was already halfway down the hallway.

"Hey! Dark! What the hell's going on?"

"Sibby," Dark said.

chapter 59

Constance raced to catch up to him, winding through the halls of 11000 Wilshire. "Dark!"

He finally stopped and turned. "What?"

"Let me give you a ride to the hospital. We can keep sorting out the murder poem in the car. What good is a flashy rental if I don't use it to fly through the streets of Beverly Hills?"

Dark turned it over in his mind for a minute, then nodded. "Okay. Fine."

The rental was far from flashy. It was a downright dowdy Chevy Uplander minivan, which Constance picked because she didn't know whether she'd be transporting a half dozen agents around town or just herself. She hadn't expected to be in this thing alone with Dark.

And now that he was headed to his wife, and now that they had a moment alone, away from the insanity of the War Room, she felt like she had to say something. Finally. After all of these months.

"You said Sqweegel's looking to judge people—to send a message," she said. "He's on a mission of moral righteousness. Trying to punish the sinners."

"Yeah," Dark said.

"So I have to ask."

"What?"

"Why's he trying to punish *you*?"

"I don't know. Riggins and I have tried to puzzle that one out. We think it's because of my prior involvement in the case, but that doesn't make much sense. He's reading way too much into our relationship."

"Interesting choice of words," Constance said.

Dark just stared at her.

Constance started to make a right turn onto Wilshire, but an SUV sped up before she could get far. It was basically the middle of the night, but the street was surprisingly alive with traffic. She looked at Dark, then decided she had to say something before it was too late.

"You don't think it has anything to do with you and me?"

Dark didn't respond at first. He didn't do anything, in fact. He didn't even seem to have exhaled. He could do that, and it drove Constance insane with frustration. Give her a little something. *Anything*. Especially putting it all out on the line like that.

She finally made the turn onto Wilshire.

Dark said, "That was a long time ago, Constance."

"Almost a year."

"And only you and I know about it, right?"

"Of course."

"Then that's not it."

Okay, then, Constance thought. Problem solved. Guilty mind wiped clean. Gee, that was easy. She should have done this years ago.

A short while later, they arrived at Socha.

Dark had thought about it, too. Ever since he'd asked Riggins *why me*.

232

There were plenty of stains on his soul, but the only one he felt an ounce of guilt over was what had happened with Constance.

He wasn't himself then. He was a hollowed-out ghost of himself. He was a walking corpse who fooled himself into thinking he was human one night.

What had happened was in the past, and it was going to remain there.

Right?

"Hi," Sibby said.

She had been vaguely worried that, after all of this waiting, her vocal cords wouldn't work, that the words wouldn't come out.

"Hi," Steve said, and reached out to hold her hand.

The past day or so had been fuzzy and dreamlike—doctors and clipboards and IV tubes and beeping machines and then hearing about the crash, and racing to save the baby. It all seemed a bit removed from her physical self, like she was watching a medical TV drama about these horrible things happening to someone else.

But none of that mattered now, because Steve was here.

She was reaching out now and touching his hand with her fingertips, and his skin was blissfully real. So real. She could smell his shampoo. The fabric softener they used on their clothes.

"Welcome back," he said. "The doctors say you're okay, your liver's stable, and the baby's going to be fine. How do you feel?"

"Like I was hit by a car," Sibby said.

Steve looked down at her, brow furrowed; then he laughed.

Truth was—even though the doctors and nurses had told her what had happened, about the crash on the I-10 and her liver damage and everything else—she didn't remember a single second of the accident, or its aftermath. It was as if her brain had mercifully erased it from her short-term memory. Maybe later she'd deal with it.

What she did remember was horrible enough: that text message from her stalker. She remembered every word, and what they implied. She had to tell Steve now because she didn't believe in coincidences. She'd been desperate to tell Steve the moment she woke up.

But Steve leaned in close, mouth open, like he had a big important thought that he just couldn't seem to force out of his throat. It was killing him.

"I have to tell you something," Steve said. "Something that happened when we first met. Something I never told you."

Constance watched through the small glass window set high in Sibby's hospital-room door. Tears welled in her eyes at the sight of Dark and his wife speaking their first words since the accident. Knowing no one would hear her say it, knowing no one but Dark could understand what she meant, Constance mouthed a few short words and hoped their meaning would find its way to Sibby somehow.

I'm sorry.

chapter 60

Sibby heard what Steve was saying, and didn't hear him at the same time. She was too focused on the texts and the need to say it right so Steve wouldn't freak out.

"You don't owe me any explanations about anything," she told him. "It doesn't matter."

"No. You need to know."

"Whatever it is, Steve—it can wait. There's something I didn't tell *you*."

Sibby felt his grip on her fingers loosen a bit, like he was already distancing himself.

"What are you talking about?" Steve asked.

"I lied to you the other morning. I thought it was just me overreacting, and you were so freaked out—"

"Just tell me," Steve said.

"When I woke up, I did feel strange. Groggy. Sore."

Steve stopped breathing, then lowered his head, which confused Sibby. She'd expected him to go ballistic, but instead it was like he already knew.

Did he know? Did they examine her for rape without telling her?

Steve pulled his hand away entirely. She reached out, caught his thumb.

"Wait. That's not everything. There were also these text messages."

Now Steve looked surprised. "Messages?"

Sibby told him as many as she could remember. How they sounded like vaguely dirty Bible verses, and how they'd always seem to arrive when he was out of the house, or she was off by herself shopping.

"I'm so sorry I didn't tell you. I didn't want you to worry. Please don't be angry."

"God, of course I'm not angry," Steve said. "Don't think that."

"I don't know if that has anything to do with this thing you're chasing, but if it does . . ."

"It does," Steve said quietly.

"But why us? Why me, all of this time?"

"It's me. It's my fault. You're with me, so he's hurt you, too. And the baby. He'll keep on hurting you. He's not going to stop."

The revelation hit Sibby hard. All of this time, their entire relationship, Sibby had assumed that Steve's stoicism was just who he was. But now it was clear that it wasn't a personality trait. It was a survival tactic—a wall he'd built to separate their new life from the life he once led. Now the wall had crumbled, the old life was seeping into the new, and there was nothing he could do about it.

That is bullshit, Sibby thought.

"Well there's only one thing you can do," she said.

"What's that?"

"End this."

Steve looked at her, almost stunned—like a child who'd been scolded. Then he recovered. Tried to put some of the wall back in place.

"You don't understand," he said. "I haven't told you everything. We have a history."

"I don't care. You're the best at what you do, even if you haven't done it for a while. Why else would they come to you? Why else would the FBI want you on this case so badly?"

"I've tried before," Steve said. "Once officially. Once unofficially. But both times, it ended the same way. I couldn't catch him. I'm not the man for the job. No matter what the FBI thinks."

"So what are we supposed to do? Run away and hope this thing doesn't come looking for us? You can stop him, Steve."

"You really don't understand."

"Stop saying that. After all of this time together, you think I don't know the real you? The one you try to hide?"

"It's not that."

"Then what?"

"The only way to catch him is to become like him. To think the sick little things he does. To climb inside of his diseased mind and try to make sense of it all. But I can't do that. Not now. Not when I climb into bed with you at night. Not with the baby we're about to bring into this world. That's what you don't understand. If I try to catch this monster, I'm absolutely fucking terrified I'm not going to come back the same man."

Sibby reached up from her bed and touched his face. Lifted it up so that she could look directly into his eyes. So that they could touch like they'd touched countless times before—naked soul to naked soul. The kind of touch when words and physical sensations and everything else fall away, and you're left standing in front of each other, completely exposed.

"I know you," she said calmly. "And I know that's not a possibility."

There were two brisk knocks. More nurses? *Now?* Sibby thought. They had to interrupt us now?

But it wasn't the Socha hospital staff. It was Steve's former boss—Tom Riggins.

"I'm sorry to do this," Riggins said, "but Wycoff's plane just touched down, and he wants us over there pronto for a status report."

Steve lowered his head again, but Sibby wouldn't let him.

"Go stop this freak," she said. "No matter what happens, I'll be here for you when you get back."

"Dark," Riggins said. "Look, I know this is shitty timing, but we really do have to go."

Steve lowered his head, sighed, then stood up slowly, like a child being forced to leave a safe, warm bed for a cold, hard, yellow bus.

Sibby reached out and grabbed his fingers one last time.

"I love you," she told him.

Steve opened his mouth as if to say something, but then changed his mind and leaned over to kiss her instead.

"I'll get him back to you safe and sound, don't worry," Riggins said.

Steve looked back at her once, longing in his eyes. Then he was gone.

chapter 61

Inside the depressurized cabin of Air Force Two, Secretary of Defense Norman Wycoff was waiting for Riggins and Dark. He looked like a caged animal preparing to pounce on his keepers the first chance he got.

Dark studied Wycoff carefully. The man didn't look right. Granted, Dark didn't know him personally. But you didn't have to know someone to tell they'd been having a bad day. His button-down Oxford looked like it had endured sheets of perspiration, then had been air-conditioned dry again. There were dark circles under his eyes, which flittered around nervously. His hair looked slightly greasy, as well as the tip of his nose and ears—like he hadn't bothered with a shower in a while. His lips and tongue seemed dry, and his splotchy, pink skin gave off a bracing odor. Wycoff had been drinking. From the looks of the small wastebasket next to his seat, he'd been knocking them back all the way from D.C. No cup, no ice, just a bunch of little plastic spirit bottles.

He was also picking his teeth with a thumbnail, as if he was trying to dislodge a fragment of steak.

"Well?" Wycoff asked. "Are we almost ready to apprehend this monster?"

Riggins sighed. "I've transported my best people here, and we're actively pursuing every lead—"

"Oh, fuck you," Wycoff said. "Don't give me that bullshit you give reporters. What have you got? Have you uncovered a single piece of evidence we can use?"

"Maybe," Riggins said. He didn't want to mention the bird feather until it turned into something real. Last thing he needed was Wycoff here demanding the feather himself, taking it to his people, and more or less getting the hell in the way.

"Maybe?" Wycoff said. "Riggins, I swear to God if you don't start giving me real answers—"

Dark coughed. "Sorry. Been a long night. Mind if I help myself to some water?"

"Knock yourself out," Wycoff said, jamming a thumbnail between two front teeth and scraping.

Dark found a small plastic bottle of springwater in the fridge. He fumbled with the cap, dropping it on the floor. He crouched down to scoop it up and deposit it in the wastebasket.

Wycoff straightened himself, as if someone had whispered in his ear that a CNN camera had swung in his direction. "Listen to me. I'm not going to rest until this son of a bitch is apprehended and executed for what he's done. That means I'm not leaving L.A. until that happens. Consider me an active part of your investigation."

Just then one of the flight attendants wandered by and distracted Wycoff, who leaned toward her and, with his hands all over her, whispered a request in her ear.

As she returned and handed Wycoff the toothpick he'd

asked for, Dark felt the object he'd just palmed and slid it into an official Air Force Two vomit bag, then into his pants pocket.

An active part of the investigation? You got it, Dark thought. *More than you know.*

chapter 62

New York City / Hell's Kitchen

6:37 A.M. EST

Wandering the early-morning streets of Manhattan, Sqweegel did a little shopping.

This was truly a novelty to be savored. So many things he procured through online orders, real credit accounts assigned to fake identities, post office boxes and pieces of real estate set up for the sole purpose of receiving packages. This was essential to his mission.

And that's how he'd done the majority of the shopping for this excursion to New York City. It was too risky to drop in and, say, rent a white van in person. Better to set it up online, then take advantage of one of the automated kiosks that made the rental experience completely anonymous.

But there *were* a few things on his list that he could pick up in person.

Especially when you were wearing a disguise that made you look like most residents of the city—completely unremarkable.

Cap pulled down over your forehead. Lightweight black jacket on your back. White sneakers on your feet.

So during this trip he took advantage of the opportunity.

First stop, last night: one of the last independently owned hardware stores in Hell's Kitchen. The floors were wooden slats, and some of the merchandise was displayed in wooden barrels, not UPC-coded shelves stocked by computer. He smiled at the counterman and purchased his blowtorch, metal starter, garden spade, and garden shears. Just another New Yorker going home at night to do a little DIY on his place.

Next stop, this morning: a corner grocery store, opening for the early-morning commute. Manhattan was still full of these; the chains hadn't quite figured out how to successfully infiltrate the island. He wandered the narrow, crowded aisles until he found what he was searching for: cardboard containers of table salt. He also helped himself to a plastic container meant for take-away salad-bar items and filled it with cherry tomatoes.

The final stop before retreating to his Manhattan hidey-hole—he had hidden dungeons all over the world—wasn't a store at all. Instead, he returned to the banks of the Hudson, to one of the few nonindustrialized, nonprivatized chunks of land near the river. He took his new garden spade from the bag and started digging.

After a few minutes he found his thick, squirming prize. He placed it on top of the dirt, then dumped his container of tomatoes. Let the scavengers of the Hudson enjoy them.

Then he gently lowered the snail into the container. It struggled to make sense of its new surroundings. Sqweegel thought it was an abnormally beautiful specimen, with markings in varying shades of brown and green.

What did you do to God to deserve a life that was essentially a living burial?

243

He used the garden shears to poke holes in the top of the container, then placed his snail into the brown paper shopping bag with the rest of his grocery items. Good thing, Sqweegel thought, the snail was unable to read. Otherwise, it might really start to worry. Especially if the snail was able to intuit what Sqweegel had planned for it.

His hunter, Dark, on the other hand, *could* read. He could read extraordinarily well.

Sqweegel peered down into the bag and watched the snail pulse and slither mindlessly against its plastic prison. He thought of Dark struggling against his own barriers, especially the ones Sqweegel had erected especially for his hunter. Dark was a mortal man gifted with the ability to see the things few could. But was he starting to understand the messages he'd been given?

Yes, Sqweegel thought. *I think he is.*

To play with snails, log into LEVEL26.com and
enter the code: getout

Four a day

chapter 63

Under the cover of night: a gloved hand lifted the glass cutter out of a small zippered bag, along with a suction cup. The cup sucked glass, the blade did its thing in a perfect circle. Pop went the disc of glass.

The hand reached in and unlocked the latch to the sliding door.

He was inside.

Inside the house again.

Then he crawled up the staircase, headed for the master bedroom, leaving his clothes behind like a butterfly shedding its chrysalis. He moved at an agonizingly slow rate.

The intruder paused at the door and looked inside at the empty room, completely stripped of furniture and any sign that a couple had once lived there. He remembered when it was full of things—a king-sized bed, flat-screen TV, sleeping dogs—everything. He imagined them now, as he crawled into the room on the tips of his fingers and the balls of his feet.

No deductive logic. No reasoned guesses. No gut. No hunch.

I am the monster; what am I thinking?

He wormed his way to the imaginary bed. He stayed there for a long moment, trying to put his mind in the right place.

Dark wanted to know what it felt like to hover about a defenseless, sleeping woman.

He imagined Sibby curled up on top. Only it's not Sibby. Not his Sibby. No, this is just someone close to his adversary. A woman he can use. A woman he can have *a little fun with.*

He unzipped the imaginary hood at the top of his head, then removed an imaginary washcloth, already soaked with chloroform. He pressed it down over her mouth. He felt her fight back. Struggle.

And then the screen goes blank.

But what's happening now? What's the monster doing to her?

It hurts to think about it, but fuck your pain. You want to catch this creepy son of a bitch, you're going to have to think like him, then think better than him. You can't shy away because it's too painful.

Stop him, Sibby had said. *I'll be here when you get back.*

Go ahead.

Be the monster, then.

You've got a beautiful, pregnant, unconscious woman sprawled out on the bed before you, naked and helpless. You're the monster loose in the bedroom. You can do anything you want. What do you do?

Do you hurt the baby? Do you feel up inside of her because you're curious? No, you're not curious. You know everything about babies, because sometimes you leave them alive. You wouldn't hurt the baby inside, because the baby's innocent, free of sin. For now.

This woman, on the other hand; what is her sin? Why are you running your fingers over her moist clit and pulling apart her labia

248

and examining her like a doctor? You don't leave any visible bruises or cuts or scrapes, but you make her sore. You make her confused. You make her wonder the next morning what happened. You make her lie to her husband.

So is she one of the two who will cry?

The four who will sigh?

You're the monster; you're trying to tell the world something—so what is it you're trying to say? What do you want more than obeying your primal urge to slice and fuck and squeeze and rip and break and suck and lick and punch and slap this woman before you?

Why have you come here tonight, Monster?

Dark padded carefully into their master bathroom and turned on the hot water. Allowed the room to be overwhelmed with steam. Then he traced the phone number on the mirror, exactly the way Sqweegel had done.

Once the steam cleared, he began his search. The tiled floor. The walls of the shower. The sides of the sink. Every inch, methodically.

And then there was a soft tone from his phone at the foot of the stairs. There was a text message waiting for him.

It was from Josh Banner. The results were in.

chapter 64

5:45 A.M.

Riggins had imported Special Circs' top DNA man to L.A. But instead, Dark had called on Banner again. They spoke each other's language. And Banner wouldn't get caught up in Special Circs procedure. He would just focus on the work, to the exclusion of all else. To Banner, the work was everything.

Dark was with him now, awaiting the results. Just another minute, Banner assured him. He'd already taken a pair of surgical scissors and snipped away samples of the floor from the seventeen-year-old mother's bedroom—the murder victim from the clip he'd watched—then placed them in a test tube. Added saline to loosen the DNA, then let the G mass spec have at it. The tube spun and rotated under the guided light.

And finally, a few hours later:

Ping.

Dark was not entirely surprised when the sample, compared to the records in the Special Circs database back in Quantico, brought up a blinking screen:

LEVEL 5 CLEARANCE REQUIRED

Banner looked back at Dark questioningly. A message like this meant that the sample came from someone high up in the federal government. They needed the okay from someone quite a few pay grades higher to go any further.

"Nothing to worry about," Dark said. "I know who it is—I'm just eliminating people from a scene. Got something else for you to run, too."

"Yeah?" Banner asked. "Something cool?"

Dark reached into his pocket and pulled out a small Dewar's bottle in a paper vomit bag.

"Oh," said Banner, disappointed.

"If you can match this against the previous sample, it'll set my mind at ease a bit."

Banner smirked. "You've got a man on your team who likes to drink and exercise proper dental hygiene. Sounds like a real winner to me."

"You have no idea," Dark said.

A short while later the results were back; yes, the same man who had used this toothpick had also knocked down this mini-bottle of scotch. He didn't share, either—not the toothpick or the booze. There were no other traces of DNA on either.

There was a final sample Dark needed matched. This was easy; it had already been entered into the system. All he'd needed to do was import the file from the Special Circs central files. It was a blood sample.

"Finally," Banner had said. He enjoyed working with bodily fluids a little too much.

The blood was another match.

Dark thanked Banner and stepped out into the hallway and opened the file. One he couldn't share with Banner.

The file contained crime-scene photos—which Riggins had finally shaken loose from Wycoff's people—from the Charlotte Sweeney murder. That was the teenaged mother's name. The one whose baby boy watched her die. *Sounded so sweet,* Dark thought automatically, then realized that no, it didn't. *Charlotte* was close to *harlot. Sweeney* sounded like *sweet. Sweet Charlotte the harlot.* The cunt. The unwed mother, who needed to be taught a lesson.

Dark flipped through the photos, which told the story in flashes:

A patio door to a suburban D.C. town house. Nice place for a teenaged unwed mother. Furniture from a high-end catalog. One phone call, and everything is delivered for you. No books. No knick-knacks. No idiosyncratic collections.

Now closer on the door. Trademark circle made with a glass cutter. Fragments of ground glass on the carpet below.

Blood splatters along the carpet.

Through the hallway and into the master bedroom. Charlotte Sweeney's room.

And now more stains between a mattress and box spring that had been stripped of their sheets. The box spring was heavily stained, and the blood flow ran down its side. Blood hadn't flowed cleanly; it had issued out in urgent gushes.

The bloodstained comforter. The teddy bear. The dental pick.

Ordinary items, now part of this nightmarish tableau. Items that belonged in this town house . . . except for one.

Dark remembered watching Wycoff picking at his teeth on Air Force Two just a few hours ago. The man was OCD when it came to his teeth.

A dental pick wasn't something a seventeen-year-old girl would keep around; it had bothered Dark when he first saw it on the video a few days ago, but it didn't click until earlier that morning when he met with Wycoff.

Still, it was just a hunch. Which was why Dark grabbed the liquor bottle and protected the evidence in a barf bag. Now the DNA testing had confirmed the worst. Finally, Dark understood the urgency. The threats. The fury.

And while it didn't excuse the secretary of defense's actions the past few days, Dark could understand them.

It was abuse of power by reason of insanity.

He'd do anything to protect his Sweet Charlotte the Harlot.

And punish her killer.

Dark needed to make his next move carefully. And for now, this meant not bringing Riggins or Constance into it. He thumbed a number on his BlackBerry and waited.

"I need to speak with Secretary Wycoff immediately," Dark said. "Tell him I've got his answer."

chapter 65

Within twenty minutes a black SUV had scooped up Dark from 11000 Wilshire and deposited him in Beverly Hills. Now he was standing in Norman Wycoff's plush, woody room at the Beverly Wilshire Hotel. The inside smelled like fast-food hamburgers and cigar smoke. Apparently the man liked to be located in the heart of things at all times. In this case, the heart of the most expensive real estate on the West Coast.

Wycoff had managed a shower since the last time Dark saw him, on Air Force Two. He had a towel draped over his neck, and tiny beads of water still clung to his red peach-fuzz hair, as well as his solid frame. Dark had never seen him out of a suit before and was surprised to see that Wycoff kept himself in shape.

"Where's Riggins?" Wycoff asked.

"I came straight to you, Mr. Secretary. Figured you'd want to know first."

Wycoff seemed unsure how to respond. With gratitude? Annoyance? He went with a little of both.

"I appreciate that, Dark. But why wouldn't I want Riggins to know? We're all on the same team here."

"Are we?"

"What kind of a question is—"

"Riggins was right," Dark said. "Sqweegel's never left a single piece of physical evidence in the three decades we've been tracking him. But I should qualify that statement. He's never left pieces of evidence *by mistake*. Sometimes, he leaves things on purpose."

"So you're saying he left that toothpick thing on the ground for us to find? I'm lucky my men even saw it."

"That's what I'm saying."

"To what end?"

"To point us in your direction."

Wycoff went pale, then sat down on the overstuffed couch in the middle of the room. He looked down at his thumbs, then back up at Dark. "Tell me what you know."

Dark returned his stare for a few moments, then walked to the other side of the room and grabbed the back of a dark wood chair with leather pads. He positioned it a few feet in front of Wycoff. He didn't want this to be an interrogation. He wanted them looking eye to eye, colleague to colleague.

"Riggins gave me the files on the slaughter of Charlotte Sweeney. It was a heinous crime, even for Sqweegel. And her infant son witnessed the whole thing."

Wycoff flinched, then did his best to recover. "I *know* what's in the file," he snapped angrily. "Where are you going with this?"

"That child is yours, which explains the sudden pressure on Special Circs to find the animal who killed his mother. Your *mistress*, or whatever word you'd prefer, Mr. Secretary."

"You're out of your fucking mind. She was fucking seventeen years old."

"Yes, she was."

"I'm not going to listen to this bullshit—"

"Sqweegel pressures you, so you pressure us," Dark said. "Don't you understand, Mr. Secretary? He's pulling our strings, and we're all dancing like little fucking puppets. There's nothing we're doing that he didn't plan out in advance, ten moves deep. You have us playing checkers, and he's playing three-dimensional chess."

"I have children," Wycoff said. "But not by that poor girl. My son and daughter attend Sidwell Friends with the daughters of the president of the United States, for Christ's sake!"

"It wasn't difficult to match your DNA to the dental floss."

"My DNA . . . ," Wycoff started, then shook his head. "How did you get my DNA? That's supposed to be classified!"

"Classified? There's no such thing, Mr. Secretary. Unless you wear a suit like Sqweegel, you and I and everyone we know leave DNA *everywhere*. I could scrape up enough from your toothbrush to clone you."

Wycoff took the Lord's name in vain again, then suddenly vaulted up from the couch. Dark almost felt bad for him. This was not going the way he'd planned.

But then again—fuck him. He was hiding behind the president and using them all to carry out some elaborate mission of vengeance against the monster who'd tortured and killed his mistress and left his bastard son to watch. The one who, in all likelihood, *wouldn't* be attending Sidwell Friends.

Dark didn't care about any of that, though. What mattered was that they stop playing into Sqweegel's hands. And that meant everything coming out in the open—at least among the team hunting him.

Sqweegel had been escalating, but he didn't leave it to the federal government to step up the search on their own. No. He ensured that retaliation would be swift and crushing. He went right to the top. Even beyond the Justice Department.

Sqweegel liked to send messages. His message to Wycoff was crystal clear: *If you can't keep your self-indulgence safe, how are you supposed to keep the country safe?*

"Where's the boy now?" Dark asked. "At least tell me you've got him under police protection."

"Charlotte Sweeney's baby is fine."

"You don't fucking get it, do you?" Dark asked. "I need to know everything. How he contacted you. What he said. It's the only way I can catch this monster. You want him caught, don't you? Caught and punished for his crimes before he kills and kills again?"

Wycoff said nothing at first. He clenched his big hands until his knuckles turned white, then unclenched them. The secretary of defense was not used to being at a loss for words or a clear course of action. He was not used to being caught up and strangled in his own lie.

Then finally he stood up wordlessly and went to the phone. Tapped a few digits.

Dark watched him calmly.

Finally, Wycoff said, "You came to me first, right?"

"Yes, Mr. Secretary."

"Good. Then you're out, you cocky son of a bitch. *Gone.* Breathe a word of this to anyone, I'll have you fucking erased. Tell anyone on your team, same goes for them. Ask Riggins. He'll tell you how easy it is. One fucking phone call is all it takes."

Dark paused, realizing that this man could make good on his threats.

"You're making a mistake."

"Look into my eyes and tell me if I give a shit."

Dark looked at him.

Then he stood up, nodded, and left the hotel room without another word.

257

chapter 66

Dark didn't have the world's easiest face to read. But even Riggins could tell something had gone very wrong.

"What the hell?" Riggins asked as Dark walked into the Special Circs War Room.

Dark moved to the desk he'd occupied and started gathering his things.

"What happened?" Riggins asked.

"I've been removed from the investigation."

"By who? That asshole Wycoff? Listen, Dark—"

"It's better if you don't know. I'm going to work this on my own. If I come across anything I think can help, I'll be in touch."

"No," Riggins said, shaking his head. "If you're out, I'm out, too. I pulled you into this. I'm not about to leave you dangling."

"No, I need you to stay on this," he said. "I can't do this without you on the inside. There's no one else I trust."

Problem with Wycoff was, he had a rather extreme definition of the word *removed*.

It wasn't just about being removed from your job. It was about removing you from the face of the earth.

"Of course you can trust me," Riggins said. "But what are you going to do? Where are you going?"

"I've tried it the old way, the by-the-books way," Dark said. "But all of that is bullshit. I have to do it my way, or this is never going to end. There are a few lines left in Sqweegel's little poem, and I want to slice his throat before he finishes."

Constance caught him on the way out of 11000 Wilshire. "Dark, wait a minute—I just heard what happened."

Dark paused in the hallway. "It was good working with you again, Constance. I know you and the team will catch this son of a bitch."

"No, we won't. Not without you."

"If you heard the news from Riggins, then you already know. I'm out."

She closed the gap between them and leaned in close. Dark was struck with a flash of memory: the other time that Constance had leaned in close to him, on the couch in his Venice apartment, pushing the bottle away from his face and pressing her lips against his . . .

"I know you're not really out," she said. "And I think I've caught Sqweegel slipping up."

"What do you have?"

"Give me a little time to sort it out. But I think it's the break we've been looking for."

"I don't think I'm going to be here much longer."

"Well, don't go vanishing just yet," Constance said. "I promise you, it'll be worth the wait. I'll page you when I've got something nailed down."

Dark studied her eyes for a moment, then nodded and walked away.

Constance jumped out of the driver's seat of her rental car the moment the shop owner slid his key into the chunky silver lock on the front door. He was a short man, fidgety, and bald on top—looking as if the hair had kindly pulled away from the top of his head to give any passing birds a nice target.

Which was appropriate, since he illegally sold them.

And if Constance was right about her hunch, the guy deserved the crap she was about to bring down on him.

The owner finished unlocking the door, pushed it open. The sign above read NEUROTIC EXOTICS—it was a pet shop specializing in rare, exotic animals. Mostly birds. The door hadn't completely swung shut behind him when Constance pushed through it and entered the shop. It was claustrophobic, cluttered, and full of tiny fluttering creatures that chirped nervously, beating their fragile wings against their cages.

"Oh," the owner said. "We're not open quite yet."

Constance smiled and closed the distance between them.

"You don't mind if I just look a little, do you?"

The owner seemed flustered, so she reached out to touch his forearm. To reassure him.

"I won't be long," Constance said. "I'm running late for work anyway. I'm just looking for a present for my mother—she's a total bird freak."

Reluctantly, the owner waved his hand in the air, muttered something to himself, then quickly moved behind the counter and fidgeted with some papers. Constance pretended to browse, but she knew exactly what she was looking for.

"This one here," Constance said. "This bullfinch. Does the *AZ* mean it's from Arizona?"

The owner gulped as if he'd accidentally ingested a small field mouse. Papers dropped from his hand. "You'll have to leave now," he said. "As I explained, we're not open."

"But it's so cute."

By this point the owner had pulled the keys out of his pocket and was already nervously ushering Constance to the front door. That was fine; she already had the evidence she needed.

On the way back to her car Constance paged Dark.

To hear about Constance's breakthrough, log into LEVEL26.com and enter the code: finch

chapter 67

They say Manhattan never sleeps, but at the right time of evening, there are pockets of dead silence everywhere. Especially in the neighborhoods, where life winds down as the clock approaches the night proper.

A neighborhood like this.

Dark moved quietly down a tree-lined street. He was still a little surprised he'd made it here without anyone trying to detain him. Constance had managed to scrounge up the identity of a Special Circs operative who was currently on family leave (read: going insane and trying to claw his way back to normalcy with lengthy and expensive therapy). The man looked vaguely like Dark, but nobody would mistake the two for cousins, let alone brothers.

Still, a plane carried him from LAX to Newark, and a private car had taken him here, to this block, without incident. Dark's head was fuzzy from the travel. His body still felt like it was midafternoon; his surroundings told him otherwise. It had been a long time since Dark had traveled to New York, dealt with the jet lag.

Now he was standing on the front stoop of a three-story brownstone, pushing the pearl door buzzer with a bare fingertip.

Dark had started out his career this way—pressing door buzzers, hoping someone would answer. Too often, no one did.

No answer now, either.

Dark tried pushing the door with his fingertips. The door creaked open, allowing a few millimeters of space between it and the frame. This was not good. People hadn't left a door unlocked in Manhattan since before they incorporated Brooklyn.

"Mrs. Dahl," Dark called out, then edged his way into the brownstone. "FBI!"

Nothing.

Inside, you could tell it was a woman's apartment—or at least, a woman was in charge of the décor. Flowers in vases. Porcelain figurines of animals. The faint sent of freshly burned candles. The only thing masculine about the place rested in a gold frame on top of a credenza—a photo of a burly firefighter. A legend on a small tag read, THE FALLEN WILL NEVER BE FORGOTTEN, followed by the date—September 11, 2001.

Deeper in the apartment were more photographs. The walls were lined with snapshots of an active life. A couple kissing at a wedding—the older bride presumably Barbara Dahl. A candid from the sidelines of an NYPD-versus-FDNY football game. A backyard picnic with a smoking grill and a cooler of ice-cold beer. Soon Dark noticed the unifying thread: the swatches of red, white, and blue. In some photos it was a flag; in others, a streamer. But it was clear these were all post-9/11 photos, when the country was swimming in its colors, because it was one of the few things you *could* do.

"Mrs. Dahl?"

Barbara Dahl had remarried since the fall of the Twin Towers had taken her first husband. As Dark moved through the house, he could find no evidence of that earlier marriage. If she couldn't wipe it from her memory, she'd managed to erase it from her home.

Dark turned a corner and saw a doorway leading to the basement level. He descended quickly, quietly, down the cement stairs and into the dimly lit room. In a second he would know why she hadn't answered.

It was the smell that hit him first.

He turned the corner and saw the body of Mrs. Dahl hanging from a leather belt affixed to overhead pipes. Her tongue poked out of her open mouth, as if she'd died in the middle of a sentence. Her bowels had voided themselves, which accounted for the smell. One shoe was on the floor; one shoe still clung to her foot, which was two feet above the ground.

But Dark didn't get caught up in the gruesome sight of her corpse. There was a sound above him—the creak of the front door opening.

Dark swung around and pointed his gun into the darkness, then slowly made his way across the basement floor. Above him there were three steps, pressing down on the floorboards . . . then nothing.

Did the person upstairs hear Dark downstairs? Is that why he stopped?

Was it Sqweegel?

As Dark moved toward the stairs, he heard more footsteps. But they were quiet this time, cautious, so that all you heard was the wooden floor straining a little under the weight of each step.

Dark's mind whipped back to the last time he had been creeping around under wooden boards—the church in Rome. Almost every night since then he'd fantasized about aiming his gun high and blasting away through the boards themselves. A full clip, emptied at random into the scaffolding above, would have more or less guaranteed that one of the bullets would find the monster. And one bullet was all he would have needed back then to prevent the nightmare to follow.

The temptation to raise the gun and start shooting was strong. But of course Dark wouldn't. Not until he was sure it was his quarry.

Now Dark would just have to move as silently as possible and meet him halfway, and pray that he saw that slithering body encased in white latex. . . .

The footsteps ceased at the top of the basement stairs. Dark raised his gun at the vertical coffin of the doorway.

A shadowed head leaned into it.

"Don't move," Dark told the shadow.

The shadow seemed to nod, then sniffle and clear its throat.

"Hands up—fucking now," Dark said, reaching up for the pull cord that would turn on the single lightbulb above him.

The shadow complied just as light washed over him. He was a middle-aged man, still in his navy fire department slacks and white T-shirt. He stepped forward, hands in the air. There was a small piece of stationery in his raised right hand.

His cheeks were red and streaked with tears.

"I couldn't touch her," he said, voice trembling. "I couldn't pick up the phone and I couldn't touch her. Oh, God, Barb . . ."

Dark called it in, then patiently drew the story out of the man—firefighter Jim Franks, who turned out to be Mrs. Dahl's second husband. He'd just finished up a shift in the Bronx and had raced home to be with Barbara, who'd been having a tough time of it lately. He'd found her body, then the letter, and went into a kind of shock. Franks was a firefighter; he knew the symptoms all too well. Knew that it was happening to him. Somehow he'd made it upstairs and into the tiny courtyard behind their house to catch his breath and put his mind back together again. A lot of time went by—exactly how long, Franks didn't even know—before he thought to look down to read her note. And then he'd gone into shock all over again.

"Can I see that note?" Dark asked.

Reluctantly, Franks handed Dark the letter he'd been clinging to.

I miss my husband. I'm sorry, Jim. The money is yours.

"What money?" Dark asked.

chapter 68

Brooklyn, New York

Across the East River, in front of a hospital in Brooklyn, the
four widows waited patiently in the oversized white van.
Tonight was something new—a field trip. They'd received the calls earlier in the day, instructing them to meet him
in front of the hospital instead of their therapy group's usual
space in the basement. Most of them seemed to welcome the
idea. It was a break from the overly bright room that reeked of
disinfectant.

It was also a distraction from the tragedy of the horses.

The senseless slaughter had hit them all in different ways, but
none of them could just shrug it off. Symbols take on a life of
their own, and when someone destroys the living symbol of
someone you dearly miss, it's almost like experiencing the original pain all over again. And once again, the city seemed to mourn
with them.

Why would someone shoot those poor horses? It went beyond
the realm of a sick joke. There was no financial motive. There
were only victims, no beneficiaries.

The site of tonight's field trip hadn't been revealed, but some of the widows guessed it involved the mounted police stables. Their therapy mentor was all about confronting your grief head-on. *Stick it in your face*, he once said, *and you'll be able to put it in its place.*

Some of the widows would like to stick something else in his pompous little face. . . .

Still, the approach seemed to help. And as a result the widows trusted him, which was why they waited patiently for their mentor inside a stuffy white van.

After a while a thin man—clean-cut, nondescript—opened the driver's-side door. He pulled himself into the seat, then turned to face the women. Big smile on his face.

"Hi, ladies. I'm Ken Martin, and I'll be your driver. Dr. Haut asked me to take you to the site; he'll meet us there. We all ready? Any questions?"

No, there were no questions. They could guess what Dr. Haut had in store for them; they were steeling themselves to dive head-first into their grief, yet again. None of them wanted to see the stables, or the plaques on the wall that would remind them of their husbands. But if that's what eventually would make them feel better . . .

"Okay, then," said Martin, whom the FBI knew as Sqweegel, as he keyed the ignition.

"I didn't want the money," Franks said. "I told her it was never about the money."

"What money?" Dark repeated.

Franks looked at Dark, then sighed. "After 9/11, I was sent out by my battalion captain. A bunch of us were. We were sent to knock on doors and talk to the widows who had lost their husbands. It was meant to be a good thing. For some of us, it was a

269

way to find some peace. For others, it was a six-month ordeal. And some of us found . . ."

Dark finished for him. "You found a wife."

"Yeah," Franks said.

"Were you married at the time?"

"Yeah, I was married. Two kids. Marriage is tough, especially in this line of work. You get a wife who doesn't understand what the job entails, and you're just fucked, no matter what you do. You can't force someone else to be happy. So imagine finding someone who wanted to be happy again. Who you could make happy. That was me and Barb."

Dark nodded. "And the money?"

"A lot of the wives after 9/11 got these million-dollar insurance policies. So it was especially hard to turn down a new life when the old one sucks and you spend most of your time trying to dig yourself out of the hole, you know what I mean?"

Another piece clicked into place for Dark. Moral righteousness, yet again. Sqweegel wasn't commenting on the institution of the police force; he was making a statement about the institution of marriage.

"I know what you mean," Dark said.

He reached into his pocket and pulled out a printed list of the widows, then handed it to Franks. "Do you know these women?"

"Yeah, I know them. They're friends of Barb's. They're in some kind of group together."

Speaking her name seemed to send Frank close to the edge again. Dark needed him to pull back for a just a few more moments; he'd have all the time in the world to sort through the rubble of his choices.

"We need to call them. Now."

chapter 69

Debra Scott's cell phone chimed. She dug through her purse—past her wallet, Mace, and a few small toys her eight-year-old daughter dropped inside on a regular basis to tease her. *Geez, Mom, I have no idea how that stuff got into your purse. . . . Maybe you need a bigger one . . . so you can give me your old one.* Debra's "old one" was a $350 Kipling. The daughter could have that in her dreams.

She finally found her cell and held it to her ear. "Hello?"

"Debbie, it's me, Jim."

"Oh, hi, Jimmy," a voice replied. "Where's Barbara tonight? We waited as long as we could, but then—"

The woman's voice was drowned out by an anguished cry from Jim Franks, who had broken down into tears. Dark reached for the phone, but Franks couldn't see him through his tear-filled eyes.

"Jimmy, are you there? What's wrong?"

Exasperated, Dark took the phone out of Franks's hand, then gestured for him to be quiet.

"Hello, Mrs. Scott? Listen to me carefully. My name is Steve Dark, and I'm working with the FBI. It's very important that you—"

"Working with who? Hang on, I can't hear well. Lemme call you right back."

"No! Mrs. Scott, whatever you do, stay on the—"

But then, in an instant, Dark was talking to a dead connection.

Debra knew something was wrong the moment the white van made a sharp right after exiting the Brooklyn Bridge, turning away from the Manhattan skyline back down to the riverfront.

"Hey, this isn't the way to the mounted stables," she said. "Sir? I think you're going the wrong way. Sir? Hey, buddy!"

"I never said anything about the stables," Ken Martin replied quietly.

"Isn't that where we're going?"

"No," he said. "Dr. Haut will explain everything."

This made no sense to Debra or the other three widows. There was nothing down here but the underside of the East River Drive. Why would Dr. Haut want them there?

Dark turned to Jim Franks, who had buried his face in his palms. "Mr. Franks, unless you want the deaths of four more women on your conscience, you're going to pull yourself the fuck together and help me."

"I'm sorry," said Franks. "I know I'm trained for this, but . . ."

That was a macho lie right there, Dark knew. You might be trained to deal with the pain and suffering of others, and trained to perform certain functions that may save the lives of strangers. But no one—absolutely no one—is trained to deal with the sight of their own loved one dangling from a joist in a dank basement, shit running down her legs and a suicide note nearby.

But Dark needed him to pretend for now, and to believe his own lie. It seemed to be working. The sniffing stopped, and Franks took a cleansing breath.

"If we act fast, we might be able to catch the guy who did this to your wife," Dark told him.

"What do you need?"

"Do you have a car?"

chapter 70

Debra watched the driver's eyes in the rearview. He caught her looking at him, then quickly turned his eyes back to the road.

The van was winding down a ramp now, headed toward the waterfront. At first Debra thought Dr. Haut might be trying to take them to Ground Zero—something she told him she would *not* be doing, his whole *face it and place it* bullshit or not. She wasn't ready to go there. She wasn't sure she'd ever be.

Debra stared at the phone in her hand. Since the morning of September 11, she had never been without it. It had been her last link to Jeffrey, who tried to soothe her best he could, saying he was headed into the towers to pull out whomever he could, not to worry, the worst was over, he'd call her as soon as he could, but he had to go, baby.

Baby was the last word she'd ever heard him speak.

Debra had clung to her phone as the towers fell, praying to God that Jeffrey had made it out before they collapsed and was scrambling for a phone now to tell her he was okay, not to worry, and that he'd saved a bunch of people, too. She had waited for his call . . . and continued waiting in the days and weeks that followed. She knew it was stupid now, but she swore to never be without her cell phone again.

And she was glad now, because something was totally wrong with this driver and where he was driving them. She saw the Brooklyn Bridge loom high above them. It was a beautiful shot that appeared in many movies, but now it just filled her with terror. Dr. Haut wouldn't bring them down here for nothing. Something was very wrong.

Had that guy on the phone a few minutes ago said he was from the FBI?

It didn't matter.

Debra pressed the REDIAL button on her phone. Heard it connect. Heard a tinny voice ask:

"Mrs. Scott?"

Debra cleared her throat and said aloud, "Why would Dr. Haut have us meet under the Brooklyn Bridge? Does this make sense to anybody else?"

The driver, however, paid her no mind. His right hand went to the air-conditioning controls, while his other hand seemed to bring something to his face. What was he doing?

"It's stuffy in here," the driver said, his voice muffled. "Let's cool things off a bit while we wait for Dr. Haut."

The cool mist blasted from the multiple vents that ran through the entire ceiling of the van. The air was redolent of sweet almonds.

"Mrs. Scott, are you there?"

A lot of thoughts went through Mrs. Scott's mind—the strangeness of this sudden field trip, the guy on the phone saying he was from the FBI, Jeffrey, *baby*, the almonds. But she forgot all about it because the air was syrupy thick, and suddenly she felt very, very sleepy.

chapter 71

I t didn't take much knockout gas, really. Just enough to give Sqweegel time to park the van, remove the widows' unconscious bodies, arrange them on the ground, strip them, hog-tie them, prepare the blowtorch, and wait for them to wake up again.

Sqweegel took a perverse delight in using the bare minimum of materials. In this case, just a small vial of knockout gas, which he had fitted directly to the intake tube of the car's coolant system. He'd tested it on multiple vans over the years until he found just the right cubic-volume-per-body-weight balance. It had taken a lot of time to perfect, but it had ultimately cost pennies.

The rope and the blowtorch came to about twenty dollars.

You didn't need reinforced rope. You just needed to know how to tie knots that would tighten the more the victim struggled.

And now they were waking up and struggling. Cursing at themselves. Cursing at him.

They couldn't see much . . . yet.

Sqweegel twisted the top of the blowtorch, then took the metal starter from his belt and clicked the flame to life.

Now they could see where they were. A small concrete patio directly beneath the bridge, down a steep grade from street level.

A tiny piece of Manhattan that was completely forgotten, except by the rats and pigeons. Their white droppings covered the floor. Sqweegel wondered whether the ladies could feel the grime and shit beneath their naked tits and bellies.

"Where the fuck are we?" one of the widows cried. "What did you do to us?"

Sqweegel weaved around them as he spoke.

"Your husbands fought fires for a living. Swept you off your feet, worked their fingers to the bone to build a lifestyle for you. But the second their bodies were destroyed in those towers"—he kicked at the knees of the closest widow, opening her legs a little more—"you spread your legs to strangers. Cashed those nice fat insurance checks. Tore husbands away from their families. Now it's time to feel the same thing your husbands felt. Without a single shred of *hope*, and the knowledge that the flames of hell are about to rain down upon you."

Sqweegel moved down the line, whipping the bright blue blowtorch flame over the tops of their heads. It *whooshed* and flared momentarily. The dank air was now full of the bitter perfume of singed hair.

Then he used a boot to flip one of the widows over on her back—the one who had answered her cell phone. Of course, she couldn't lie on her back, with her ankles and wrists bound together. She came to a stop on her right arm and leg, and she tried to squirm out of the way, her limbs straining against their binds. He could see her milky white skin flush as she struggled.

Sqweegel stopped her with a gloved hand on her left elbow. When limbs were tied right, it took very little force to render someone completely immobile.

Then he used the lit torch like a flashlight to illuminate her body. She jolted as if she could already feel the intense heat.

"Fuck you," Debra snapped. Her voice echoed from the concrete and metal.

"The world shouldn't have to look at that," Sqweegel continued, pointing down between her legs. "So let the flames of justice burn away thy offending parts."

She screamed, but he pretended not to hear. He lowered the torch so that its bright blue flame rested in the space between her knees—then slowly he lifted it toward her body. He could feel her buck and writhe, completely unable to move away . . .

In the near distance, a cell phone rang.

It was coming from inside the van, which was parked next to the patio.

"Oh," Sqweegel said. "You left your phone on? You're going to get it the worst. Who could that be, calling for you?"

"Why don't you answer it and find out," Debra said.

Sqweegel's curiosity was too great. The burn could wait a few seconds. He had to see who was calling. Quickly he made his way to the van. Found the cell phone on the floor as it rang a fourth time.

He lifted the phone to his face. This might actually be fun. "Yes?"

"Sqweegel," the voice said. "This is an old friend. Can you see me?"

Confusion washed over Sqweegel's face. His hunter? Where?

"No," he whispered. He couldn't help it.

"Good."

Then the naked widows screamed as the blast of a gunshot echoed beneath the bridge.

chapter 72

The bullet spun Sqweegel around. The cell phone and blowtorch fell out of his hands. The torch rolled across concrete. His back slammed into the side of the van. The widows screamed for help.

Up on the horizon, at street level, Sqweegel saw Dark clearing the top of the ridge, gun in hand. Now running down the grade, firing at him.

Sqweegel flipped himself to the right as two bullets smacked into the van. There was a loud metallic clang, and then a spray of glass.

He dropped down and shuffled forward, feeling the agony in his left shoulder.

Ignore the pain. It is nothing but a warning signal from a set of wires that run through the body. Focus on the body. The body will help you escape, not the pain. The pain will only distract you.

Sqweegel speed-crawled toward the bridge. He had a space picked out in advance, in case of an emergency like this. He always planned ahead. There hadn't been a need for his emergency spot in well over a decade. How had Dark found him so fast?

The phone. The bitch had left the phone on.

As Sqweegel cleared the side of the bridge—out of view—more shots rang out, slicing through the air around him.

He took a moment to implement a part of his contingency plan, one that should throw the hunter off track for a precious moment—perhaps enough for him to make good his escape. Or perhaps not.

Then—even though his shoulder was throbbing with red-hot pain—Sqweegel thrust his fingers around the rusted metal lip of the door, then pulled hard. The movement sent fresh agony coursing through his nervous system—

Nothing but a warning signal from a set of wires . . .

And he pulled again—

The body will help you escape, not the pain . . .

And pulled until he'd opened the way to his little hidey-hole.

Dark rounded the corner of the bridge in time to see the expanding impact circles on the surface of the East River.

He shuffled to a stop in the rocks and dirt, aimed, and fired four times at an imaginary clock on the water: nine, eleven, one, three.

Nothing.

Eyes trained on the water, Dark walked down the incline, reloading as he went. He knew at least one bullet had hit the bastard. Where the fuck was he? Didn't he need to surface for a gulp of air? But the blank surface of the East River revealed nothing. Dark scanned the water until he caught himself.

He was being the rational investigator again.

He wasn't thinking like the monster.

chapter 73

Dark turned around and saw the masonry foundation of the bridge—a thick slab that supported thousands of cars and pedestrians moving back and forth from Manhattan to Brooklyn every day. It would look like a dead end to anybody else. Anybody else running from the law would run the fuck away from the bridge.

Not the monster.

Not, Dark realized, when the monster saw the faded yellow and black fallout-shelter sign bolted to the brick next to a door that was acned with rust.

Dark reloaded, then pulled open the door and moved inside. The nauseating odor of mold filled his nostrils, and it was as if a hood had been dropped over his head. Complete and utter blackness. He felt glass crunch under his boots as he moved forward, gun out.

He tried not to worry about the pitch black. He tried to imagine that he was in the gloomy Mater Dolorosa in Rome again. It hadn't been his vision that brought him close to Sqweegel that time; it had been another sense altogether.

He would rely on that now.

Sqweegel could barely contain the joy pulsing through his veins, even as the blood continued to spurt from his shoulder. He moved deeper into the vault, around the heavy-duty cardboard boxes and rust-flecked metal drums. This was an old fallout shelter, more or less forgotten by the city of New York after the cold war ended. Sqweegel, an avid reader of history, hadn't forgotten. He never did his holy work without a strong sense of his surroundings, and the base of the bridge presented him with a perfect hiding place.

He never imagined that Dark would be here at the scene so quickly—or even follow him into this dank vault.

Dark was truly starting to listen to the messages.

Dark was stretching beyond his human limitations, toward his full potential.

Dark was beginning to be fun again.

Dark was tempted to reach for his cell phone; there was a setting on the phone that doubled as a makeshift flashlight. But the monster was in here. The monster didn't have a light. The monster knew where to go instinctually.

Moving forward a few steps, Dark felt something sharp rip across his shirt, right near his belly.

No, not a knife. He reached out and felt the rounded lip of a metal container. And over to the left, the ridge of a box. He was in some kind of storage room.

Dark crouched down, his back to the row of cardboard boxes. He guided himself along them, resisting the urge to think about his surroundings in a rational way and instead thinking about the *whores* tied up outside.

The filthy bitches who had taken the money and come, Dark

thought, *while the rest of the city still breathed in the atomized ash of their dead husbands. They must pay for their sins. . . .*

There was sudden movement to the right of Dark. A twitch. A faint stretching of latex.

"How is she?" a voice asked.

Dark snapped to the right, gun up, but resisted the urge to fire. A room this big would be full of strange acoustics; the voice could be coming from anywhere, and the blast of gunfire would give his position away. The utter blackness was working to his advantage for the moment, and he didn't want to lose it.

"How's my little baby?"

Dark was close now. Sqweegel was impressed with how far he'd come.

But his mission wasn't meant to play out here, in this vault of moldy crackers, out-of-date medical supplies, and canned water. No, this was just a way station on the road to their final destination.

Sqweegel silently climbed a stack of five boxes and felt the corners of the masonry wall with his gloved fingers. Ah, here it was. A small vent that led up into the innards of the bridge base itself. The bridge designers had probably thought it too small to be accessible by any human being. But the designers had not considered the divine.

Despite the pain, Sqweegel reached up with both hands, and his fingers found purchase in the vent. It would be difficult climbing with the strength of only three limbs, but far from impossible.

Sqweegel was about to insert his head into the vent when the room was flooded with light.

chapter 74

D ark held up his cell phone and saw the monster's lower half right away—two spindly white legs perched on top of a box marked CIVIL DEFENSE ALL-PURPOSE SURVIVAL CRACK-ERS. The limbs were clad in Sqweegel's holy vestments—the white latex that covered every inch of his flesh.

Dark aimed and squeezed the trigger.

The legs pulled up toward the ceiling and disappeared. Bullets snicked off the wall, spraying tiny chunks of concrete everywhere. Dark could taste the centuries-old stone dust as it settled into his nose and mouth.

Dark raced through the room, avoiding the drums and boxes and blankets and wooden planks like he was running a football play. He was running so hard that he slammed into the opposite wall and scraped the back of his right hand lifting the gun until it pointed straight up into the vent where Sqweegel had disappeared. Dark squeezed the trigger again and again and again, hearing the hollow clang and seeing the sparks as the bullets ricocheted up inside the bridge.

He looked for the tiniest flicker of white.

He hoped for the splash of liquid red.

He prayed for the telltale scream and the echoing thud of a body falling back down to earth.

But nothing.

The monster had scurried away again, like a white spider retreating into a sliver of a crevice the naked eye couldn't even see.

Back outside the bridge, Dark saw that Jim Franks had temporarily forgotten about his own problems and his firefighting training had kicked back in. The women were already free from their binds and draped in the torn remnants of their clothes, along with some old blankets Franks had pulled from the trunk of his car. The widows, in turn, comforted one another, as they had since the dark days of September 2001. They cried. They talked in low voices to one another, reassuring one another, crying to one another, reminding one another that they were alive, and that was all that mattered. Dark looked at them, and a line from Sqweegel's poem echoed in his brain:

Four a day will sigh.

Sqweegel was high, impossibly high, above the vault room now, where Dark's bullets couldn't reach him. Fortunate that the crevice had widened, giving Sqweegel room to maneuver. If it had been an ordinary vent, rather than an architectural quirk of the bridge, his holy mission would have indeed ended down in that vault.

But there was no time to reflect on close calls. Dark was

ascending, and Sqweegel had to leave the bridge immediately if he was going to prepare for their final meeting.

He had a plane to catch, a bullet wound to sew. There was an important appointment Sqweegel had to keep, and first he needed to pick up his special instruments.

To enter the mind of a madman, log into LEVEL26
.com and enter the code: practice

"Come on little one. Let's get dressed"

chapter 75

Dark sat in his window seat, trying desperately to control his breathing. He had caught the first available flight back to L.A., which was at 8:20 A.M., and the logical part of his mind was trying to talk sense.

Sqweegel was shot just a few short hours ago. You saw the bullet strike his body. He's not stepping onto a commercial aircraft—no matter who he is under that mask—with a gunshot wound. You'll make it back to Sibby long before he's even touching down in L.A.

So why was Dark having such a hard time breathing? Why was his heart smacking the inside of his rib cage?

Because the logical part of his mind was full of shit. It hadn't helped find Sqweegel then, and it wasn't going to help now. Because the monster inside his head kept taunting him:

How is she? How's my little baby?

The flight crew made their sweep of the cabin; the plane was about to take off. Dark looked down at his cell; he had just texted Riggins for an update and was waiting for him to reply.

Don't worry. She's safe. Riggins has it under control. You used to trust Riggins with your life; why not trust him now? Why this cold ice ball in your guts? Why this urge to take over the controls of the plane yourself and fly faster, fuck flight patterns, faster, faster, goddammit, all the way to the West Coast . . . ?

A text message arrived, just as a flight attendant who looked too tall for the aircraft walked by.

"I'm sorry, sir, I'm going to have to ask you to turn off your phone in preparation for takeoff."

Dark looked at the screen. The message wasn't from Riggins. It was from an unknown caller. He thumbed the OK button.

"Sir?"

The image was hard to understand at first. There was blood and stitching . . . on a human shoulder. But where? The top of the building behind the shoulder looked familiar. The white letters ENCY ran along a patio.

Emer*gency*.

Socha Medical Hospital.

Oh, fuck.

"Sir, did you hear me?"

"Shut the fuck up."

Dark speed-dialed Riggins, got his voice mail, and began to talk fast.

Socha Medical Hospital
Thirty Minutes Later

Riggins walked behind the plainclothes team. He spoke into a palm mike.

"Subject on the move. Back of house elevator. Stand by."

Then, inexplicably, the lights flickered out.

290

"We've lost light," Riggins snapped. "All of E-Wing. What's going on?"

There was a click, then a mechanical hum. The backup generators had kicked back on; the yellow lights returned.

"Proceed. Let's get her out of here."

Riggins had no idea if that was just a fluke, or friggin' California blackouts, or something worse. But he wasn't going to waste any time standing here trying to figure it out. He needed Sibby safe, and for Dark to know she was safe.

What gave him hope was that Sqweegel seemed to be human after all. Dark had winged the creepy little fucker in Manhattan. And now, for the first time, they had a tiny sample of his blood, now on its way to the satellite Special Circs War Room here in L.A. Probably it would reveal little . . . but it was something. It proved the thing was mortal, not some supernatural entity set on pissing in their Cheerios the rest of their days. That alone gave Riggins something he hadn't felt in a while.

Hope.

Especially now that Sibby was under the watchful eye of three plainclothes officers—handpicked by Riggins. They would escort her to another private residence—again, one hand-selected by Riggins, and known to Riggins alone—where she would be guarded until this was over.

For the first time, Riggins believed it could be over. He even told Wycoff as much, and the man sounded relieved, then effusive, promising Riggins whatever New York support he needed. Riggins told him he'd let him know.

Now he watched his men lift Sibby into the ambulance. Two climbed in after her; a third slammed the double doors shut and made his way around to the driver's seat.

The plan was simple: Riggins would lead them up the 405, then out the 118 all the way to a town house out in Simi Valley.

The place he'd chosen had no obvious connection to Riggins, let alone Dark or anyone he knew. Sibby's guards had no idea, either. Which was why Riggins would lead them.

And then Dark would return, and they'd finish this fucker off for good.

We have some of your blood, you little prick, Riggins wanted to tell him.

Your dead body soon to follow.

The patient opened her eyes and recoiled from the red flashing lights of the ambulance.

"Hey, you're okay, Ms. Dark," the EMT told her. "We're taking you someplace safe and your husband's going to meet us there."

She nodded and seemed to drift off again.

He busied himself in the stainless-steel supply cabinet near the floor of the ambulance, shifting clean bandages into the staging area in case the worn suspension on this old crate opened any of her sutures. This was some strange shift. The EMT prided himself on never leaving Los Angeles County, and now here he was on his way to Simi Valley of all places, a couple of creepy Feds riding behind the patient, conferring in low voices and ignoring him altogether. At least he was getting double-time for his trouble. A couple of hours of L.A. traffic and the nurses at the new location could take over; maybe the EMT could even get home in time to catch the Dodgers game.

He checked again on his patient and then bent back down to the low cabinet. That was odd; the white bandages were stacked differently than he'd left them.

And then they started to move.

He figured he was imagining things; there was no reason the pile of white bandages should have two soulless black eyes. Wait, no; that was just a reflection in the door from the stainless-steel cabinet behind him. . . .

The EMT thought he heard a faint click and a rush of fluid just after two pale arms grasped the sides of his head and twisted, and as the light faded his last thought was that he'd just heard the sound of his snapping spinal column.

Sibby nodded awake as the ambulance hit some kind of pothole—at least she assumed that's what had happened, since something heavy seemed to have hit the floor behind her. Sibby felt the reassuring hum of the tires on asphalt beneath the gurney. Riggins had explained quickly what was happening, but it was all so dreamlike and fuzzy. What mattered most to her was that Steve was on his way; he had gone somewhere, it had been very important, but now he was on his way back.

There was the clack of metal beneath her gurney, but Sibby assumed that was normal, too.

Until a hand reached up and placed a mask over her nose and mouth.

And two straps tightened, and the mask cut into her face.

Sibby reached up with her fingers, feeling the butterfly IV needle pull from the back of her left hand. She scratched at the plastic mask, but her fingers felt fat and formless, partially numb. Why was this so difficult? Goddammit, it was happening again, and here she was unable to do something as simple as pull this fucking thing away from her own fac—

chapter 76

Socha Medical Hospital

S qweegel had needed only three seconds of darkness to slip into the tiny space beneath the hospital gurney.

He'd flittered across the linoleum floor like a spider and fitted himself in place before the light returned.

They hadn't suspected a thing.

Arranging those brief moments of darkness had been easy, too. Simply a matter of placing an inexpensive remote fuse-blow in one of the many circuit boxes on the bottom level of the hospital. It was even easier to slip into the hospital unnoticed. All you needed was patience and a map.

Traveling west across the country hadn't been easy or cheap. But Sqweegel had realized the importance of ultrafast travel decades before. Under multiple aliases, he had set up accounts with half a dozen private carriers, and $20,000 bought him speedy passage from JFK to Burbank in a little less than four hours. He used the time to stabilize his shoulder and practice a few new techniques. The flight crew let him be. Wear the right fabric over your skin and present the correct series of numbers on a piece of plastic, and the world can be yours.

All of which put him into position to take the woman and the precious cargo she carried inside.

The rest was just executing a ballet that he'd practiced in his mind a hundred times.

A second after pushing the mask down on her face, he threw the first flash grenade. The concussive blast knocked her two guards to their knees, moaning, hands over their ears. The ambulance rocked on its tires as they hit the floor.

Then the choking gas had them gasping for air and reaching for their guns at the same time. That would keep them busy for a few seconds.

Sqweegel used the opportunity to slide out of his hiding space and remove his own gun. He wore a mask, too—and earplugs.

The ambulance driver, by this time, knew something was horribly wrong. The blast produced by the flash-bang would have roared like a cannon. Sqweegel felt him steer the ambulance to the side of the 405.

Just as Sqweegel had expected.

By the time the ambulance had ground to a screeching stop, Sqweegel had already placed a bullet in the back of both guards' heads, *pop-pop*, nothing fancy. A low-caliber bullet meant the slug would stay within the cavity of the skull and scramble their brains.

This left enough time, too, to place a third bullet into the back of the driver's head. The small caliber was especially important here, as blood spray on the windshield would only attract attention. The bullet did what it was supposed to: shatter skull on the way in and spend the rest of its short life span cutting through gray pulp and veins.

These steps completed, he walked back over to the woman and ripped away her mask. She began to choke.

"Relax," Sqweegel purred from behind the mask. "Sleep. We've got quite a drive ahead of us."

. . . *quite a drive ahead of us.*

She was not going to fall asleep.

She was not going to fall asleep.

She was not going to fall asleep.

Sibby dug her nails into her palms until her skin burned and she could feel blood dripping from the cuts.

She was going to pay attention and look for landmarks. Signs. She knew the highways of Southern California better than anybody else. She was not going to be a frightened little girl, helpless in the back of a goddamned ambulance driven by a monster in a white suit.

She couldn't afford the luxury of being the frightened little girl, because she was about to become a mother—the person who was supposed to chase the monsters away.

She pressed her nails deeper into her palms until she thought she'd ripped all the way down to her bones.

She was *not* going to fall asleep.

Riggins had slammed on the brakes, skidded to the breakdown lane, pulled his gun, and found himself running up the 405 . . . but he was still too late.

The ambulance rocketed forward, blasting by him in a flash of spinning reds and gray exhaust.

He cracked off three shots at the vehicle, but his aim was off— mostly out of fear that a bullet would pierce the metal body of the vehicle and find its way into Sibby.

Oh, Christ, Sibby.

What had he missed? If Dark had wounded Sqweegel in New

York City, how had he made it back to L.A. in a matter of hours? Riggins wondered whether Sqweegel wasn't a supernatural creature after all. Able to resist gunshot wounds. Endowed with the capability to spout thick, leathery wings and flap his way across the continent.

Even as he ran back to his car, Riggins knew it would be too late. Sqweegel had her. And they were long gone.

Thirty-five thousand feet above Pennsylvania, Dark squeezed his armrest until he felt the plastic shatter beneath his grasp. It would be three hours or more until he'd get cell reception again. Something had gone wrong; he felt it.

And there was nothing he could do about it.

chapter 77

Somewhere in Southern California
Several Hours Later

All she saw, at first, was a small red light in the corner of the room.

She felt something touching her right foot.

Sibby jumped but realized she couldn't move. There were restraints on her wrists and ankles. If she squinted, she could make out her binds, bathed in red light. Thick cuffs made of leather and metal, keeping her arms pinned to the sides of the gurney and her knees bent and spread to an unsettling degree.

"Who's there?"

She heard a tittering sound, then cold plastic fingers gently touching her left ankle. Was she still in the hospital? Sibby looked down over her pregnant belly and saw a ghostly thin form. She must be hallucinating from the painkillers, she thought. None of this made sense.

The thin little ghost began to undo the restraint around her right foot.

And then it all came back to her. The texts. The almond smell. The soreness. Her cut and bleeding palms. The landmarks. The ambulance.

The monster behind the wheel.

So this was him—the creep who'd been tormenting them.

The ghost-thin man froze midactivity, as if someone had pressed PAUSE on his central nervous system. Not a single part of him moved. He seemed to stop breathing. Even his skintight bodysuit betrayed no movement—no moving bulges or wrinkles.

Then he slowly craned his head to face Sibby. Those horrible dead black eyes peered at her through the holes in the mask. Sibby tried hard not to react to it, but there's something fundamentally terrifying about a face that chooses to hide itself.

"Stay away from me," she said.

"Oh, but it's so much fun when we're together, Sibby." He reached out and placed his gloved hand on her belly, and she tried hard not to flinch. "Can't you feel the connection between us?"

"Don't you dare touch me!"

"I'm not doing anything I haven't done before," Sqweegel said. "We have much to discuss, so much to *catch up on* . . ."

HE HAS SIBBY

Dark felt his heart race uncontrollably as he ran through LAX. The words of Riggins's last text message were still imprinted in his mind.

That hadn't been the only message. Riggins had sent him a bunch, rapid-fire, that arrived in his in-box during the descent beginning the moment his cell phone had started getting reception again. Each had been like a metal spike jabbed straight into his heart, scraping rib along the way.

The first had been a warning:

DA ON YOU

In other words: Dark Arts was onto him. All the while, Riggins had been keeping tabs on the fake identity Dark had been using. All had been fine on the trip out to NYC, but halfway through his flight back, the name—"Gregg Ridley"—had been flagged on a Homeland Security watch list. This could mean only one thing: Wycoff had found out about the fake identity and made that phone call to Dark Arts.

Dark knew the fake identity wouldn't last long. The incident under the Brooklyn Bridge had probably tipped Wycoff's goons off. It was only a game of elimination to come up with a list of who'd flown to NYC then back again during that time frame—and then poke holes in each until the flimsy identity was revealed.

The second was brief but chilling:

SQ STOPPED AMBULANCE ON 405

And then:

3 DEAD

And finally:

HE HAS SIBBY

So what line in the murder poem would this be? Sqweegel had taken the two most important people in Dark's life. Would they cry? Would one of them die?

Dark felt like he'd heard this poem all of his life—background noise he'd managed to ignore until it was too late. Now it was impossible to unhear it, to pry it out of his mind long enough to think clearly. It was just a fucking childhood taunt. A silly rhyme from a sick creep who wanted to pretend his words had some kind of totemic power over the world. They were *nothing*. He was *nothing*. And when he was dead, the words would fade away.

Yet he still heard the voice of his enemy whispering his poem in the middle of his brain . . .

> *One a day will die.*
> *Two a day will cry.*

Soon the black bondage tape was cut from her wrists and ankles, and her tormentor was yanking her by the arm, forcing her onto her swollen feet. She desperately hoped the pins keeping her left femur and her right fibula together would hold.

Sibby hadn't moved since the accident, and she felt an uncomfortable, dizzying head rush as she went vertical. Her insides were beyond sore. Her entire torso felt like it was throbbing.

Resisting would do no good. She could tumble to the ground and hurt the baby.

"Walk," the freak in the mask said, draping her arm around his hard, wiry neck. She was repulsed to touch him, even through the latex, or whatever the hell he was wearing.

"Walk," he commanded again, a bit more angrily now.

No, she couldn't walk. She could hardly move. She was only a few days removed from major surgery; she hadn't walked on her own in days. The exhaustion was like four heavy slabs of concrete affixed to each of her limbs.

But one nudge of his foot to her left leg forced it to take a step. It held her weight while he nudged the other leg.

"Why are you doing this?"

"Walking has been shown to induce labor," he said.

"No. I am not having my baby down here in this dirty base—"

"*Walk*," he bellowed, then nudged her left foot. Then her right. Sibby wished she could smash one of the concrete slabs attached to her forearms right into this freak's face. But it was all she could do to avoid falling over.

"That's it," he said.

The left foot. The right.

"Just focus on walking," Sqweegel replied. "It's going to be a long night for all of us. Oh, but *what a night*."

chapter 78

Dark hastily formed a plan as he rushed through the airline terminal, past the fast-food shops and bookstores and luxury-travel-item kiosks and public art displays. He would clear the terminal doors, throw himself into the back of a cab that would take him to the garage where he'd stashed his Yukon . . .

No. Wait. Not his own car. It had a GPS unit. Traceable. He'd need to steal something. A car that wouldn't be missed for the next twelve hours.

Then he saw one of Wycoff's men lurking by a rent-a-luggage-rack machine, right near the exit. There was no mistaking him. Dark remembered him hanging out on the Santa Monica Pier, circling around him like a seagull over bread scraps on the beach. He had a gray buzz-saw haircut. And somewhere around here was probably his friend with the missing fingers.

No suit for this babysitter—not now. Dark assumed they had to be professional chameleons. The one had donned some average business casual—button-down shirt, short sleeves, pleated slacks. The very image of your basic cubicle jockey picking up his buddy at the airport before hitting the nearby titty bar for a few lagers and maybe a basket or two of spicy wings.

Dark had no weapons on him. Nothing that even resembled a weapon. He'd left the gun he had behind in NYC—he was in too much of a hurry to check it and declare it as a member of law enforcement. He hadn't counted on needing a gun the moment he stepped off a plane here.

As he stood by the spinning luggage carousel, stalling until he could think of an exit strategy, Dark saw the Dark Arts operative with the buzz cut look in his direction, his eyes widening slightly.

Apparently *he* had an excellent memory for faces, too.

Sqweegel leaned forward and tapped Sibby's chin with a bony knuckle. The walking was over; she had drifted off, despite her desperate attempts to stay awake.

"The second method to induce labor is to drink castor oil," he said, his breath hot in her face. "It causes spasms inside the intestines. Drink up."

He handed Sibby a small dark bottle, but she refused to take it. "No."

Sqweegel reached for a knife on the small table behind him. He pressed its sharp point into the corner of Sibby's eye, right near the tear duct. She groaned, then caught herself. *Don't give him the pleasure.*

"Take it," he repeated.

She felt the point so sharply, it was as if it was already in past her eye, stabbing her brain. With trembling fingers, she took the bottle.

"Now, drink it."

She opened the childproof cap, messing it up the first time, then pressed the bottle to her lips and drank. Some of the castor oil dribbled down her chin. It was like swallowing oily liquid metal.

Sqweegel made a small chuffing noise, then flicked the knife's edge down, away from her eye. She knew immediately that he'd cut her. The damaged nerves beneath the skin relayed the message in a burst of white-hot panic—even before it relayed the pain. She waited for the warm flow to confirm it.

"Drink it," Sqweegel said, "or I'll cut the baby out of your cunt."

Now the blood flowed down her cheek, tracing the cheekbone and running to the corner of her lips. *Drink the castor oil, not your blood. Because if you taste your own blood you're going to be sick. And that might hurt the baby. Swallow it and forget it, and close your eyes and try to think of a way out of this nightmare.*

As the buzz-cut operative approached, Dark glanced down at the sliding metal scallops carrying the suitcases from his flight around an endless loop until their owners retrieved them. He also checked his peripheral vision. He could see the babysitter taking something out of his pocket, casually, as if it were nothing more than a pack of chewing gum.

But Dark knew better. Buzz-cut would be using his fingers to flick away the protective plastic cap, freeing the business end of the syringe.

Buzz-cut wouldn't want a scene. He'd just want two seconds to jab Dark, depress the plunger, wait for the ketamine to work. Then he'd lead his drunk friend out to his car, where he'd give him a ride home, and *boy would he be keeping him away from the little liquor bottles from now on. . . .*

Buzz-cut was steps away. Syringe in hand, out of sight.

Dark reached down and grabbed—more or less at random—a round fabric makeup bag with a rubber handle riveted to the top.

Buzz-cut made his move.

Dark twisted and quickly lifted the bag up. The needle slid into the side of the bag.

Then Dark smashed his forehead into the babysitter's nose.

The castor oil wormed its way through Sibby's digestive system, and all that kept her from vomiting was the reassuring kick of the baby every few moments.

"Spicy food," he said next, after a while. "You're going to love what I prepared for you."

Then she was forced off the gurney again and walked over to a small table covered in an off-white tablecloth—laced around the border, as improbable as that seemed. Is this what monsters used to entertain their guests? It didn't seem right. Sibby almost wanted to laugh. But she couldn't. Because the moment she did she'd start crying, and she wasn't going to do that. Not in front of this freak.

The aroma of harsh cayenne peppers and thick tomato sauce and greasy beans and congealed cheese made her immediately sick. She fought back a heave.

Sqweegel was already plunging a fork into the mess— something that looked like an enchilada—and was cutting off a large portion with the edge.

"Try. You'll like."

He held the forkful in front of her mouth.

Sibby spat in his face.

The freak didn't flinch. Instead, he stabbed the tines of the fork into her quivering lower lip. The spices mixed with her blood and burned.

"I have a metal jaw spreader I could use," Sqweegel said, "but that makes chewing difficult, and frankly, the food doesn't reach the tongue effectively. You have to taste the spices for it to work."

She took the food into her mouth and tried to swallow it fast, but already his hands were on her face, working her jaw up and down. She wondered whether she had enough strength to snatch away the fork and bury it in his eye socket. Improvise from there. As his hands pressed into her face and jaw, she realized how strong he was. How fast. She was drugged, pregnant, and recovering from surgery. She didn't have the reflexes to beat him: She had to think of something else.

"Chew," he said. "Savor. I worked hard on this dish."

As he ran, Dark reached up and touched his forehead. *Blood*. Didn't know whether it was his blood or Buzz-cut's—or both. Didn't matter now. He was up and moving, and Buzz-cut was temporarily down, fumbling around on the luggage carousel, scaring the crap out of people who'd come to L.A. for a little sun and fun.

Now Dark was clearing the large sliding doors, and he was propelling himself up the sidewalk, scanning the roadway for an open door. Any open door. Even a rental bus that would put some distance between himself and his hunter.

Behind him, Dark heard a series of screams, followed by the crack of a gunshot.

chapter 79

I t was later. Maybe a few minutes. Maybe an hour. Sibby wanted to throw up but couldn't seem to muster the energy for even that. She hated being so weak. Inside, she felt like all fire and fury, but none of that translated to her useless limbs.

And then this ghost-freak was standing in front of her again, hand extended, showing her a group of fat pills that look liked insect sacs resting in his palm.

"Blue and black cohosh," he announced, as if telling her tonight's specials. "These are herbs that have been proven to induce labor. Try some and then we'll check for dilation."

Sibby took the pills. Swallowed them with water, robotically. Then she snapped to life and whipped the glass at Sqweegel's head. It made a bonking sound and fell to the floor and shattered.

She knew it wouldn't work, but she couldn't sit there and do nothing.

Sqweegel grabbed her hair and yanked back hard, exposing her neck.

She had to fight him with the only thing she had left—her mind.

"That's number four, my dear. But we don't have to sit around waiting for those pills to kick in. No, no, no. Better to charge forward. Want to know what number five is?"

"No. Why don't you go strap on an apron and cook another enchilada, you pansy."

"Tsk, tsk, tsk. Step five is *sex*, of course," he said, spitting out the word like a fourth grader trying to shock his classmates.

"You're not coming anywhere near me."

"But we've done it before," Sqweegel cooed. "And, oh, how I've dreamed about this encore."

"That the only way you get any? Drugging your women? Tying them down?"

"So you remember. We've done this before. It'll be so much more interesting with you awake. Do please try to fight."

The freak moved her body again, half pulling her from the gurney before flipping her body over. Her pregnant belly wouldn't allow her to turn all the way over, so she found herself in the uncomfortable position of resting her upper-body weight on her right hip.

Then he was on her, over her, his fingers skittering up her arms. Cold metal brushed her skin. An instant later her hands were cuffed to the rails, her legs immobilized by the need to support her own body weight. Her bare feet pressed against the cold floor, her toes flexing at the concrete as if they could help her dig her way to freedom. She could do nothing else.

Nothing but lash out with the only weapon she had left.

"I fucked you and created this child," Sqweegel said. "Now I'm going to fuck you and bring it out into the world." Sibby heard the sound of zipper teeth grinding open.

"Is that what you think?" she said, trying to pack as much mockery into the words as she could. "That you fathered this baby?"

309

His hot, stinking breath was at her ear. "You know the truth."

"You're just a *boy*." She laughed. "You have no idea about the connection between a mother and her unborn child. I *know* this baby isn't yours. It just isn't a possibility. Because my body would have rejected anything having to do with you. It would have aborted itself in the womb. *I would have flushed it down the toilet.*"

She looked over her shoulder. The freak froze in place, as if someone had hit his PAUSE button again. His eyes just stared at her through the holes in the mask.

Then he tilted his head to the right.

"Well, then, *Mommy*," Sqweegel said. "How about I just fuck you and help the process along anyway?"

"Wait," Sibby said. "It's happening."

"Oh, what's that?"

"No, the baby. It's coming. . . ."

The freak in the mask looked at her suspiciously.

But Sibby wasn't kidding.

Oh, God, *now*, of all times, and of all the horrible places on earth . . .

The cramping was blinding and painful, like someone had wrapped a giant blood-pressure cuff around her stomach and wouldn't stop pumping, pumping, pumping . . .

"I suppose we should skip to step six," Sqweegel said. "The stripping of the membranes."

Sibby was re-strapped to the gurney now. Her feet were apart again, legs stretched wide. Hands fastened at her sides.

Sqweegel looked down at her, pulling a plastic rubber glove over his already-gloved hand. Was he being funny? Teasing, in the middle of all of his torments?

"Stripping the membranes is when I separate the amniotic sac

310

from the lower part of the uterus," he explained carefully and slowly, as if he expected her to nod. Maybe even thank him for the explanation.

"I hate you, you piece of shit," Sibby gasped. The cramping was intense now, and she barely had the strength to whisper. But she kept on fighting, desperate to say something that would get her out of this. "You're going to fry for this."

"Oh? Is that all, you think? I'm counting on Dark for so much more."

chapter 80

D ark was down.

Agent Nellis approached him carefully, gun pointed at the ground. The people around him were going insane. Airport cops on their way, most likely followed by a platoon of air marshals. This needed to end quickly, not messily, tied up in law enforcement bullshit.

He needed to commandeer a cab. Dump the body in the backseat. Take it somewhere quiet for disposal. Orders from Wycoff himself.

And Agent Nellis had about a minute to make all of this happen.

Nellis knew he shouldn't have taken the shot. It was very risky, doing something like that in public. Their MO was stealth, flying below the radar at all times. But the nose thing had really pissed him off. The needle deflection, sure, fine, all part of the game. But the goddamned head butt? His nose felt like it had been crushed with a cinderblock, then set on fire. And he'd be damned if he'd have to report back to Wycoff with a busted nose and a lame excuse about Dark getting away.

He used his foot to flip the body around, prepared to take another shot if needed.

And that was the moment Nellis realized he had made two other mistakes.

He'd forgotten to check the ground around Dark for blood splatter. A shot like that would be messy.

And he'd forgotten to reclaim his knockout syringe from the black makeup bag at the scene. Because if he'd taken a second to retrieve it, he would have seen it wasn't there.

Instead it was in Dark's hand.

And now it was stabbed into the meat of Nellis's thigh and its contents would render him unconscious in about two seconds.

One . . .

Somewhere in Southern California

Now was the part Sqweegel had been looking forward to ever since he'd first conceived it.

Pun very much intentional.

He measured her vaginal cavity—six centimeters dilated. He told her, but she didn't seem to be listening.

He turned toward a tray of new tools. One glowed with a faint blue light. But not yet.

He slithered closer to her. The final step required just the right touch.

He lifted a bony finger, rubbed it over a stick of butter a few times, then placed it on Sibby's nipple, tracing its circumference. Round and round. Round and round.

Oh, she bucked against her restraints. Moved her chest. Tried to break free.

But he continued to rub round, round, round, round, anyway.

She wanted to stop pushing. She wanted to forestall the inevitable. But he wasn't going to let that happen. After a while he stopped to peer between her legs, and then retreated to the corner and bowed his head as if in prayer.


```
To confirm practice makes perfect, log into
LEVEL26.com and enter the code: delivery
```

PART THREE

the heavenly virtues

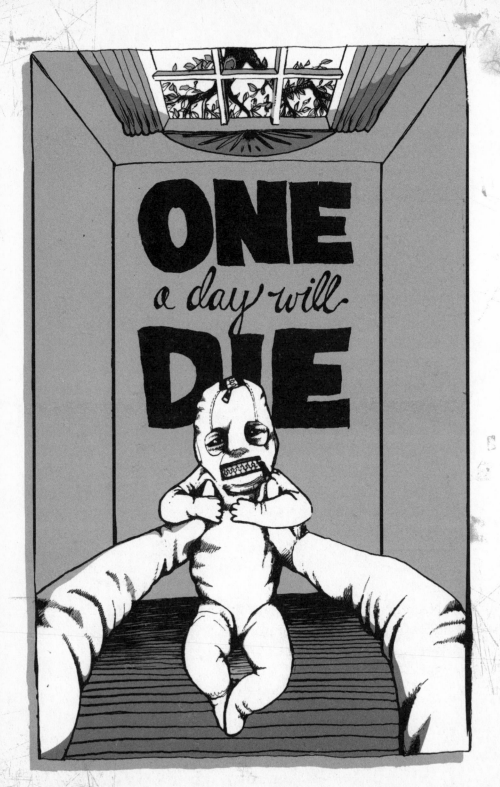

chapter 81

Constance Brielle found Sqweegel.

She was reasonably sure she had, anyway.

She'd traced the bird feather found at Dark's house to its specific species: an Azores bullfinch, the rarest of its type. Not found, or legally sold, in the United States. It was also on the critically endangered list—only two categories away from total extinction.

There was only one shop in the entire Southland area known for dealing in bullfinches; Constance found the name of the Woodland Hills shop—Neurotic Exotics—on a finch discussion group online.

Neurotic Exotics, naturally, didn't advertise that it sold critically endangered birds. Instead, Constance soon learned, bird traffickers used code names.

Such as this one:

Bullsore Finch, Arizona, $1,110

After making a trip to Neurotic Exotics to confirm they sold "bullsore finches," Constance met with Dark to tell him what she'd learned. The code was an anagram, simple enough for any bird fetishist to figure out.

Arizona's state abbreviation was AZ.

Take the *bull* out of *bullsore*, and you're left with enough letters to spell *Azores*.

Then simply add the *bull* to the *finch*, and presto . . . an illegal and highly desirable bird.

The question was: Who'd purchased a "bullsore finch" recently?

And had they paid with a credit card?

Special Circs isn't supposed to be able to look into the private financial records of American businesses. No law enforcement agency is, without a warrant. But since the introduction of the Patriot Act, there was a bit more gray area to these issues, and Constance liked to take advantage of the gray areas from time to time.

There was a computer security expert named Ellis on staff; he was especially gifted at prying into credit card statements. People were often defined by what they purchased. It was a nice tool to have when profiling someone.

"Ellis," she said.

"Connnstannnce," he replied. He sounded a little giddy. Constance realized she might be the only female he had spoken to in the last few weeks.

"I'm going to give you the name of a pet shop," she said.

"And I'm going to break the law," Ellis finished for her. "I know, I know. Go ahead."

Constance gave him the name and address; she heard the superfast plastic *click-clack* of a keyboard. Soon they learned that a number of "bullsore finches" had been sold in the past three months, all to the same customer.

"I guess you want me to check his account and get an address, right?" Ellis asked.

"If you don't mind," Constance said.

"Sure, but you've gotta tell me—is this about Sqweegel?"

"Don't worry about it."

Ellis did some more superfast typing—too fast for even Constance to follow.

"Okay, the guy has a PO box. But want to know the address on file?"

"That would be great," Constance said.

"This *is* Sqweegel, isn't it? Come on, you can tell me."

"Yeah, and I'm going to send you in after him alone once you give me the address. Come on, this is just background stuff. You know that."

He gave it to her, finally. Constance thanked him before he could ask about dinner, or maybe a couple of martinis at the Standard. She'd made the mistake of palling around with him for a few days early in his career—thinking a computer geek would be a good ally. She was right about that. Only, Ellis didn't seem to get the hint that this was the extent of her interest in him. Their professional relationship had been one long, awkward dance ever since. As if her job wasn't difficult enough.

But finally she had a name: Kenneth Martin.

And she had his home address.

Never mind what she told Ellis—could it be Sqweegel?

chapter 82

T he maniacal pecking thundered in the basement dungeon:
> *ThwakwakwakwakwakwakWAKWAK.*

WAK.

WAK.

WAK.

Sqweegel's foot pushed the pedal. His delicate hands coaxed the zipper cloth forward, directly into the path of the throbbing metal head as it applied the stitches. It had to be right.

After all, it was for the baby.

Sqweegel continued his work in the nude while the cunt suckled her newborn. She was still tied down, save one arm—to hold the child.

He'd watched them for a while. Making sure the newborn took to the nipple. Some don't. That would have required other methods. Nothing, however, beats the first few sips of breast milk.

The colostrum—that first hit from a mother's teat—is a potent cocktail of vitamins and hormones, like one last hit of the divine before settling in for a life of pain and toil on the mortal plane of existence. It's a brief sip of temporary invulnerability, including antibodies for every cold, flu, and disease the mother has ever fought off in her life. Sqweegel had been tempted to dribble a little on his tongue, just to see what had been denied him at birth. But no. The baby would need its strength if it was to endure the trials to come.

Sqweegel had gazed down upon the newborn and saw that it was perfectly at peace. Still graced with the divine, most likely. The shock of the earthly plane hadn't set in.

Sqweegel had looked at its tiny features and, oh, yes, most definitely saw the resemblance.

Now, though, he focused on finishing the baby's first present.

He lifted it up with both hands so he could admire it.

The baby's suit.

Two little eyeholes. Mouth zipper—for when it cried too much. Two tiny nose slits, so it can smell everything. A bone-in zipper from the top of the head to the crack of the baby's soft behind.

"Come, little one," Sqweegel said. "Let's get dressed."

chapter 83

He was coming for her. And there was nothing Sibby could do about it except stay alive and protect her child.

Her sweet, sweet baby.

Her limbs were bound to this stupid gurney, except one—her left arm. But that was useless, because it held her precious little daughter as she took her first sips of breast milk. She'd dreamed about this moment of absolute peace, having only read about it or heard how it had happened to some of her friends. She never imagined she'd be spending it in a dank, disgusting basement with a madman.

A madman who was now standing next to the gurney, reaching out for the baby.

The only weapons Sibby Dark had right now were her voice and her will to survive—for her baby's sake.

"You're not going anywhere near my baby," Sibby said.

"*My baby, my baby,*" he mocked. "Listen to how selfish you sound, Sibby. Not even a thought about the father."

"You're not her father, you freak. And I'm not letting go of her."

"I'm sure you think you mean that," Sqweegel said. "But here's the reality. Either you hand it over gently, or I sever your wrists with a hatchet and lift it myself from your bloody stumps. Do you want your baby's first sounds to be your anguished wails for mercy? Do you want it to reach out and taste the tiny droplets of *mommy blood?*"

Maybe this twitchy, herky-jerky monster in the white suit was one of those abused kids who grew up to dish out abuse on the rest of the world. He couldn't be bargained with, but maybe he could be frightened.

"You stop this right now," she bellowed, looking him dead in his black little eyes. "I'm not afraid of you or your threats. I know your type. Skulking around because you're too fucking petrified to step into the real world. I've laughed at people like you. I'm *laughing at you now.*"

The freak looked at her for a moment, then cocked his head slowly to the left, as if his neck muscles were on a time delay.

Then without warning a gloved fist whipped across her face. Sibby had never felt pain this savage or intense. The blow was hard enough to loosen teeth and fill her mouth with blood.

She felt the weight on her arm lighten . . . and then disappear. *Oh, God, no.*

When her vision cleared, she saw that the monster was holding her daughter.

"Don't hurt her," she said, tasting the salt-copper of her own blood on her tongue. Her mouth felt thick and fat. The pity in her own voice shocked her. "Please, I'll do anything you want, just don't hurt her."

"I'm not going to kill it," Sqweegel said, shaking his head. "If I wanted to do that, it'd be dead already."

"Don't hurt my baby."

The masked freak snorted and walked away with the infant in his arms. Sibby watched him leave and was surprised to see how

323

tender he was with her. This stick insect of a man who had punched, stabbed, cut, and tried to rape her. Infants were something else, apparently.

Then he made his way to a minifridge and removed a small stick of butter. After placing her on a table, he proceeded to grease the newborn all over its pink body.

The baby didn't cry. She simply looked up at the man curiously. Was this what happened next? Was this the way the world worked?

"See?" Sqweegel told Sibby. "It likes its father."

chapter 84

Constance stepped outside into the late-afternoon California sunshine with a bottle of water. She twisted open the cap, took a swig, then recapped the bottle, which was mostly full.

Then she pitched the bottle into a metal recycling receptacle and walked back into the building.

After a minute or so, a teenager zipped by on a skateboard. He snapped the latch on the receptacle, flipped open the plastic lid, then removed the heavy-duty liner from the receptacle before snapping the lid back down. Then he was on his way, bag in hand. Anyone watching would assume the kid was on his way to an automated recycling machine, where he'd get maybe a buck or two to put toward his beer/weed/amplifier fund.

Actually, it was going to Dark, who'd paid the kid $20 for the run—about two minutes of his time. Which would go a lot further toward procuring beer, weed, or an amplifier.

With Wycoff and his Dark Arts goons watching their every step—both in reality and in cyberspace—Riggins, Constance, and

325

Dark quickly agreed that the only safe way to communicate would be through old-school spy methods. Stuff nobody used anymore.

Like the hidden message in the full water bottle trick.

The bottle wasn't really full; it had a false middle, which Constance had quickly assembled with a second bottle, some rubber cement, and a pair of scissors. The bottom half is full of water, just like the top half. But the message inside stays dry.

Dark unscrewed the bottle, feeling the separation under the plastic label. He retrieved the handwritten note, which contained a simple address:

6206 Yucca

He knew the street; it was just off Hollywood Boulevard. It also made sense. The address was just a few blocks from the Methodist church Sqweegel had torched. Had he been in their backyard this whole time? It would explain why he moved about Los Angeles so easily.

Maybe Sqweegel didn't move here just to torment him. Maybe this was already his home.

chapter 85

5:10 P.M.

D ark returned to his rented room—a Super 8 on Western—
and walked into the bathroom. He closed the door behind
him and snapped off the light switch. With no outside
window, there was a bare minimum of illumination.

Dark didn't have forever; he knew that Constance would soon
be asked about her progress on those credit card receipts, and
then Wycoff would have this address.

And a man like Wycoff would not be interested in saving
Sibby, no matter how good it made him look. He was beyond PR
now. He wanted his tormentor erased, along with everybody else
who knew about it.

That included Dark and Sibby.

Already he could hear the choppers overhead, whupping in
the warm evening air as the sun fell down over the Pacific. They'd
be making time, waiting for intelligence. Dark had to act faster.
Think faster. Constance and Riggins could work only so much
subterfuge.

He'd stolen a car—something a few years old, shitty, nothing

327

that would be missed—and abandoned it around the corner on Vista del Mar.

There weren't many single homes on this stretch of Yucca. A lot of apartment complexes, lofts, all within eyeshot of the famous Capitol Records building. Probably a lot of musicians here, needing to fix their eyes on that totem every so often, if for no other reason than to keep their dreams alive.

Was that Sqweegel—a failed musician? Somebody wanting to outdo Manson? His creepy little poetry told Dark he had a musical ear, of sorts.

No. It wasn't about fame. This was beyond the trivial cares and concerns of mortal man. This was the business of God. Sqweegel was teaching mankind a lesson, one dead body at a time.

Would Dark find another parable here?

The house at 6206 was a single, painted eggshell blue, and in dire need of a new coat. There was no car out front. No lights inside the house.

Dark leapt over the small wrought-iron gate surrounding the property and moved across the brown lawn quickly, dropping down when he reached a set of basement windows on the side of the house. Totally out of view.

He listened. Nothing from inside the house. Just the ordinary hum of Los Angeles all around him.

The basement window was plate glass. Dark felt the seconds ticking away in his blood, and he had an impulse to smash, unlock, and pounce.

But no. Play this right. *Like he would.*

Dark pulled the glass cutter from a small pouch attached to his waist. He rotated the blade, suctioned out the cut piece. Reached in. Unlocked the rusty latch. The window dropped open. Dark slid in.

The cement floor was covered in feces—animal. Cobwebs in the corners. Upstairs, more of the same, only with a complete array of Chinese food menus piled by the front door, along with a healthy selection of real estate agent cards.

The kitchen—nothing but a foul-smelling refrigerator. A container of salt on the counter. A pair of garden shears.

The living room was empty except for a series of built-in bookshelves that were still packed with dusty volumes. From a quick glance at the perfectly arranged spines, Dark could tell the shelves contained nothing with a copyright date past 1970 or so. One book, however, caught his eye, because it was sticking out a fraction of an inch.

The book was called *Sinners and Sadists* and was a cheapo compilation of short entries about famous murderers throughout world history. Sick reading for sick minds. Dark blew dust from the top, then cracked it open and saw that one of the pages had a bent corner. That page contained a short entry about Lizzie Borden, the woman long accused—but never convicted—of chopping her father and stepmother to bits with an axe. Borden was the O. J. Simpson of her time, the stuff of pop culture before there even was pop culture.

Everything, from the book sticking out ever so slightly, to the dog-eared page, to the collection of books itself, was too weird to be coincidence.

But to what end? What was Sqweegel trying to tell him? He'd never been this overt before. It was like a mass murderer leaving behind a copy of *Helter Skelter*.

Dark continued searching the house.

Closets, bathrooms, bedroom—nothing. No signs of habitation or life, except for a single bed left in a back upstairs room. Otherwise, it had been completely denuded of furnishing. But maybe that wasn't the point of this place. Maybe this wasn't where he lived. Then what was it for?

Think like him. Would you live out in the open? Or would you use a house like this to practice squeezing yourself into little hidey holes?

Yeah. Maybe.

Dark started checking every space that had hinges or could be pried apart. No floor or ceiling was trusted until he tested it with his fists or fingers. No space was considered too small.

Still nothing. No sign anyone had been here.

And he heard the choppers in the air—seeming to be closer now. Maybe Constance hadn't been able to hold them off any longer, and they were moving in.

He returned to the back bedroom to the only clue. A single bed. Meant for a child? Small enough for him? But why? Dark ran his fingers over the thin, threadbare fitted sheet that wrapped around the mattress. No visible hair or stains. He dropped to one knee, checked under the bed.

Where Dark saw a small piece of tan parchment paper, with a small pink bow knotted around its center, resting on top of a book. He imagined the patience it took to craft an object of beauty and hide it in such an ugly place. Evil of this magnitude would take the craftsmanship of an artist. Dark realized that he was nothing more than one element within a masterful performance, the equivalent of a musical note whose purpose could only be deduced from those around it, the end result a terrifying crescendo rung out by a hundred instruments playing a melody made up of tiny, inconsequential notes. Notes that were only inconsequential until they were arranged by a virtuoso.

To read the birth announcement, log into LEVEL26
.com and enter the code: noprints

chapter 86

6 P.M.

Sibby couldn't see much. Just some flashes of silver in the darkness. The monster had a thing about light. Too much of it, or too little. Never just enough.

There was a metallic click, followed by another, and another. She could see the shape now. A tripod.

And his sticklike arms were affixing a video camera to the top.

At one point, he paused to turn his head—slowly, always slowly—to look in her direction. His beady black eyes made her blood freeze. *Please look away. Go back to whatever it is you were doing. Just leave me alone already.*

Even though, clearly, he wasn't finished with her.

Sibby's neck was fastened to the hospital gurney with a studded leather strap. The cold metal buckle dug into her chin. It was too tight to turn her head. Her wrists and ankles, meanwhile, were refastened to the gurney. Her hands and feet were starting to turn numb.

Nor was he finished with the baby.

Where was she?

What had he done with her?

Sqweegel was setting up something else now, something much taller than himself. He unraveled a dirty extension cord and affixed it to something on the ground, then—

Bright lights stabbed Sibby in the eyes.

chapter 87

Dark made it out of the Yucca Street house just as the first Dark Arts van pulled up to the front. Three agents leapt out, all dressed in black. Dark wondered whether the broken-nosed babysitter was among them. Or had they made him pay the ultimate price for his ineptitude at the airport?

Dark was wearing black, too, so he crept along the lawn and made it over the fence without being noticed. It wasn't long before he was back in the basement lab at 11000 Wilshire, alone, looking for trace of any kind on the parchment paper the monster had left for him.

One a day will die has moved to another theater near you.

Fingerprints? None. Touch DNA? Nope. Bodily fluids? Zero.

Dark slammed his hands on the desk and nearly knocked a ten-thousand-dollar microscope onto the concrete floor. He wanted to scream, he wanted to run, he wanted to find any tiny little piece of evidence that could lead him to Sibby.

Instead he crept quietly out the basement door and crossed the parking lot to his car. He knew he couldn't stay in the lab long without word getting back to Wycoff. Something had to break soon and he wanted to be mobile when it happened.

As he keyed the ignition, his cell phone vibrated. The display told him the call was coming from Sibby. Of course, he knew better.

"I'm coming for you," Dark said.

"I know, Steeeeeeeve," Sqweegel said, drawing out the syllable. "Find a laptop. Our final conversation is about to begin."

"Listen, you son of a—"

But the line went dead.

Three seconds later, a text appeared with an IP address and a two-word message: "30 MINS."

There was no time for subterfuge. Dark needed Constance and Riggins in on this *now*. Sure, he needed the Special Circs computers and their signal-hunting capabilities, but he needed their brains even more.

Whatever Sqweegel was planning, he wanted Dark to be watching alone. Dark was through playing this monster's twisted games.

Constance kept up the ruse on her end when she answered. "Brielle."

"It's me."

"Make it fast. We're swamped here."

"I'm going to text you an IP address," Dark said. "Hide it if you can, but that's not important right now. Track the feed any way you can."

"Yeah," she said, then paused. "I'll see what I can do. Like I said, we're swamped."

"Patch me in, too."

"Yeah, yeah. Isn't it approaching midnight out there? Go the hell home already."

"Thanks."

"Stop bothering me. *Good-bye.*"

chapter 88

Back in his dim hotel room, Dark opened his laptop, fired up the browser. Instantly, a gray box appeared and he was remote linked to the Special Circs service. Constance had been waiting for him to pop up on the network.

If anyone from Dark Arts was paying attention, they could probably find him in seconds using his signal. Dark hoped they were busy elsewhere. At least for a little while. Depended on how much Wycoff and his goons were leaning on the Special Circs team.

A video image filled the browser screen. A live, shaky Webcam image. At first there was nothing but a blank wall, shifting lights, some digital distortion.

The screen shook a little more, then panned over to focus on a wooden chair. Three minutes passed—Dark watched the time tick by on his laptop clock—and then there was a noise. A sharp cry. A baby's cry.

Dark's fingers clenched the sides of the computer. He had to be careful not to break the plastic housing, destroy the machine, lose the feed.

Lose his mind.

There was more crying from the baby now, along with soft rustling and then . . . footsteps. Soft padding on a concrete surface.

Then, like a ghostly apparition, a white form appeared onscreen.

Sqweegel, in his white latex murder suit.

Holding a baby, also dressed in an infant-sized white suit to match.

"I'm going to hurt you in ways even God doesn't know about," Dark said.

Sqweegel shook his head. Leaned in close to the camera. His voice popped out of the laptop's tinny speakers:

"You don't have to shout, Steeeeeeve. We can hear you just fine. Can't we, honey?"

Saying his name like that. Mocking him. No one called him "Steve" except Sibby. *He knows that. He's been watching. Listening. He knows the buttons to push because he flipped open your skull and examined the circuitry.*

So flip open his skull, Dark told himself. *Then rip out every fucking wire you see.*

On-screen, Sqweegel's white hand reached toward the camera, and for a moment it was as if he would be able to reach out of Dark's laptop and wrap his cold, thin fingers around Dark's throat. But instead the palm just filled the screen, and between the white fingers, Dark could see Sqweegel was moving the camera.

Aiming it at Sibby.

She was bound to a gurney. Naked. Helpless. Pale. Terrified. Trembling.

"Go ahead, honey," Sqweegel said, off-camera. "Say hello to your man."

Sibby looked drugged. Lost. In pain. She moved her head around like a blind woman, trying to find something—*anything*—to focus on. Then she locked eyes with the camera. With Steve.

"Don't worry about me," she said. "Save the baby from this mani—"

With that, Sqweegel quickly moved the camera back in his direction. His face filled the browser screen.

"Like she said, Steeeeeve. Don't worry about *her*. Worry about *the maniac with the baby*."

chapter 89

11000 Wilshire

Constance put both hands on the operative's shoulders. He was recording the Webcam feed and analyzing it at the same time. He flinched at first, then relaxed when he saw it was Constance. He'd been up way too many hours and his eyes hurt from staring at a screen.

"What?" he asked. "Did you see something?"

"Roll it back to the woman," she said.

The operative froze the image, then rewound it to the brief segment featuring Sibby bound to the gurney.

"Right there," Constance said. "Freeze it."

"Hey," Riggins said, looking over at them. "You got something?"

"There . . . above her head. Do you see it?"

Riggins squinted. "Is that a framed painting on the wall?"

"No," Constance said. "I think it's an actual window. You can tell there's some natural light coming through it. It's dim, but I can make out something . . ."

Meanwhile the rest of Special Circs was busy attacking the IP address on all fronts, tracing it back to the service provider and approximate location. Someone shouted out, "He's in the general Los Angeles area."

And this is where most IP searches ground to a halt. To go any further meant a court order or an illegal hack into the files of the Internet provider itself. This IP address, however, was unusual. It seemed to lead to a kind of straw-man Internet provider, which leeched bandwidth from a dozen other providers. Like a man stealing pennies a day from a thousand banks until he had enough wealth to open his own bank.

"Where in Los Angeles?" Riggins asked.

"Working on it . . ."

"Work harder." Then he turned back to Constance. "What have you got?"

The operative had zoomed in on the window, then digitally enlarged it. You could plainly see the top of a snow-covered mountain.

Riggins shook his head. "Hey," he shouted. "I thought you said this was coming from Los Angeles."

"It is," someone shouted back. "We know that much."

"Where's the nearest ski resort?"

A few names were bandied about—Bear Mountain. Mount Baldy. Mountain High. Snow Valley. Snow Summit—all to the northeast of the city, up in the mountains beyond Antelope Valley.

"No," said one of the operatives tracing the IP address. "Wrong direction. We think this is south of the city."

"Can't be," Constance said. "That's definitely a snow-covered mountain. If we identify the peak, maybe we could triangulate . . ."

Hollywood

Dark stared at the blackness on his screen, waiting for something to happen. This couldn't be it. Sqweegel wanted something. He wanted to play his little endgame.

So why the silence?

Then, through the black digital haze, her voice:

"Steve?"

"Sibby, I'm here. What's happening? Is he there with you?"

"I'm moving . . . rolling . . ."

"I'm right there with you. Remember that. Even if we're cut off and you can't hear my voice anymore, I'm with you. I'll be talking to you. I'll be coming for you."

"I know you will," she said. "And then we'll go to Disneyland. All of us."

"You know it, baby."

"Oh, God, Steve, you should see the baby, I've never seen something so beaut—"

Then nothing. The squeaking of wheels rolling across a concrete floor.

Dark pressed his face up against the screen, looking for any hint of an image, any clue to what was going to happen next.

There was a chuffing sound that gradually turned into a guffaw. The fucker was *laughing*. And then the screen twitched and turned completely black.

The feed was gone.

But it didn't matter. Sibby had given him what all of Special Circs, and their operatives and analysts and protocols couldn't.

A clue.

Disneyland.

Were they near Anaheim? It was a start, but it was so vague as to be useless. If only that creepy motherfucker hadn't cut off the feed, Sibby could have dropped another hint.

But it was something.

Dark texted Constance:

TRY ANAHEIM AREA. DISNEYLAND.

11000 Wilshire

"What the fuck just happened?" Riggins asked.

"We lost it . . . ," mumbled an op hunched over a keyboard.

"Well, get it back."

"Got the log-in box, but it keeps locking me out."

"Try again."

"I am."

"Fucking try harder!"

Meanwhile, across the room, Constance read Dark's text and looked at the screen again. Snow-covered mountain.

Anaheim.

And then she experienced one of those beautiful moments that she lived for but went unappreciated—the pure sweet hit of a connection being made.

The snow-covered mountain wasn't real. It was the top of the Matterhorn, in Disneyland. Her parents had flown her out every summer to visit the park—well, every year until they got divorced.

Sqweegel's house was somewhere near the most wholesome fucking place in Southern California.

chapter 90

Dark punched the wall of his hotel room. The drywall disintegrated beneath his fist, caving in a foot-long portion of the wall. Not the smartest thing to do—a curious manager could have heard it. Could knock on the door at any moment.

But his rage had to go somewhere. It couldn't ride his nervous system forever.

Dark was itching to kill something, and his rational mind was barely able to stop him.

Dark hadn't felt this way for years. Not since his foster family was taken from him. From that point on, his heart had gone supernova, the center of his soul turned into a superdense ball, an unfeeling mass of iron. He'd heaved that iron around the world, smashing it into whatever he thought was separating him from the spindly little monster who'd done this to him. And after that, after a year of bloody, frustrating, black, sick failure, everything else burned out of his body, all of his senses gone white-hot and then cold dead . . . burned to *nothing*.

Sibby had stirred up the ashes, found some flecks of heat in a place he'd long considered barren. She'd turned the ashes around, slowly, cultivating the fire, making him feel human again.

Now with her in the hands of a maniac, it was as if someone had dropped a bunker buster into Dark's chest. He felt his insides burn, shake, collapse.

There was nothing he needed more than to destroy Sqweegel . . . and all he could do was stare at his dead browser and resist the urge to hurl the laptop across the room and rip the lid off the machine and scrape out the keys with his fingers. . . .

"Hold onnn . . . Yes! Third time's a charm. We're back."

Riggins and Constance rushed over to the screen, which was filled with Sqweegel's face. His zippered mouth looked like a tear in the screen itself, and any moment, his fat wet tongue would come poking through.

"Constance Brielle," he said. "I know you're with us. This involves you, too."

Everyone turned at once. But she ignored them. Stayed transfixed on the image of his mouth, like the mouth of God, ready to read her sins out loud.

"We have a lot to talk about," Sqweegel said. "All of us."

And then Sqweegel's face was gone, and the camera was pointed at Sibby.

"Steve?"

"I'm here," Dark said, touching the LCD screen with his fingertips. Feeling the faint warmth of the pixels, pretending it was her.

"We're all on, then?" asked Sqweegel, who swung the camera back to him. He was cradling the baby, still in its white bondage suit, in his right arm.

"It's important we get a few things out of the way before we finish."

The more Constance stared at Sqweegel, the more she knew he could see them. It was in the thousand small ways he reacted. This wasn't a man acting to an imaginary audience. He could see them all.

He must have some kind of surveillance camera in this room. Maybe even more than one.

How?

Constance kept her eyes on the screen but found a pen and Post-it note with her hands. Scribbled on it:

Keep triangulating QUIETLY. Need this locale ASAP. My eyes only.

She handed it to the op next to her, her fingertips lingering on his hand to make sure he understood.

Sqweegel smoothed out imaginary wrinkles on his latex body suit, then cranked his head up to face the camera like a television anchorman. Confident. Stiff backed. Completely at ease in front of the audience.

And with his audience gathered, he began to speak.

chapter 91

Just After Midnight / Father's Day

"I am here on earth to rid men of their sins and remind them of the heavenly virtues," Sqweegel told the camera. "Be it greedy cunt widows who've lost all hope and fuck for government hush money. Or faggot priests who have forgotten their faith and abuse children, think they'll be able to confess their way out of the eternal flames. Be it over-privileged juvenile delinquents who look for thrills but are unwilling to deal with the consequences. Or the hypocrite defender of the country who can't even defend his bastard child."

"I'm going to destroy you," Dark told the screen.

Sqweegel looked up at him. Smirked from behind his mask. Dark could tell by the way the latex scrunched up.

"Or a washed-up federal investigator who couldn't protect his foster family from one little mortal being."

"You have nothing on me," Dark said. "You see nothing but sin around you, but you don't see your own sins. You want to kill

348

everyone in the world? Send everyone to hell? Do it. But I hope your bags are packed, because when I get my hands on you, you'll be joining them."

Sqweegel tilted his head to the side. "I'm not afraid, Steeeeeeve. There are two reasons I wanted us to speak this evening. First, I want to forgive your sins."

"Fuck you," Dark said.

"That seems to be your answer for everything. Fuck *it*. Fuck *me*. Fuck *her*. But you know what happens when you *fuck*? Did your foster mother teach you this, maybe reaching her hand down the front of your underwear to make her point? Did it give you a little rise? Do you still fantasize about her, Steve?"

"Get to the point."

"When you *fuck*, you make a baby. At least, that's what God intended. And you made a baby."

"Yeah. It's in your cellar. And I'm coming for her, you twisted little fuck."

"*Your* baby?" asked Sqweegel. "Are you sure?"

Sqweegel snickered. He couldn't help himself. Once he started it was hard to stop. His was an animal laugh; he'd had it since childhood. It bubbled out whenever he let his emotions get away from him. So *hard* to contain himself sometimes. He'd managed a rarified level of control for decades. But now the journey was almost complete, and it was as if his body knew it.

This was serious now. It's not every day you're able to destroy your mortal enemy with just a few words.

"What are you talking about?" Dark asked.

"The baby isn't yours," Sqweegel said. "It's mine."

"Liar."

"No, no. You see, I put Sibby to sleep the night you forgot the virtue of restraint when you stuck your hungry cock into Constance Brielle."

The blood in Dark's veins turned to ice.
Oh, God. *He knew.*

chapter 92

Constance felt like she was standing naked in this control room, surrounded by men who could see her every flaw, every bulge and dimple.

How did he know? She'd told no one. Not even her mother in Philadelphia. This had been a secret she was completely willing to take to her grave, and deal with the judgment later. But it seemed she was being judged now.

"She aborted it, Steeeeeeve," Sqweegel said. "But you knew that already, didn't you? Even offered her a check, what was it . . . ooh, right, check number 1183, to help pay for the . . . *services*? But she ripped it up and threw it away where *anyone* could find it. Well, anyone with a little roll of tape and a lot of extra time."

Constance remembered doing that now. At the time, the sting of Dark's indifference, the coldness of him, had made her furious. But she got over it. Moved on.

She couldn't see Dark's face right now, but she wondered whether he was reacting at all.

"Ah, don't be sore," said Sqweegel on the screen. "Constance wanted to keep everything quiet. She didn't want to cause you any trouble. You know, an extra life chasing you around, mewling for attention. It'd be very bad for you, wouldn't it, Steeeve?"

Constance heard Dark's voice reverberating in Sqweegel's lair. His voice boomed so loud, it overwhelmed the tiny laptop microphone and distorted.

"Shut up!"

"If I'm lying, I'm dying," Sqweegel said. "I'll cut my tongue out at the *root*—all on camera. I'll accept the punishment for my sin. I will never be able to lie again. But I'm *not* lying, am I, Dark?"

This was a madman telling lies. Nothing more. Sibby tried to block out the words and focus on the baby. All that mattered was that their little girl made it out of this hell house alive. The rest didn't matter—not her, not Steve, not any of it.

But the words squirmed their way into her conscious mind anyway.

. . . stuck your hungry cock into Constance Brielle . . .

She aborted it, Steeeeeeeeve . . .

And she thought about the night she told Steve the news about the baby. She'd been so cautious—more cautious than anything she'd ever done. When she saw the happy flicker of light in his eyes, she knew everything would be okay from that moment on.

This is amazing, he'd said then.

Sibby, I tried to tell you, he said now.

Constance's voice, now, too:

It was my fault, Sibby. It was one night. I know it was a shitty thing to do. I got rid of it because I didn't want to screw you guys up. I take total responsibility.

Steve again:

I do, too. I tried to tell you.

"Shut up, shut the fuck up, all of you, just rescue my baby from this nightmare," Sibby screamed.

"See how hateful we can be to each other when we forget the lessons of heaven?" Sqweegel told the camera. "We all have little secrets. *I* kill people; *you* kill people. At least when I kill, I don't keep it a secret."

Then he pulled the camera off its tripod; the screen was now full of nothing but his naked face.

"Every person I sent to hell deserved it," Sqweegel said. You and Constance got rid of a life, so Sibby and I are going to do the same. An eye for an eye, and the world will go blind.

"I must admit . . . it's going to be hard to abort this one. I've become rather attached."

And with that, he killed the Internet connection.

The Special Circs techs went into a frenzy trying to isolate the problem, but they quickly realized it was the power, fluctuating on and off, on and off, like a thunderstorm had rolled in to wreak havoc on their circuit breakers.

But after a few seconds the power resumed, and a new, pixilated, black-and-white image appeared on all of the monitors.

```
To view this "live" film, log into LEVEL26.com
and enter the code: run4fun
```

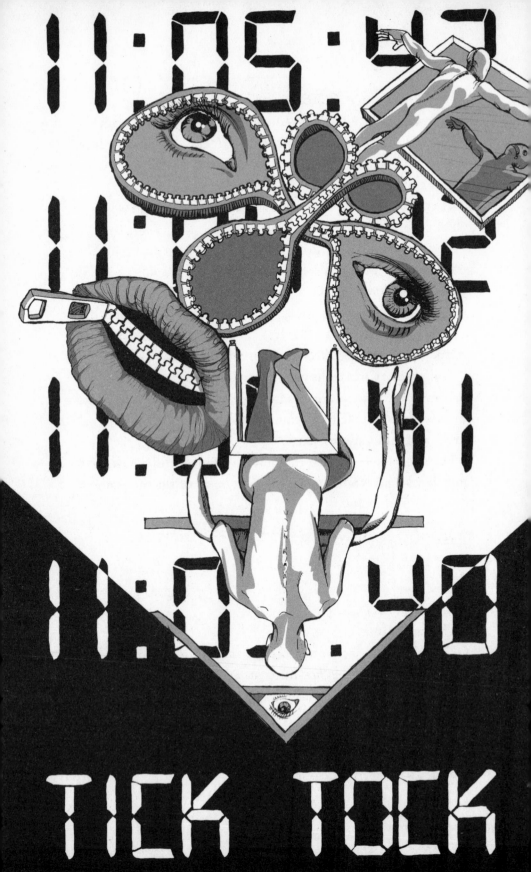

chapter 93

The images were nothing less than surveillance footage from the heart of hell itself.

Latex hands lowering a baby into an open metal crate. The baby is cold. Crying. Reaching out for her mother . . .

The image twitches.

The mother is freed from her wrist binds and taunted with a razor. Over her chest. Her legs. Her toes. Cruelly, mercilessly, like a butcher tormenting a chicken he's about to chop. The mother lies frozen in fear, but it is no use. The butcher is determined.

The image twitches.

The mother is freed from her ankle binds, knees the monster in the face and scrambles off the hospital gurney, blind, limping, scrambling, spitting, screaming . . .

The image twitches.

The mother screams at the camera, screams at all of us, and we see the butcher pursuing her, razor in hand, bobbing and weaving and chasing, through the butcher's nightmare dungeon and down a long hall until the butcher finally overcomes the mother. . . .

The image twitches.

The butcher holds the razor in the air now. He, it seems, is determined to strip the skin from this sacrificial chicken. . . .

The image twitches, as if it can't bear to watch what it's been forced to record.

And now the butcher has the baby in his blood-soaked hands, holding it up like an offering to some ancient and forgotten god. . . .

"What the fuck *is* this?"

Everyone in the Special Circs War Room turned to face Secretary of Defense Norman Wycoff. The man's shirt was untucked and he had dark bags under his eyes. Little hairs stuck up from the top of his head, making him resemble a duckling who'd just kicked its way out of the shell.

The op heading up the computer search spoke up first. "We think he's in Anaheim."

Riggins had been dreading this. He'd hoped that Wycoff would do what all figureheads should do—stay the fuck away and let them do their jobs. Wycoff loved snapping off commands, but he never stuck around and plunged his hands into the meat of it. The fact that he was here confirmed that Dark was right: This was so totally fucking personal.

And a serious abuse of power.

"Think?" Wycoff asked. "You got something real, or is he just jerking us off, like that Yucca Street address?"

The operative brought Wycoff up to speed quickly, making sure to note that the Matterhorn breakthrough had, in fact, *sir*, been his idea. Constance muttered something to Riggins about needing the ladies' room and started to edge her way out of the War Room.

Wycoff saw her. "Agent Brielle. A *word*."

Constance exhaled, then walked back over to the secretary of defense. He leaned in so close, he'd be able to tilt his head and bite off her earring, if he wanted to.

"I told you I wanted the latest intel the *nanosecond* you received it," Wycoff said. "What do you think you're doing?"

"Our jobs," Constance said. "We literally just pieced this together seconds ago. Do you want this monster caught or not?"

Wycoff looked her over for a moment. Her hair, her lips, then her tits. He was drunk. She could smell the scotch radiating from his pores. Wycoff's eyes flittered around in their sockets, unable to focus on any one thing for very long.

"We got it!" an op shouted.

Oh, shit, Constance thought. Could she pull it off?

"Bring it here," Wycoff said. He was already pulling his Black-Berry from his pants pocket.

"Just let me confirm," Constance said, and made her way over to the op. She made him write it down quickly on a piece of paper—so there could be no error, she told him. Then she took the slip of paper to another desk, wrote something else on the note, then brought it over to Wycoff.

"Come on, already," he said. "You can file all the paperwork you want when this little motherfucker is dead and buried."

"Here," she said, handing him a slip of paper. "We just wanted to lock it down. You don't want to bring the wrath of God down on John Doe and his two-point-five kids living in the shadow of Disneyland, do you, Mr. Secretary?"

"Disneyland?" he asked, then looked down at the slip of paper, which read:

1531 Playa Del Rey
Anaheim

Wycoff stormed off without so much as a *hidey-ho* or a *fuck you*, cell phone pressed to his ear. He read the address over the phone. "You got that? Send the fucking cavalry. Execute all targets. Yes, fucking now. If it has a heartbeat, it *dies . . ."*

The op who'd found the address stood up, confused. "Wait—Agent Brielle, I think the secretary has the wrong—"

Riggins glided over to run interference. He put his hand on the op's shoulder and guided him back down to his rolling desk chair. "Agent Brielle knows what she's doing," he said. "Now, get back on the machine and get me any kind of surveillance you can on the address you found."

A few moments later Constance walked into the ladies' room, chose the stall on the end, lifted her skirt and pulled down her panties, then sat down. For a moment she caught herself staring blankly at the gray metal stall door, a little confused about how her career had brought her to this point.

Then she snapped out of it, pressed a key, speed-dialing Dark.

"What've you got?" he said.

"Did you see that little window in the corner of the screen?"

"No," Dark admitted. "What was it?"

"The best lead we've ever had on this case. We were able to triangulate and somehow got an address. But here's the problem: Wycoff's goon squad is moving in."

"I need more time."

"And you've got it," she continued. "I gave Wycoff the wrong address. The real one is 1531 San Martin Drive in Anaheim. You've got about fifteen minutes of me jerking them around before they figure it out. Go."

"Thank you, Constance. If I haven't—"

"Just *go*."

Dark hammered the accelerator of his stolen car, blasting south on the 405, headed for Disneyland.

chapter 94

1531 San Martin Drive, Anaheim, California

The house looked like it had dropped out of the wrong decade and accidentally landed here, in this decade, in the middle of this sunbaked suburban sprawl. Unlike the ranch houses around it, 1531 San Martin Drive was a grand folk Victorian, with brackets under the eaves and a trellised porch ringing the front. The home appeared to have been built before people realized what homes in Southern California should actually look like, its style imported from turn-of-the-century New England.

Inside, every piece of the décor was white. Floors, walls, ceilings— even the windows were smoked white. Dark, clad completely in black, crawled along the white carpet, pistol with a laser-sighting rig strapped to his right side and a small bag of gear strapped to his left. Dark thought of a line from Raymond Chandler—*he stood out like a tarantula on a piece of angel food cake.*

Clearly, Sqweegel had a thing for light and dark. So be it. All Dark needed was for that little red dot to land on a vital piece of his twitchy body—his forehead, maybe. Then one squeeze and it would be over.

There was a white wooden door with a smudge of blood near the knob. Only a RIGHT THIS WAY sign would have been more obvious.

Sqweegel, clearly, was waiting for him.

White marble steps led down. Dark followed a set of bloodied footprints—messy and smeared. They were headed in both directions, as if someone had marched up to the doorway, changed his or her mind, then headed back down.

Were those Sibby's footprints?

Dark paused at the doorway. The light was scant down here. He quietly fished out a mirror attached to a thin metal rod—a sniper's snake mirror—to look around the corner.

Sibby was in the reflection, tied to a hospital gurney, covered in blood. There were so many wounds and gashes, it was hard to tell where they began and ended.

Do not think of your foster family. Do not think of what the monster did to them. Sibby's alive; that's all that matters. No matter what he's done, she can heal. We can all heal together.

All you have to do is slay the monster, take your family, and go home.

Dark dropped the mirror, not giving a shit about stealth anymore. There were no rules now. No more games. He drew his gun and rounded the corner to see Sqweegel.

Holding the baby up in front of his chest.

"I didn't *think* you'd want to miss this," he said. "Are you ready to fulfill your destiny?"

chapter 95

Dark aimed his gun at Sqweegel's forehead. It was dim in here, but not so dim that he couldn't see his white, wormlike writhing body. While Dark had stood out upstairs, Sqweegel's white costume made him practically glow down here. All of his joints pumped like pistons, as if tuned to some song playing only in his head.

The baby glowed, too.

"Put the baby down or I'll—"

"You'll what, Steeeeeve? Kill me? You wouldn't dare shoot. A stray bullet might hit my precious little baby."

"That's *not your child*," Dark hissed.

"Why don't you shoot us and find out? Give us *both* blood tests. Watch the truth wriggle its way to the surface. The truth always comes out. *Always.* You know that now. God is always watching us."

Dark struggled to find a shot. The red tracer dot bounced erratically around Sqweegel's body. He was itching to shoot.

But the moment the tracer sight found a clear shot, Sqweegel would inch back and move the baby into a different position—using it as a human shield. This basement was too dark. The margin of error too high.

The baby was crying now, too. It didn't like being bounced around, lifted up and down. It was cold and smelled like death down here. What was going through its tiny mind?

Jesus, there he was, thinking of the baby as an "it." Dark didn't even know the gender—he and Sibby had decided to wait to find out. Most fathers were treated to the news two seconds after the birth. Their baby had come into the world inside the basement dungeon of a madman. Its first sounds the tortured cries of its mother, along with the lies of a sick little freak.

And now the bright red laser sight from a gun held by its father.

Welcome to the world, little one. It's a stranger place than you ever could have imagined.

"Having trouble?" Sqweegel taunted. "Would a little light help?"

His elbow tapped a hospital-style metal plate, and instantly the dungeon was bathed in fluorescent light. And a hundred monitors, mounted in the walls, flickered to life.

Illuminating Sqweegel's secret place—the one he'd success-fully hidden for three decades.

The one he'd spent his entire adult life burrowing and constructing.

For years Special Circs assumed that Sqweegel had some kind of home base, a lair where he could bring his victims with relative ease. They speculated that it had to be well equipped with a variety of gear and, most important, soundproofing.

Now that Dark was finally seeing it, his mind boggled at the horror.

chapter 96

The place seemed to have been constructed with two types of building materials: video monitors and human corpses.

Squint and if you were lucky you might see only the video monitors, each linked to a hidden camera in a different location: Air Force Two. Quantico—the Special Circs War Room. Dark's Malibu home. Sibby's empty hospital room. And dozens of random interiors—homes, apartments, offices—all offering a visual portal into a space Sqweegel had already defiled. Clearly, he liked to keep tabs on things once he'd visited.

Sqweegel liked to bring back souvenirs, too.

And that's what filled the spaces between the monitors—the remains of human bodies. Skulls, bones, joints, veins, pink muscles, cloudy eyeballs, spongy gray brains, all preserved through plastination. They served as the mortar holding the monitors and computer gear in place, Sqweegel's final mockery of the human form.

"You're the first to see my life's work, Steeeeeeve," he said. "Go ahead. Look around. Explore. You might recognize the fragments of a tiny skull somewhere in there. Maybe some of your own DNA will tug at your blood. I'd be interested to know. It took a lot of searching through medical waste to find the right one, and I wouldn't want to be wrong."

"You've killed . . ."

"Far more than anyone's ever imagined," Sqweegel said. "I only leave the occasional body to send a message. But nobody seems to understand my work . . . except you. You were close, you know, when you were talking to Constance. I liked how you put it—Saint Peter, right? Not perfect, but close."

"You've been watching everything."

"What, with this? No, no, no. This is just the compound eye of a common fly compared to the almighty vision of the Father. No, Dark, I was just watching you and those in your orbit. I've had your life on tape for years. I've seen your every move. Heard every conversation. Watched every second of every hour of every day. There is nothing I don't know about you, or her, or Riggins, or Constance, or our traitorous Secretary Wycoff."

Dark moved closer to Sqweegel. "You're not God."

"No," Sqweegel admitted. "But He sent me. Don't you realize that by now?"

"You're fucking delusional."

"No, I'm merely telling a parable. Cast aside your mortal shell and listen with your soul," Sqweegel said. "I know at least part of you can hear me. You wouldn't have come this far if you hadn't. And we wouldn't have met up again in Rome."

Met up again? Dark thought. No. Rome was the first time. *He's trying to confuse me. Keep it simple. Flip open the monster's skull. Follow the wires running around his diseased brain. Pull the wires. Pull them all out and strangle him with them.*

"You're trying to show us sinners the errors of our ways," Dark said.

"No, I'm not interested in punishing the sin," Sqweegel replied. "Instead I serve as a beacon of God and all of His heavenly virtues."

Something clicked in Dark's mind. Seven. Not the sins. Everyone knew about the sins. But who considered their opposite—the seven heavenly virtues?

"Surely you remember them," Sqweegel said. "After all, your fake family enrolled you in that so-called Catholic school. Come on. Recite them with me. *Prudence* . . ."

Dark's mind spun through the past in the present. The definition of the virtue, matched against the recent carnage. He couldn't help it. He couldn't not think it.

Prudence was all about showing proper judgment. If Sqweegel held himself up as an example of prudence, then he'd taught that lesson in New York City.

"The 9/11 widows," Dark said softly.

"Ah, see—I knew you were listening! How about *justice?*"

The guilty will be punished. And the punishment will fit the crime.

"The kids buying beer."

"*Faith?*"

"The priests. Punishing six for the actions of others who lost their faith and hurt children."

"*Hope.*"

"You didn't kill the wives, just the horses. You expected them to do better. You had hope in them."

"Fantastic, Dark! Now the virtues from this evening, starting with *charity.*"

"You helped Sibby give birth."

"*Restraint?*"

"You let our baby live."

"And finally . . . *courage.*"

"You and I. Right here in this basement. The ability to face our worst fears. Is that it? Are we here to face each other, you son of a bitch? Are you afraid of me?"

Now he held the baby close, and Sqweegel began to make a

strange hissing sound as he contorted his body—as if he held an orange somewhere in his rib cage and he was trying to squeeze the juice out of it. Black bile began to seep out from between his teeth. It dripped on the infant's masked head.

"I've waited for this moment for so long," he whispered. "You have no idea."

chapter 97

Above Sqweegel's head, on a series of video monitors, Dark saw a flurry of running bodies in uniform. He recognized them. Wycoff's Dark Arts team, swarming out of their vans, rifles in hand. Moving in for the kill. Only now there were more than two. Easily a half dozen, from what he could tell.

And they were here in much less than fifteen minutes.

"Face your fear, my brother," Sqweegel said.

"Don't!"

But he did. Sqweegel used both hands to toss the infant in a high arc over Dark's head.

No no no no no NO . . .

Dark dropped his gun, spun, and made two giant strides across the floor, hands out. The baby was moving too high, too fast, too far away—

Behind him he heard a quick shuffling and a metallic clicking noise, but *forget that; focus on the baby*—

Which was plunging now, way too fast, toward the cement.

Dark lunged out with both hands, blindly, without any thought to how he might land—because how he might land didn't matter. Saving the baby did. Sibby's baby. *His* baby—

His fingers brushed the back of the baby's soft head, and they both slammed into the ground.

Somehow, his hands protected the child's fragile head from the fall.

Dark's lungs struggled to recover. The breath had been pounded out of his body when he hit the ground. But that didn't matter, either. Breathing wasn't important. He would breathe later. The important thing was taking Sibby and the baby out of here now.

He scooped her up and climbed to his feet. Newborn in one hand, he picked up his gun with the other. Where was he? Where was that slippery son of a bitc—

There.

A slithering, squirming flash of white.

Dark aimed, squeezed the trigger. He felt the baby jolt in his arm, recoiling from the gunshot blast.

But no direct hit; he could hear Sqweegel chuckling to himself.

"You missed," he said.

Dark charged forward. He wasn't going to let history repeat itself—this was not a church in Rome. This was not scaffolding. He had the monster trapped in his own lair, and Dark was going to kick and shoot and pursue and punch until he found the monster no matter where he tried to hide—

There.

Twisting under what looked like a heavy wooden worktable. Spindly leg retracting itself, tucking itself away behind a paneled door—

Dark raced forward and slammed the edge of the table with the heel of his boot, sending it tumbling over on its side. He fired, then fired again, directly into the open door of the table like he was firing into the mouth of a beast, and the baby started crying and—

Nothing. Sqweegel wasn't inside.

Fuck!

And then—

Over there. The white wraith twisting its way inhumanly down a corridor. Dark held the baby tighter against himself—he wasn't putting the baby down anywhere, not in here—and charged after him, praying for just one clean shot. A bullet to snap through the latex and his flesh and nerves and maybe even a bone, enough to cripple him for a few seconds, because a few seconds were all Dark needed . . .

Dark took three steps before something exploded.

He felt a sledgehammer blow to his right biceps, causing him to stumble. Dark caught himself, turned.

Sqweegel was moving toward him, smoking gun in hand. Sqweegel had a gun, too.

"Uh-uh-*uh*," Sqweegel said, singsonging, then fired again.

The bullet this time hit Dark's leg and sent him tumbling to the ground. The baby fell out of his arms and began to scream-cry, face flushing bright red. Dark fumbled in the bag strapped to his side. His fingers scrambled for the sharp edge he knew was in there . . .

"It's not fun unless you're fighting," Sqweegel said. "So, come on. Fight! The world will be watching!"

Dark turned around. The baby let out a plaintive wail from somewhere on the disgusting floor nearby. Sqweegel was in his face now, fetid breath invading his nostrils, beady pinpoints of black just inches away . . .

"Shut up," Dark said, then hooked three fingers into the open mouth zipper of Sqweegel's mask and pulled forward. As the latex-clad freak tipped toward him, a ghastly smile plastered across his face, Dark whipped the business end of a carbide glass cutter across his throat.

The blade sliced through latex and Sqweegel's neck, opening a wicked gash that seemed to unleash the very vapors of hell from within. Black blood spurted twelve feet or more across the room.

Sqweegel tried to scream, but all that came out was a thick, syrupy *gurgle*.

And now Dark ripped the monster's mask from his head, tearing the material at the neck. The latex peeled apart in a neat circle all around his writhing, bony neck as bright black blood gushed across the virginal white suit below.

Dark looked at Sqweegel's naked face.

And saw that it was completely . . . unremarkable.

Dull black eyes, which didn't seem as menacing now. A shaved bony head. A narrow forehead devoid of eyebrows. Bad teeth. Mottled skin. A geek grown up. An abused little boy who never outgrew his hate and as a result grew up hateful.

A hate so powerful it turned his blood black in his veins.

"You like poems?" Dark asked. "I've got one for you. Maybe you've heard it before. In fact, I know you fucking have."

The monster's fingers pushed at the gash in his neck as if he could seal the wound by hand. His arms trembled. His black eyes rolled around in his head.

Dark stood up now, even though the bullet wounds in his biceps and leg were agonizing. He scanned the torture room for a moment and immediately saw what he wanted. Sqweegel could only choke and hack and spit in reply.

Dark turned to stand over Sqweegel's writhing body now, and held up the small silver hatchet in his hands.

"Lizzie Borden took an axe," Dark recited, "gave her mother forty whacks. And when she saw what she had done, she gave her father forty-one—"

And on the *one*, the hatchet blade swung down and chopped through the monster's right shoulder.

Dark lifted the hatchet again and slammed it down into Sqweegel's left shoulder this time, cleanly severing his toothpick

370

arm from his body, which rolled off to the side and rocked slightly before coming to a stop. Black blood spurted from the wound, splattering the blade of the hatchet before Dark had a chance to lift it up again and choose another place to bury it.

The right leg joint, right below Sqweegel's hip.

Then the left.

The monster's spindly legs, which had allowed him to slither and crawl and hide and contort, were no longer part of his body. They were useless hunks of meat and bone now. They would not grow back. They would just cool and spurt and eventually rot away to nothing.

Dark whipped the hatchet up in the air and felt the warm dots of fetid blood dribble on his face. The smell was unholy, almost like the monster had liquid sulfur pumping through his veins.

He glanced down and saw that Sqweegel was staring back up at him, complete calm on his face. Black eyes boring into his own. Like he was expecting something.

Here! Here's what you've been expecting!

What you've been begging me for—

Dark heard a gleeful scream escape his own throat.

—this—

he turned his wrist to get the angle right

—whole—

and slammed the hatchet down into Sqweegel's neck

—time!

and the force of the blade chopping through hard spine sent Sqweegel's head spinning across the dungeon floor.

As Sqweegel listened to Dark recite his little nursery rhyme, a holy peace came over him—even as the blade took off his right arm at the shoulder joint. Then his leg, midthigh. Dark was a strong man, even with two bullets in him. The blade had no prob-

371

lem slicing all the way through the meat, the bone. Sqweegel watched a dollop of his own blood escape gravity and explode in the air above him.

The hatchet took the other leg, then the other arm, but he was *still alive.*

Which was so fortunate. He didn't want to miss a minute of this.

He was even conscious for a little while after the blade cut through his neck, all the way to the floor. It was strange; he could hear the sound of his spine snapping not with his ears, but in his skull. Consciousness faded in and out for a while, and Sqweegel struggled to stay on the mortal plane just a few seconds longer.

He'd worked long and hard on his heavenly mission and he knew he deserved to rest, but he wanted so desperately to cling to this world just to see it all end.

It was too bad Dark had sliced his throat. Sqweegel honestly hadn't seen that coming. In those early moments of his death, Sqweegel thought it might be possible to close the hole in his throat and form the last few words. But all that came out were the awful hacking sounds of an animal. Which was too bad.

He'd been trying so hard to tell him one last thing.

He'd been trying to *thank him.*

chapter 98

Upstairs there was the thunder of broken windows, pummeled doors, boots on the floor. Dark listened, if only to figure out how much time he had left with Sibby. How long before they found the bloodstained knob, the marble steps. And then . . .

Sibby didn't have much time left at all. The maniac had savaged her body, sliced at it with surgical precision. Her breasts were gone. Her legs and stomach streaked with slash marks.

"We're going to get you out of here," Dark lied as he placed the baby on the gurney and went to Sibby. The skin around her wrists and ankles was pale white. He kissed her wrists, pretty much the only place on her that wasn't bleeding.

Sibby shook her head and looked up at him. She tried to speak, but a dollop of blood came out instead.

"Hey, it'll be okay," Dark murmured softly, knowing full well it wouldn't be. She was going into shock. Pupils narrowing.

"No," she said, "it won't." Her voice was a gurgling rasp at first, but she gave him a sweet smile anyway, then cleared her throat of the blood that was pooling there.

"Don't talk that way."

"Your worst nightmare's come true," Sibby said. "You're the father of a beautiful baby girl."

Even Dark had to smile at that one. They'd joked about it when Sibby had first learned she was pregnant. Dark told her he was praying for a son because a girl would be the end of him. He'd be posted at the door on a permanent basis to frighten away any potential suitors.

"If she takes after her mother, I'm in serious trouble," Dark said.

Sibby smiled, then cleared her throat again.

They stared at each other now, all joking and pretense fading away until there was nothing but two souls, connected at a level that lay beyond the normal senses. Words didn't mean much anymore. They both knew what they were, what they had been, and what was going to happen. A perfect and heartbreaking understanding passed between them. Dark felt his heart surge and implode at the same time.

"You take care of her," Sibby said finally. "I decorated her room, I hope you like it."

Her. The baby was a she.

They'd had a daughter. Congrats, Daddy.

"Hold her with me in your heart."

She inhaled again . . .

And that was it.

Before Dark Arts burst into the room.

Sibby Dark had a dream once. She'd met a man in a supermarket aisle. They lived together by the ocean and they got married and they were going to have a baby together, and then one day the man of her dreams asked her to dinner at her favorite restaurant and she smiled at him over the candlelight and was overwhelmed with gratitude, gratitude for this life of hers, and this life they were going to bring into the world together, and that's all that mattered.

And the dream never ended.

chapter 99

"Oh, no, you fucking don't."

Everyone turned—Dark included.

He hadn't bothered to turn around when the two agents burst into the room. Dark could only assume they were Wycoff's babysitters—Buzz-cut and his friend with the missing fingers. They had their guns out, barking commands to freeze and get down with his hands locked behind his head.

Dark also hadn't turned when the retching started as they saw what surrounded them. The bodies. The monitors. The stench. The pool of black blood seeping from the broken body of a monster who used to hide under people's beds and in their closets.

"Jesus fucking Christ, what the fuck *is* this . . . ?"

But a few seconds later there was another voice. One Dark recognized.

Riggins. And he was telling the Dark Arts agents no, they fucking didn't.

And with that, Dark finally turned.

Riggins had his hands up, palms out, showing that he wasn't holding a weapon. He looked the agents in the eye.

"Before you do something foolish," he said, "look around you, boys. This look like a normal op to you? Look at the baby in that man's arms. Look at the woman next to him. Her name's Sibby Dark, and she woke up this morning fighting for her life. That's her husband, and in his arms is their baby girl, who was born in this fucking dungeon a few hours ago. I know you've got orders; I know this is what you do. This is what I do, too. But I'm asking you to think about it, and look around you. Is this something you really want to do?"

Nellis had spent enough time watching this middle-aged burnout to know that he was quite possibly serious. Their orders had been to erase everything in this house. But a baby? Born to a woman who'd been captured and tortured here, in this charnel pit?

No, there were such things as too fucking dark for Dark Arts.

The horrors in this basement . . . Hell, he'd be lucky to ever scrub the images from his mind, let alone off the face of the earth. There were too many questions here, too many uncertainties.

And after the last few days, he'd grown a little fond of the broken-down agent in front of him, although he'd never admit it to anyone.

"Stand down," Nellis told McGuire.

Dark watched Constance approach, holding out her arms. She was something out of a dream from another lifetime.

"May I?" she asked.

At first Dark didn't know what she meant. Then he looked down, realizing that, yeah, he was holding a baby. His little baby girl. He'd scooped her up from the floor at some point. Funny he didn't remember when. Was it before he'd gone to Sibby? Or after? With Dark Arts already stomping around the room? The past few minutes were a blur. The edges of his vision swam.

He felt Constance lift the child out of his arms, but somehow, the weight remained. Dark's chest felt like huge pieces of granite had been laid on top of it. He stumbled backward until he reached a wall, then slid down slowly.

Constance looked good with a baby, Dark thought. She should have kept hers.

Theirs.

His.

Dark hadn't even looked at the baby. Couldn't bring himself to. Because what if he saw something in her eyes?

Something that *wasn't him at all?*

Riggins touched his shoulder. "Let's get the fuck out of here."

chapter 100

Dark sat on the side of the hospital bed. The meds had finally kicked in. They didn't take away the pain. Not exactly. They pushed the pain aside and encouraged him to focus on something else. Here, look at this. A giant scrambled fuzz of nothing. Isn't that interesting? Pay attention to this here now. Not the pain. The pain will always be there. You can get back over to it at any time. He was set to be discharged soon. He'd insisted. Better finish his recovery at home than here, in the hospital that only reminded him of Sibby, and the horrors she'd endured.

Somewhere in the gray fuzz a thought stabbed at his mind. He felt himself jolt. The flexing of his muscles tore at his stitches. But that didn't matter.

"The baby," he said.

To his surprise, someone answered him.

"With Child Services," Constance said. "They wanted a full evaluation. She'll be released tomorrow, they said."

There were two visitors standing in the doorway of his hospital room—Constance and Riggins. Constance came to his bedside now, put her soft, cool hand on the side of his cheek and smiled at him.

"It's a girl, right?" Dark asked. "I didn't imagine that, did I?"

"Yes, Steve. A beautiful, healthy little girl."

Then this wasn't all just gray fuzz. There was a point to it, after all. Beyond the carnage and pain and the poems and lies and the blood, there was this. There was still *life*. Sibby was not dead. Sibby would live on forever in their daughter. The monster couldn't take that away.

But with those words something again stabbed at Dark's mind, and he realized what had pained him even more than the surgeries and stitches. It was the words of the dead monster, booming over the gray fuzz:

Why don't you shoot us and find out. Give us both blood tests. Watch the truth wriggle its way to the surface. The truth always comes out. Always.

"I need a favor," Dark said suddenly. "Get a nurse. Draw some blood."

"For what?" Riggins asked. "You feel like something's wrong?"

"No. It's not that at all. The baby. I need to know if she's mine."

"You need to rest, buddy—"

"I need to know."

Riggins nodded. The look on his face told Dark that he understood that any argument would be futile and that rest and recovery would have to wait until he knew the truth.

"I'll get the nurse."

To confirm the paternity test results, log into
LEVEL26.com and enter the code: father

chapter 101

Ordinarily there are rules about these sorts of things.

Bodies of captured serial killers are kept on ice for a certain period of time. Often, various agencies want to claim pieces of them—especially certain scientific divisions. They view hunters of men as a slightly different species, and in need of further study. News of Sqweegel's demise leaked throughout the scientific community, and everybody clamored for a piece of him.

After all, he was a new kind of predator. A monster the world had never seen before.

A Level 26.

But Dark wasn't going to let that happen.

It wasn't just the nightmares—which were bad enough. Images of the dismembered hand, still in its glove, flittering across the basement floor like a white tarantula. Dragging its own severed arm toward the torso. Veins whipping out like worms, desperate to reattach themselves to their host. His eyes—his awful black eyes—coming to life again through the eyeholes. And then his reanimated body crawling out from under the baby's crib, reaching up for her, and the baby cooing, and not understanding at all what was coming for her . . .

Yeah, the nightmares were bad.

But it was also the idea that Sqweegel would somehow live on, even if it was just in a petri dish in a government lab somewhere. That was a kind of immortality, and Dark couldn't allow that. Every piece needed to be obliterated. Flesh burned, bones charred into dust. Every cell burst out of its membrane and dissolved into nothing.

Sqweegel spent his adult life leaving no trace of himself behind. Dark thought the little bastard's wishes should be carried out in death as well.

Which is why they were standing here now, at a private crematorium, with a heavy-duty cardboard box containing the mortal remains of Sqweegel. Riggins had broken at least a dozen laws to make this happen, but what was he going to say at this point—*no can do, Dark?* No, he made the arrangements without complaint or discussion. Dark suspected that Riggins wanted to fry the little fucker as much as he did.

Sqweegel had claimed that he had fathered Sibby's baby. Thankfully, the paternity test had proven otherwise. And after today, no mortal trace of the monster would be left on earth.

Dark nodded, and the crematorium employees pulled the lever. The box began its slow roll into the furnace. Inside, the flames blasted away.

The workers had stared at the box suspiciously at first—who the hell brings a corpse in a cardboard box? Not only that, but a dismembered corpse, thrown into the box like scraps of meat. Severed arms and legs. A hacked-up chest. A decapitated head, with the eyes still open.

But Riggins showed him his badge and the employees were all business after that.

The box bobbled a little as it made its way toward the mouth of the furnace, which radiated eighteen hundred degrees of heat.

The flames lapped at the box hungrily.

The box curled and twitched and burned first, but the body parts inside seemed impervious to the heat.

The workers made a move to slam the furnace door shut with metal poles, but Dark raised an arm to stop them.

He wanted to watch every last detail.

He needed to *know*.

Dark stepped closer to the furnace, so close he could feel the heat baking the pores on his face. Sqweegel's dead black eyes looked up at him—as if taunting him, refusing to yield to the fire.

But then finally they did, bubbling into little dark pools of nothing. Scraps of meat that had been his body turned black under the intense blaze. Bones charred and crumbled under the heat.

About an hour into the process the crematorium workers re-positioned the remains, using metal rakes and poles to ensure a proper and thorough burn.

Another hour later, all that remained were ashes and stubborn bits of calcium, which would be raked out and ground into tiny white particles.

Sqweegel was gone.

The Level 26 killer flensed from the face of the earth . . . forever.

Even his dungeon had been scrubbed clean of all physical traces, including the decaying remains of his victims.

But the scent of acrid burned meat would cling to the inside of the employees' nostrils for days to come, no matter how much they tried to use sprays and tissues and finally saline solutions to flush away the odor. Dark and Riggins had the same problem.

Scent is not a mist and not a smoke. It is actually particles of the thing you're smelling, which travel into your nasal cavity and bind themselves to your nasal receptors.

Dark would be feeding his infant daughter, or washing his face, or staring at himself in the bathroom mirror, holding a shaving razor to his cheek . . . all he would have to do was breathe, and Sqweegel would return.

In the middle of the night, just hours after the cremation, Dark woke up and realized he'd made a terrible mistake.

He *should* have kept some of the DNA. Just a sample to keep for future reference to match against unsolved crimes. If the world was to ever be rid of Sqweegel, his actions needed to be cataloged, understood, filed away. You don't pretend the boogeyman doesn't exist; you drag him under the scientific spotlight and show the world that this was just a fucked-up man, nothing more.

Some hours later, while staring at the ceiling, Dark realized there *was* one place where Sqweegel's DNA might still be found.

Riggins volunteered.

He'd seen the look on Dark's face as he explained what he needed to do. Dark tried to sound all detached and clinical about it, but Riggins knew what was going through his mind. Dark was steeling himself for the task of collecting DNA from the corpse of his wife. That was an experience no man should face. Especially after what Dark had already been through.

So Riggins went instead.

Inside the morgue he lifted Sibby's hand and gently ran the stick under one nail, like wiping a tear away from the corner of a baby's eye. He thought of the strength it had taken this woman to fight back, to ensure she took a piece of her killer with her into the afterlife, to tear her fingernails through the freak's latex suit and bring a piece of his flesh out of that basement to ensure it was waiting for them now, when they needed it most.

He ran the sample personally and sat in the empty trace lab, waiting for the results. He didn't know whether they'd find an identity, but he figured they had a pretty good chance of finding a relative. The results came with a digital *ding*.

Seven of eleven alleles were a match.

No, Riggins thought. *Can't fucking be possible.*

A short while later, Dark asked about the results.

"Nothing," Riggins said. "No hits. Fucker was a real no-where man."

Of all the lies Riggins had ever told, this one was the most difficult.

chapter 102

Hollywood Cemetery / Wilshire Boulevard

Sibby's funeral was a blur of black suits and white crosses and pungent flowers and churned-up dirt, its sweet smell hanging thick in the summer air.

Her family was here from northern California. Dark couldn't bring himself to look at them. Riggins was here, too, of course, along with Constance and most of the Special Circs team, from what he could gather. Dark wasn't keeping track or paying much attention. All he could focus on was Sibby.

Their daughter, Sibby, named for her mother.

The baby held a rose in her hands, completely unaware. Dark was sure she was able to smell its perfume, but that would be it. To babies in their first few days of life, the world was a frenetic blur. Thank God for that.

Baby Sibby pressed her face into Dark's chest, nuzzling him through his dress shirt. It took Dark a moment to realize what she was doing.

She was hungry and looking for her mother.

It was Sibby who should be here. It was Sibby the baby wanted.

The priest talked about salvation and love and the Kingdom of Heaven, but Dark honestly wasn't listening. He couldn't listen, because listening to the words now and unpacking them in his mind would be a disaster. He wasn't going to fall down to his knees here. Not with Baby Sibby in his arms.

But he knew that the priest had stopped talking, and the crowd looked to Dark, so it was time. He stepped to the edge of the grave, on the green Astroturf the graveyard crew had thrown down so mourners wouldn't get their shoes dirty. He took the rose from Baby Sibby's little fingers, which were pale, soft, and wrinkly. Then he placed the rose on top of the casket. The late-morning sun baked the back of his head with warmth.

"Rest in peace, Sibby."

Dark looked down at his daughter, whose tiny face was still pressed up against his chest. He knew she couldn't understand, wouldn't recall a thing years later. But Dark knew he would never forget this moment, how the little child looked as her mother's casket slowly descended into the earth below her. It was a moment he didn't want to forget.

"I promise," Dark said softly, then lowered his head. He wasn't saying it for the benefit of anyone else. Not even Sibby. More a reminder to himself.

He'd lost his heart once; he'd had everything stripped away from him, and he'd retreated like a wounded child.

Dark couldn't afford that luxury now.

chapter 103

The funeral procession made its way to the black asphalt path where everyone had left their cars. Riggins walked next to him but didn't say anything. Just touched him lightly with the backs of his fingers to direct him to the correct limo.

Riggins had told him the plans for this afternoon:

Make it through the luncheon.

Leave the baby with Sibby's parents, who were itching for time with their baby granddaughter.

Then retire with Riggins to the nearest, quietest Hollywood Boulevard dive, where they would proceed to get incredibly, *massively* shit-faced.

"If we don't end up on Santa Monica beach wearing nothing but vomit and our underwear, I'll be incredibly disappointed," Riggins had said.

Dark had said nothing. He'd have a beer with Riggins, yes, and he'd leave Sibby for a while with her grandparents. But the time for numbing reality was over. He'd tried it. It hadn't worked. There had to be some other way. People who had lost just as much—and more—somehow managed to play the masquerade. Dark wanted to know their secrets.

Just as they reached the limo, however, Robert Dohman, Wycoff's number two, jogged up from the procession to stop them.

"Dark. Riggins. Brielle. I need a minute of your time."

Riggins turned red. "Now? Are you insane? Or just an asshole?"

"We gave you the time you asked for," Dohman said. "Funeral's over. We have unfinished business."

Riggins looked over at Dark, who betrayed no emotion. *Whatever. Let the man say what he thinks he needs to say and get it over with.*

"Make it quick," Riggins said.

Dohman smiled an *I'll take as long as I please* smile. "The president is an understanding man. But still, federal crimes were committed. You don't walk away from this scot-free. You should be looking at life terms in prison."

"But?" Riggins asked.

"But the president has something else in mind."

"What do you mean *something else?*" Dark asked.

"You're going to work off your charges."

Riggins shook his head. "No, no. I put my papers in. I'm out."

"And you'll be arrested right now."

"You know," Riggins said, "you're just as much of an asshole as your old boss."

"I'm sorry for your loss," Dohman said. "But make sure your affairs are in order. We'll be in touch with your first assignment within forty-eight hours."

Dohman and the rest of his DOD crew left the cemetery behind the other mourners, who were already on their way to the luncheon, leaving Dark, Riggins, and Constance in a quiet, hot field of graves.

chapter 104

Georgetown, Washington, D.C.

They'd be coming any minute now.

Ordinarily Wycoff liked this time of night. The time of night when the rest of the world was asleep—especially his complaining kids, his passive-aggressive wife. He could finally be himself. Pour himself a drink, jump on the computer. And maybe for a few minutes, forget he was the secretary of defense.

As far as the public knew, Wycoff was taking a few days to "spend more time with his family," an excuse that covered a host of sins and excesses. As far as his wife knew, Wycoff was feeling burned out. As far as his kids knew . . . well, who was he kidding? Like his kids gave a shit? They were upstairs now, plugged into their iPods or instant messaging their spoiled friends.

The truth was, Wycoff had taken the time off to tie up a few loose ends. The Sqweegel case could have been a career-ending nightmare, had he not taken certain steps.

Wycoff checked his watch.

Yeah, they'd be arriving soon.

Wycoff allowed himself to wonder about the boy. The boy

neither his wife nor his kids knew about. The bastard son who would never know that his father was once the secretary of defense of the mightiest nation on the planet . . . and his mother was a high school senior who had been slaughtered by a maniac. Wycoff had come from privilege; this boy was born out of lies, and later, horror. Who was to say the boy wouldn't do better? Wycoff had all the advantages in the world, and look where he was now.

Waiting for two silent killers to appear.

No—not at his door.

At the door of Bob Dohman, his loyal assistant.

After all, in D.C. shit always rolls downhill. Wycoff was too important a man to let something like this Sqweegel debacle derail him now. But the machine demanded a sacrificial lamb, and sadly, Bob Dohman was the best possible candidate.

It wouldn't be so bad. Dohman would feel the slight pinch near his carotid artery, nothing more. And by now . . .

Wycoff looked down at his watch.

Well, yeah, by now the killers would be there at Dohman's condo in Annapolis.

Rest in peace, Bob.

Falls Church, Virginia

Riggins keyed into his front door and heard a beeping sound—his security system. The keypad was mounted on the wall behind the door and was flashing a steady, annoyed red.

Twenty-five seconds remaining . . .

He dropped his overnight bag on the linoleum floor, pushed the door to the side. There were nine number keys—pretty rudimentary shit, really—but Riggins, for the life of him, couldn't remember the code. Two of the digits, he was pretty sure, were the year he first got married. Funny thing was, though, he couldn't remember that year, either. He remembered the cake, the booze, the band . . . the swirling chaos around a young marriage. But not the fucking year.

Twenty seconds remaining . . .

It had been more than a week since he'd been in his apartment. Thank God he didn't have any pets. They'd be half-a-week dead by now.

Fifteen seconds remaining . . .

He really needed to remember this code. Enough fucking around.

Ten seconds remaining . . .

How embarrassing was this going to be, a member of the FBI's most elite manhunting agency, flummoxed by his own security system?

Five seconds remaining . . .

Riggins stared at the keypad, still blank, still wondering how he could have forgotten something so basic as the year he was first married. That year had mattered once.

The security team showed up a few minutes later. Riggins sat on his front stoop, ID ready in his hands.

And then his cell phone rang.

Silver Spring, Maryland

Constance Brielle had mouths to feed.

Her next-door neighbor had filled in for a while, or so she had claimed. Truth was, the food and water bowls were both empty, and the cats were swirling around her feet, complaining.

Constance opened four cans of wet food and dished them out onto plates her grandmother had given her. Her parents were supposed to have received them, but that hadn't quite worked out. So now the cats enjoyed their chicken primavera on them. Better than nobody.

She thought about Dark and almost picked up her cell a few times and called, but she couldn't think of what she'd say.

And she didn't want to wake the baby.

So she sat on her couch in her calm suburban apartment, cell phone in her hand, thinking about whether she could have done anything different in the past week. Anything that would have made a difference, either way. Anything she could have done to avoid sitting here in her calm suburban apartment, alone.

And then her cell phone rang.

West Hollywood, California

Dark went to the box, dug it out, and carried it over to the wall.

There was already a nail sticking out of the wall. He felt for the wire on the back, then guided the framed photo onto the wall.

Sibby, a year ago, in her sheer yellow dress, on the Malibu beach.

Sometimes Dark stared at photos too long, and wondered whether that was what you did in the afterlife—inhabit your old photos. Because sure, you're frozen in that moment. But sometimes you have a look in your eye that you're seeing more than just your immediate surroundings. You're seeing out into the present. You're seeing your future, no matter how happy or sad it might be. You're seeing what has been, what is, and what could have been . . .

Dark went back to the box and found his other favorite photo: a black-and-white shot of Sibby on the beach—arms gracefully lifted above her head, hips swaying to one side, the shadows so intense she's almost a silhouette. She's on the edge of the Pacific, which seems to extend out into infinity.

And she's preparing to dance.

```
To remember what might've been, log into LEVEL26
.com and enter the code: sunset
```

EPILOGUE

the second gift

chapter 105

Two Days Later
West Hollywood, California

D ark ripped open a packet of powdered baby formula with his teeth and dumped the beige contents into a plastic baby bottle. He glanced at the instructions, trying to figure out how much water he should add. They should make this stuff clear, shouldn't they?

From the reverse-osmosis tap, Dark filled the bottle exactly to the line. Screwed on the lid. Shook it. It was ready for Baby Sibby, and not a moment too soon. She was hungry.

His daughter, Sibby—as soft as a flower. Big blue eyes. Wailing so pathetically, it was enough to break Dark's heart.

And she always seemed hungry.

So Dark sat on the couch and fed her, nearly blinded by the morning sun. Riggins had picked out this apartment blind, and Dark had only used it at night. This was the first time he'd been in his new place in daylight. So strange to think about that. His life with Sibby was all about the sun, the beach, the waking hours. At night, they'd huddled together and tried to block out everything else.

Now he was here with his daughter, who was sucking happily from the latex nipple.

Dark hadn't had much time at all to unpack boxes, save for the photo of Sibby in her yellow dress on the beach. He showed the baby the photograph and explained that this was her mommy, and her mommy would always love her very much. Dark wanted to plant the memories early and never let up. The two of them would be sociologists studying the life of Sibby Dark, and Dark wanted to leave no detail forgotten.

He was done hiding from death. He had decided to revel in life for a change.

And then, there was a knock at the door.

The noise startled Baby Sibby. The bottle was finished now anyway—sucked dry. Dark gently set her down as there was another knock, more urgent. He briefly debated the merits of opening the door. He thought of the Blaise Pascal quote: "All of man's misfortune comes from one thing, which is not knowing how to sit quietly in a room."

But Dark knew better. The knock wouldn't go away.

So he quickly checked on his daughter in her soft-pink bassinet—hastily assembled two nights before—and then pulled a Glock nine-millimeter from a drawer in the coffee table.

"Who is it?" Dark asked.

"Delivery," a female voice said. "I've got a box here for you."

Dark checked the peephole in the door. There was a tall, slender woman in a courier uniform, dark hair tucked up under her cap, holding a brown box marked with the name of a diaper delivery service. Dark recognized the name; an analyst from Special Circs had set it up as a gift. The card had read: *Just because you left us doesn't mean you're finished wading through shit.*

"Hold on," Dark said. He tucked the gun into the waistband of his jeans, near the small of his back, then unlocked and opened the door.

"Steve Dark?" the woman asked.

"Yeah."

"Can I bring these in? I've got something for you to sign."

Before Dark had a chance to respond, the delivery woman took a computerized tablet from the top of the box and handed it to Dark.

Then she dropped the box of diapers on the floor, kicked the door shut behind her, and removed her cap. Her long brunette hair flowed down to her shoulders. She plucked a cell phone from her courier uniform before peeling it away with a single movement, revealing a business suit beneath. Within seconds she was completely transformed.

But by then, Dark was already pointing his Glock at her head.

"Take it easy," she said. "I'm Brenda Condor from Child Services out of Washington."

"What's with the diapers?" Dark said.

"Would you have opened the door if I said I was from the federal government?"

Dark nodded. She had a point. If she had announced she was from the government, he might have shot through the door first before opening it.

"A car will be here for you in seven minutes," she continued. "I'll be taking care of the infant while you're away."

"Oh, yeah?" Dark asked. "Where is it I'm going?"

Condor walked past Dark and into the apartment, making a beeline for the baby. She made it two steps before Dark pressed the Glock to the side of her head and kindly asked for her identification and credentials.

"You don't need that gun anymore."

"You don't have to take another breath," Dark said.

Dark watched her pupils dilate and her lovely blue eyes widen, and it distracted him just enough for her to disarm him with a move he'd never even seen before, let alone anticipated from her. Later he would blame it on lack of sleep. Instead of using his own gun on him, however, she fished inside her purse and handed her ID over, along with an open cell phone.

At first glance, the credentials looked legit. But Dark was reassured only when he heard the voice of Riggins on the other end of the line.

"Yeah, she's the real thing," Riggins said wearily. "Fuckin' Dohman called me a few hours ago. I'm dealing with the same kind of shit out at my place. I should be enjoying a perfectly good hangover, but apparently we're being pressed back into service."

"Right."

"See you in a few."

Dark pressed END and looked at his new babysitter.

"You don't have to worry," Condor said as she handed over his gun. "I'll take good care of her. I've been instructed to bring her to you wherever you are in the world—as long as it's safe. Pack your shit. The DOD is four out."

Dark walked to the wall and retrieved the yellow-dress photo.

"This is her mother. Make sure you show this photo to her a few times a day. It's important to me."

Condor took the photo, looked at it. If she had a response, she kept it to herself. She squeezed a two-way microphone inside of her blouse.

"Steve Dark, Code Four. Infant in possession. Over."

chapter 106

J ust minutes after Dark managed to transfer a few things from a cardboard box to an overnight bag, a long black limousine pulled up, bookended by two LAPD motorcycle cops. Lights were off. Two Department of Defense suits in sunglasses stepped out of the limo. His escorts.

Condor trailed him to the door, with Baby Sibby in her arms. The way she held the baby didn't inspire much confidence in Dark. The woman looked like she'd be more at home patting and burping a submachine gun.

Dark set down his bag and took the baby, pressing her against his shoulder. He whispered in her ear.

"I don't know if I'm much of a dad," he said, "but I know one thing. I love you. And your mother loves you, too. Be a good girl, okay?"

Dark looked at Condor as he handed her back. "Take care of her, okay?"

"Your car is waiting."

The limousine door opened at the curb.

Hours later he landed at Newark, where he changed planes.

Riggins and Constance were already in the lounge area, overnight bags at their feet.

"So we meet again," Riggins said, pressing his thumb between his eyes. "Oh, fuck, does my brain hurt."

"Anyone know where we're going?" Dark asked.

Constance shook her head. "I asked my lovely escort what to pack, and all he would tell me was *business attire*."

"We're going to Rome. And no, I don't know why."

chapter 107

Leonardo da Vinci Airport, Rome

The tires of their plane burned and smoked upon touchdown at Leonardo da Vinci Airport in Rome, Italy. It was night. After they'd taxied in a semicircle, Dark watched a boxy van marked POLIZIA, red lights blinking, park next to the outdoor stairway.

They weren't five steps off of the aircraft when they were introduced to a man who presented himself as General Costanza and told them he was the leader of the Arma dei Carabinieri. Dark knew this meant military police. Several of his officers gathered around him like ducklings. One of them had a brown leather briefcase handcuffed to his beefy wrist.

"Hundreds are dead," Costanza said in broken English. "Please step inside."

The *polizia* van doors slammed shut behind them, and they peeled away from the airport.

Dark knew he was jet-lagged, and on top of that, sleep deprived, as is any new father. But did this man say *hundreds*?

Within thirty minutes they arrived at the largest baroque

fountain in Rome. Orange crime-scene tape cordoned off the architectural masterpiece. Dark saw hundreds of people scattered in the street, crying and stepping over . . . sheets?

Yes, sheets. Over bodies.

Not all were covered, and Dark saw glimpses of decayed eyes, purple veins, bloated flesh. Dead open mouths caked with blood.

In the back of the van, Constance covered her mouth. Riggins sat expressionless, then shut his eyes. He was painfully sober now.

"What happened here?" Dark asked.

And now Costanza took the briefcase—still handcuffed to his assistant's arm—and unlocked it. He lifted the lid, then spun it around so that Dark could see inside.

As he glanced inside, Dark's heart nearly stopped. Just a few moments ago, the briefcase had been just that—an ordinary vessel containing papers, files, folders. But when Dark saw what was inside, everything took on an aura of pure evil that stole his breath.

"This can't be happening," he said finally.

Dark had thought Level 26 was nothing but a bad memory.

He was wrong.

To travel to Rome, log into LEVEL26.com and enter the code: zipper

acknowledgments

Anthony E. Zuiker would like to thank: First and foremost my wife, Jennifer. My muse. To the cast and crew of *Level 26*, thanks for supporting my directorial debut. I had a blast and a ton of laughs. To Orlin Dobreff, Jennifer Cooper, and Morgan Schmidt, you guys are my dream team. A very special thanks to Duane Swierczynski, Marc Ecko, Marc Fernandez, John Paine, Ben Satterfield, and Robert Kondrk. And a written apology to Margaret Riley, Kevin Yorn, and everyone on Team Zuiker for putting up with all of my disturbia. LOL! Brian Tart and Ben Sevier, that goes for you guys, too. :)

Duane Swierczynski would like to thank David Hale Smith, for showing him the way to Sqweegel's lair, Anthony Zuiker, for the thrilling and disturbing guided tour of the place, and Ben Sevier, for helping him scramble out with his soul intact (more or less). Also, huge thanks to his wife, son, and daughter, as well as the good people at Dutton and Dare to Pass, Inc., who were incredibly supportive throughout the writing of this novel.

level 26: dark origins

Starring Dan Buran as Steve Dark

Michael Ironside as Tom Riggins

Glenn Morshower as Norman Wycoff

Bill Duke as Jack Mitchell

Kevin Weisman as Josh Banner

Daniel Browning Smith as Sqweegel

Tauvia Dawn as Sibby Dark

about the authors

ANTHONY E. ZUIKER is the creator and executive producer of the most-watched television show in the world, *CSI: Crime Scene Investigation*, and a visionary business leader who speaks regularly about the future of entertainment. Zuiker lives in Las Vegas and Los Angeles.

DUANE SWIERCZYNSKI is the author of several thrillers, including *Severance Package*, which he's currently adapting for the screen. He also writes the monthly X-Men series *Cable* for Marvel Comics, and has written other titles featuring Iron Fist, Punisher, and Wolverine. He lives in Philadelphia.